ELLORA'S
CAVEMEN

SEASONS of
Seduction

ELLORA'S CAVE
ROMANTICA PUBLISHING

Ellora's Cavemen:
Seasons of Seduction I

Her Lance-Alot
Delilah Devlin

1154 England. Lady Margaret du Bary must find a way out of the marriage her king has decreed. Lord Roland is far beneath the ideal knight she's dreamed of! But how can she distract the brute from consummating their marriage?

Lord Roland is very pleased with his bride. Besides the lands and fine castle she brings, she's pleasing to the eye and has a suitably demure demeanor. The only thorn in the ointment is he has no experience tupping a gentlewoman. Bedding his modest bride will prove a true test of this knight's steel!

Dance of the Plain Jane
Lillian Feisty

Shy Jane Holliday has loved sexy Navy SEAL Michael Sky from afar for over a year. But one night the sultry beat of an exotic drum loosens her inhibitions and empowers her to seduce her dream lover.

The instant Michael spots the veiled dancer weaving her sensual magic he's stopped dead in his tracks. His hands itch to touch not just the curve of her undulating hips but every spot on her enchanting body.

Club Vamp
Allyson James

When master vampire Kenelm sees Helena Girard, he knows she's the one destined to restore him to power. He sends his lover, Adam Chase, to bring her to him. Helena is instantly smitten with gorgeous Adam, but knows she can't be with him because of the deadly electricity her body sends off when she orgasms.

But Kenelm can siphon off her power so she can make love to Adam—as long as he is with them. Helena revels in the excitement of both of them, until they reveals the truth about who she is.

Choosing Madison
Sherrill Quinn

Gaelen Brecca has to track down the errant fiancée of his world's leader. When he finds her hiding out on Earth, Gaelen has no choice but to take along Earthwoman Madison Marquette as well. Finding a mate was the last thing he and his bond-brother, Leax Ilan, expected on their mission.

When she discovers that her new friend is actually an alien princess, Madison is ready for a grand adventure with her. She's immediately drawn to Gaelen and Leax, who make no secret of their attraction for her. Can they secure her sensual surrender?

Come Howling
Denise Rossetti

Being a banshee is a lifetime Curse—and a magical pain the ass. Needing a career change in the worst possible way, Maeve O'Brien the banshee visits an employment agency. Surely someone will listen!

Luc hangs on every single word. The woman's voice is sex incarnate. A single whisper and he's got the hot chills. Two sentences and he's hard enough to pound nails. To help Maeve—Hell, Luc would do anything, even go to the devil.

Lyrael's Sacrifice
Jory Strong

Lyrael was Azzura, one those raised to be given to the Djinn. When she dreams of a panther that shifts into a bird before changing into a serpent, she knows she will be the next Azzura sacrificed. Whether she lives or dies will depend on her courage, her determination. And her trust in Asrafil, the Djinn prince who introduces her to carnal pleasure and will name her the wife of his heart, his flesh, his spirit—if she passes the tests necessary to enter the city of the Djinn.

An Ellora's Cave Romantica Publication

www.ellorascave.com

Content Advisory:

S – ENSUOUS
E – ROTIC
X – TREME

Ellora's Cave Publishing offers three levels of Romantica™ reading entertainment: S (S-ensuous), E (E-rotic), and X (X-treme).

The following material contains graphic sexual content meant for mature readers. This story has been rated E–rotic.

S-*ensuous* love scenes are explicit and leave nothing to the imagination.

E-*rotic* love scenes are explicit, leave nothing to the imagination, and are high in volume per the overall word count. E-rated titles might contain material that some readers find objectionable — in other words, almost anything goes, sexually. E-rated titles are the most graphic titles we carry in terms of both sexual language and descriptiveness in these works of literature.

X-*treme* titles differ from E-rated titles only in plot premise and storyline execution. Stories designated with the letter X tend to contain difficult or controversial subject matter not for the faint of heart.

Contents

HER LANCE-ALOT

Delilah Devlin

જી

Chapter One
England 1154 AD

ဢ

"Another flagon of ale!" The new lord of Beckwith Keep slammed his empty cup on the wooden table. A serving wench tripped in her haste to reach him, spilling more ale onto the table than into his hammered silver chalice. He ignored her dismay and planted his elbow in the puddle, tilting back his head to take a long draw of warm ale.

"Perhaps you should curb your thirst."

Lord Roland Du Bary cast a baleful eye at his friend, Dougal Fitzhugh. "Why ever for?"

"The wedding night is still to come. Are you not afraid your ardor will flag?"

Roland licked the foam from the hairs that curved over his upper lip. "A little ale has never impeded me in bedsport. Not once have I failed to rouse my staff when the occasion called." He cast a glance at his bride. The shy little miss had taken a seat further down the table. Her hair, neither blonde nor brown but all the pleasing shades of a pheasant's tail feathers, hung in a long curtain to her hips. "Besides, my wife inspires me sufficiently."

"Aye, you are a lucky man. You've a fine keep and lands — and a comely wife."

His gaze still on his young bride, Roland replied, "She seems a pleasant mouse. Although methinks she tends to overimbibe. Her cheeks are quite flushed already."

"Why say you she is a mouse?"

"She's so timid, she has not once looked me in the eye."

"Perhaps she is put off by your ill looks," Dougal said with a laugh.

Disgruntled, Roland straightened his shoulders. "My looks haven't a thing to do with it. My sword arm and my fame as a warrior are all she's concerned with."

"You only met the girl today. How do you know this?"

"Why, you heard her. When she greeted us at the steps of this keep, all she could say was, '*You* are Sir Roland Du Bary? The king's knight?' And she looked me up and down as though she could scarce believe her good fortune."

"Just how many flagons of ale had you quaffed before this scintillating conversation with your beloved?"

"Not a one, as you well know. And it is *wedded wife*. I would caution you to get that aright. There will be no *love*. Love is for weaklings and puny courtiers who fawn over a lady, read her poetry and sing, just so that they might stand close enough to stare down her gown at her tits."

"Then you've experience with that sort of endeavor?"

"I haven't the time for such nonsense. Thanks be to God, my dear wife is a more sensible sort."

"How do you know this? You spoke to the lass for less time than you took to throw your reins to the stableboy."

"I know she is sensible, even-tempered and appropriately submissive. She stared at my feet the entire time we spoke." An intriguing thought crept into his brain. Perhaps, his wife had been studying the size of his feet...

"Then have a care for your wife's tender sensibilities. She is only fresh from the convent."

Roland shuddered. A virgin. An appalling thought. "Think you I would cause her harm?"

"She's not built to take the likes of a beast like you. Go easy on the drink or you'll forget yourself."

"Bah! She's a woman. All are made to sheathe a man's sword." Roland scratched his beard then looked down the table at his meek bride. Her skin shone as lustrous as a pearl. Would it be soft and creamy to his touch? Perhaps he should trim his rough beard. He lifted his sleeve to his face and sniffed. "Do you think I should bathe?"

His friend laughed and slapped his shoulder. "You smell like your horse. What woman wouldn't appreciate the aroma of an earthy man? It has only been three months since we last bathed."

A movement at the end of the table drew his gaze. His bride rose from her seat and without a backward glance left the hall with only her nurse in attendance. Laughter and loud cheers rose from the lower tables.

Not for the first time, he admired her straight back, the gentle curve of her waist and her round, firm bottom below.

"Seems your bride's as eager for the bedding as you, my friend," Dougal said, his tone teasing.

Unbidden, the thought crept into Roland's conscience—he'd never before bedded a gentlewoman.

* * * * *

"I won't have him!" Lady Margaret Du Bary had worked herself into a high state of indignation. "You'll just have to tell the king. He can beat me, starve me, tie me to a stake and whip me 'til I'm bloody—but I won't have the brute!"

Her nurse, Grania, watched her mistress's pacing with interest. "Why ever not, milady? Lord Roland appears to be a strong man and well respected by his men and king."

"Strong? Oh yes, *strong smelling*! He reeks of horses and sweat. Why, he stood in dung when we met and he never noticed!"

Grania folded her arms over her ample chest. "His horse was last to enter the bailey. That he honors his men with such an act speaks well of him."

"That beast of a man stood in horse shite while the king's priest said our marriage rites *and he never noticed*!" Margaret's words grew louder until she shouted her displeasure.

"If it is only his aroma," Grania replied calmly, fighting a smile, "a bath will solve that problem and would likely be appreciated by your new husband."

"A bath is only the beginning of what would appease me. Did you see his hair *and his beard*? His fluff sticks out around his head like a big bear. And if he didn't eat for a week, he could live off the crumbs embedded in his fur." She stopped her pacing and stomped her foot. "*I'll not have him!*"

"Well, it isn't as if you were given a choice of husbands, my lamb. The king's instructions were quite clear. This knight will rule your keep. Your late father would have wanted this."

"My father cared nothing about me or this keep, or he would have stayed here to rule it himself instead of always following a fight."

Grania ignored her charge's familiar complaint. Her father hadn't cared enough to forge a bond with the child after the death of her mother. Thankfully, the girl didn't grieve too deeply at his loss. "Obviously, the king believes our new lord will be strong enough to hold this tiny corner of England. Roland Du Bary is your lord by *his* decree. What you make of this marriage and this man is up to you."

"I'll make nothing of him. I'll return to the convent—that's what I'll do. Before he has the chance to make me his wife in deed."

The stubborn glint in her eye worried Grania. The last time she'd seen that look had precipitated events resulting in her mistress's prompt expulsion from the convent.

"Hurry! Pack!" Lady Margaret plucked gowns and underclothes from their pegs on the wall and tossed them at Grania.

Grania paid her mistress no mind and rehung the clothing. Her lady could not return to the convent. The prioress would bolt the door if she saw who begged entrance.

The sounds of laughter and drunken shouts floated up from the hall. "Your husband will be here any moment and you're not prepared to greet him," Grania chided. "Would you shame the people of your keep? They barely know you now since you've just arrived from the convent. Will you have them thinking you're a mouse?"

Lady Margaret stomped her foot again. "The shame is not mine. *I...will...not...have...him!*"

'Twas then the old nurse noticed the sheen of moisture in her young charge's eyes and guessed the girl was afraid. "Now, lamb, perhaps he's not the man you imagined in your maiden's fantasies, but you are no squeamish miss either."

"He's far beneath the man I dreamed he'd be. Why, he lived for a time in Queen Eleanor's court." The young mistress's words cracked and her shoulders slumped. "I had hopes he would at least be clean."

"And you had hopes he would recite poetry and sing you songs."

Lady Margaret gave a dismissive wave of her hand. "I'd dreamed his hair was golden and his manner would be...pleasant. The man belched at my table!" she whispered furiously.

"Most men belch." Grania cut to the heart of what she believed was the cause of her mistress's distress. "Are you afraid of the bedding?"

"I'm not completely ignorant. I've seen animals mate." Lady Margaret's fierce expression grew dubious. "I know what is to come, but I never thought he'd be quite so...large."

"Ah love." Grania hugged her. "Every girl has fears of her first time. You're a smart one. You've only to apply your wits to ensure your husband takes care with you."

"Think you he will listen? Did you see how much ale he consumed?"

"Well, think on that. Doesn't Elspeth complain that her husband's...oak—"

"Grania!"

Grania waved her hand. "'Tis not the time for maidenly airs. The men are coming up the steps even now. Elspeth says when her husband is in his cups, he cannot sustain a..." She searched for a word other than the coarse one that first came to mind.

"Wood?"

"Yes!" Grania replied, flustered with the topic of their conversation, having never experienced a man's ardor. "You've only to ply him with more ale and get him into a hot bath. His...limb will wilt like a willow branch and he'll be unable to claim you."

"But what of the morning?"

"Tomorrow is another day, love."

Margaret's eyes widened. "We could wait until daylight and slip out of the keep." Her mistress hugged Grania. "Whatever would I do without you?"

Have children? Live a long life? Grania pushed aside her morbid thoughts. If the new lord was half the man she believed, Lady Margaret might not be so eager to leave in the morning. And she'd witnessed how her lady's gaze had clung to his tall, broad frame as he'd approached the keep—before he'd dismounted. "Quickly, now. Remove your clothing. You must appear willing. I'll order a bath brought to this chamber." Grania helped her untie the knots at the side of her bliaut and drew it over her head, and then swept away her undergown. "Now, put on this robe."

As soon as the robe was belted tightly around Margaret's slim waist, the door to the chamber burst open. Lord Roland stood in the doorway, his arms braced on either side, holding back the crowd of boisterous revelers. "Good even, wife," his deep voice boomed.

Margaret kept her gaze on the floor, afraid her intentions would be written on her face. It would serve her better to have Roland continue to believe her a submissive mouse. With a quick glance upward, she nodded her greeting, then her gaze fell away again.

That one look had her knees shaking. With the knot at the neck of his cotte undone and his hair sticking up in spikes around his head, she feared he might be too far gone with drink to fall in with her plan.

"We should inspect your bride for impediments," Dougal Fitzhugh his sly friend said and pushed his way past Lord Roland, opening a passage for the rest of the party to spill into the room.

"Aye, let's have a bedding!" "Aye!" "Take off her clothes, Lord Roland!"

Margaret bristled with rage and felt heat stain her cheeks.

"Take off your robe, wife. I'll not have any say you are not a fit bride for me," her new lord said, his voice a deep rumble within his broad chest.

Humiliation causing her hands to shake, Margaret fumbled with the belt, but finally she shed the robe, allowing it to puddle at her feet. *Please don't let the oaf be overcome with lust and take me now!*

"Her breasts are small, but even-sized and nicely placed," Dougal said.

Her husband didn't comment. She dared a glance and found his gaze fixed on the juncture of her thighs. "Turn around," he said, his voice sounding strained.

Knowing she had no alternative but compliance with his command, Margaret fisted her hands at her sides and slowly turned.

"She has fine, broad hips," the priest pronounced. "She'll carry strong sons to serve our king."

"A lovely arse she has, Lord Roland!" "Aye, on to the bedding!"

Completing the turn, Margaret lifted her chin. "I, too, would know there is no impediment to our marriage, *milord*."

"Oh ho!" Dougal chortled. "She's eager to see your manstaff."

Roland scowled at his friend, color rising from his neck to flush his face. With a glare that expunged her small flare of triumph, he stripped his shirt over his head, knelt to remove his boots and chausses and then dropped his braies to the floor.

Immediately, Margaret realized her bid to humiliate him had failed. He stood proudly before her, his body sun-bronzed, except for the pale swath at his hips, a testament to his years of physical training out of doors.

Her mouth dry as dust, her gaze swept over his broad, hairy chest and arms, noting the play of shadow and candlelight on his deeply muscled flesh. She blinked, unwilling to linger over what rose from between his legs, and stared at his large feet, at the lightly furred toes and up his strong ankles and calves to his massive thighs. Naked, he was more formidable than he'd appeared when she'd first seen him, fully clothed, helmeted and wearing heavy mail.

Calling herself a coward, she drew in a deep breath and inspected his manflesh. She'd seen other men's dangling parts since she'd arrived at the keep and had never been impressed. The part that was their pride seemed vulnerable and awkward. Her husband's, however, rose straight and strong from a nest of curly, dark brown hair. It terrified her.

"T-turn," she stammered.

Hands on his hips, he presented his backside, yet another view of masculine strength and pride. The wide V of his back narrowed at the waist, and his round, muscular buttocks looked anything but foolish. Dear Lord, and she had thought to control him. "I see no impediment," she whispered.

He turned to face her once again, and Margaret fought to keep her gaze anywhere but on his "limb".

"There being no impediment to this marriage," Dougal said, "on to the bedding!"

"Aye, give her a swive!"

Roland watched the color drain from his bride's face. He'd thought she might swoon when she'd first stared at his cock. Now, she looked terrified. Dougal's levity and the growing din from their witnesses caused her eyes to widen until the whites framed her fine gray eyes.

"Wait!" she cried out. "I haven't seen all of him. I would know there is no deformity." She swept her hand upward, pointing at his face. "I would see him beardless."

If he hadn't seen her fear, he might have laughed with the rest of the buffoons. Instead, he lifted his hand to his beard and scratched. "If it will remove the last of your doubts, then aye, I'll give up my beard, though I don't know how I'll warm my face in winter."

Her relief was not flattering.

"Move aside, you louts. Make way!" Lady Margaret's old nurse called from beyond the wall of bodies crowding the chamber doorway. When a narrow path cleared, she strode inside, followed by two burly men carrying a large metal tub and a trail of women bearing buckets of steaming water. "Your bath, milord."

Seeing another plot afoot to delay his enjoyment of his shy bride, Roland decided a bath might be just the thing to calm his rampant erection and soothe his bride's nerves. "A bath is a fine idea. My wife will attend me."

Her startled gaze told him of her dismay.

"Now the rest of you, *out!*"

"Nay!" "What of the bedding?" "On to the bedding!"

"There must be witnesses when you take your bride," Dougal murmured.

Roland watched his wife's tightly clenched fists. "We will display the sheets in the morning. My word she was a virgin and that the deed is done will be enough."

Dougal gave him a curious look and nodded. "Come, men! The ale is below. Let's go raise a cup to our lord's potency." With not so gentle shoves, he hastened the rowdy crowd's exit.

Except for the sound of water sloshing as it was poured into the copper tub by servants, silence descended on those remaining in the chamber.

His bride knelt to pick up her robe from the floor.

"You won't be needing that," he said. At her wary glance, he added, "You'll only wet your clothing. Leave it off."

"But I'm cold." Her nipples were tightly beaded, but not from the cold, he'd wager. She still assiduously avoided looking at his cock.

"We'll add wood to the brazier."

"Milord, is the temperature of your bath to your liking?" the old nurse asked, reminding him there were others still in the room.

He walked to the tub and bent to trail his fingers in the water. Steam rose from the surface. "It's perfect. You may leave us now."

"As you wish," she replied after a pointed glance at her mistress. The other servants followed in her wake.

Now that the two of them were alone, Roland studied his bride's body more closely. Dougal had thought her breasts small but well placed on her chest. Roland thought them perfect— round as apples, tipped with ripened berries. Indeed, the small nipples pointed north so that a man need only lean down to sip upon their stems. Her waist was small and neat and flared into rounded hips. The dark down between her thighs looked soft as silk, and Roland's groin tightened. He wondered whether the flesh her curling hair cloaked was as pink and succulent as her nipples.

Tonight, he'd dine on the freshest, lushest fruit in the kingdom—his bride's virgin flesh. But first, he had to overcome her maidenly fear. He had to convince her he wasn't a great, rutting bear. God's ballocks, but virgins were a true test of man's will!

"Attend me," he commanded, and he stepped over the rim of the tub and knelt in the narrow space. The water lapped at his hips and was hotter than he'd first thought, but it had the desired affect on his manroot. Almost immediately, the pressure building in his cock eased.

Lady Margaret hovered beside the tub behind him—out of his range of vision apurpose, he suspected.

"Would you care for more ale, milord? I've a pitcher warming next to the fire."

"I would be much obliged if you would pour me a cup," he replied, remembering his manners. Women seemed to prize a pretty turn of phrase or an unneeded thank you on occasion. Now that his erection no longer demanded he pounce upon her, he relaxed. The two of them, he and his unruly cock, had the entire night to woo his nervous wife.

A silver flagon was handed to him and he threw it back, draining nearly half the cup before holding it out to her. "Take it. I would have you wash me, now."

"P-perhaps, I could start with your hair."

"Whatever pleases you, my dear." The warm water and ale lulled his body. A pleasurable ease settled over him. Aye, he was a lucky man to own such a thoughtful wife. He envisioned many nights to come when he returned from battle or a hunt to find a warm bath and her lush little body ready to comfort his aches and wounds.

"Tilt your head back, milord. I can't reach you with this pitcher."

Water sluiced over his head. His indrawn breath whistled between his teeth, but he bit back the oath he would have shouted to spare his wife's tender feelings. The water was so hot his skin felt parboiled.

"Oh! It's too hot. I'm so sorry."

Before he could assure her she had not roasted him like a lamb on a spit, another pitcher of water was dumped over his head, this time so cold his fingers left their imprint on the sides of the tub. *Bloody hell!* If this was her version of a soothing bath, he'd wait until the next spring's thaw to wash his arse in the river!

From the corner of his eye, he saw her hand dip into a pot and bring out a dollop of soap. He grasped her wrist and tugged her forward. If he turned his head, her sweet nipple would brush his lips. Lord, she was a temptation. "I'll not smell like a flower," he said more harshly than he intended.

"I-it's scented with herbs only. Smell it."

He pulled her hand to his face and sniffed. The fragrance was pleasant, like green fields in springtime. "Very well," he said, releasing his hold.

"If you'll lean your head back again..."

Closing his eyes, he did so. Her hands glided over his hair, and then her fingers dug beneath to gently scrape his scalp. The sensation was so pleasurable, he moaned. "You've a gentle touch, wife," he said, remembering to give her praise.

"Thank you, milord," she said, her tight voice betraying her worry.

A smile tipped the corners of his lips. Aye, she should be alarmed. Her silken touch was countering the affects of the warm water and ale.

Margaret chewed on her lip, wondering how long she would have to wait for the water and the drink to strip his oak of its bark. In the meantime, she listened to his murmured praise and moans and wondered why his pleasure drew the tips of her nipples into hard points and made her woman's furrow moist.

Sweet Jesus! If merely touching his hair could do this, she would surely perish of ague if she were forced to bathe the rest of him!

Knowing she had already spent overlong washing his thick hair, she reached for another pitcher of water, this time testing the temperature to make sure she wouldn't cause him any discomfort—however satisfying his reactions had been with her first rinses. She poured the contents of another pitcher over his head and watched as the warm water rinsed the dirty, gray film from his hair. By the time she'd finished, she realized his hair was a deep chestnut color, with strands that glinted red in the candlelight.

"I'll scrub your back now," she said, hoping when she was done that he'd be satisfied and finish the rest himself. Her stomach was so tight, she felt as though she'd eaten a green apple.

He leaned forward and she dipped a cloth into the water, and then worked some of the herbal soap into lather before smoothing the rag over the broad expanse of his back. She scrubbed hard, partly hoping to cause him more discomfort, but mostly because she wanted the job done quickly. She didn't dare venture below the waterline. What little she understood about men's anatomy warned her that touching him *there* would render her plot useless. When she was finished, she held out the cloth to him.

He looked over his shoulder and didn't say a word. The arch of his eyebrow said it all. Blast his hide! His challenge laid down, she rinsed the cloth and applied more soap, and then circled the tub to face him.

Aware her breasts rose above the rim of the tub even though she knelt to hide the rest of her body from his knowing gaze, she laid the cloth against his chest and scoured his skin in circles. The cloth did not provide enough of a barrier between her palm and his hard chest. Everywhere she touched, she learned the hard contours of his muscles and the warmth of his skin.

Hers became so heated, she was sure she grew fevered. She knew her cheeks flushed and a glance downward confirmed her breasts suffered a similar malady.

Except for the ripples and spasms of his muscles as she cleaned his flesh, he never moved. But the heat of his gaze followed her everywhere, scorching her lips, burning the tips of her breasts, and lower, when she rose on her knees to scrub his shoulders and underarms.

She reached for his left hand, intent on digging dirt from beneath his nails, and didn't notice at first when his right hand slipped softly over the top of her breast. When she did, her breath caught and held, and then her gaze rose to his face.

His expression was hard and assessing, and then his fingers glided lower until they smoothed over her nipple.

Margaret forgot how to breathe. Her breast tightened, almost to the point of pain, but she didn't want him to stop, until his thumb and forefinger plucked her nipple. Then she jumped and placed her hand over his to make him halt.

Without saying a word, Lord Roland returned his hand to the edge of the tub and he leaned back his head, his chest rising sharply with his indrawn breath.

Taking it as a cue to resume his bath, she washed his neck and around his ears and tried to ignore the disturbing sound of his breaths and the rigid muscles beneath her fingertips.

Thankful when at last her task was done, she rinsed his chest and back and sat back on her haunches.

A small, tight smile and a shake of his head brought a surge of anger boiling to the surface. She was becoming ill, and he wanted to be bathed like a babe!

"You've missed a few spots, wife," he said, his voice like silk and gravel.

You pompous, sodding b— She bit back the retort. Her reticence was her only defense left. "I've cleaned behind your ears and under your arms. Surely I'm finished now."

"I would have you cleanse the rest of me. It will help you overcome your fear of my body. You'll find I'm made like any other man." With that, he gripped the sides of the tub and hauled himself up to stand in the center. She glanced a long way up his body and her heart stopped.

His "limb" didn't droop like a willow's.

Chapter Two

ဢ

Roland hesitated at the flare of panic in his young bride's eyes. In his experience, fear was an impediment to useful congress between two people. Having no experience with marriage, he suspected the same held true for bedding virgins—and especially for any hopes of repeating the act before dawn!

Inwardly, he sighed. Introducing his wife to her new duties would be much akin to breaking a horse to halter. He'd have to gentle her with his voice and hands.

His body leapt eagerly ahead to the hands part of the gentling process—his staff grew measurably more alert.

Frustration gripped his body hard. "Don't just gape! Gather the soap and wash the rest of me...*wife!*" *So much for gentling her with my voice.* "Ballocks!" he muttered.

Trembling as she stood, her eyes never rose above the wayward flesh straining from his groin.

"You may start here," he said, pointing to his backside, hoping to give her time to gather her courage again while he fought for control over his cock.

No use dispensing his seed into the bathwater when her lovely body needed only priming to receive him.

A frown creased the narrow space between Margaret's eyebrows, but she grabbed up the cloth once more and worked another dollop of soap into the fabric, rubbing so long, he was sure the fabric frayed. But he let her take her time to accustom herself to the idea of the task—and so that she could continue eying him thoroughly as she did now.

Familiarity would ease her fear—*and perhaps feed her desire.* After all, he was a well-formed man, or so the women he'd bedded in the past had said.

When her small hand scrubbed the cloth across his buttocks in sharp, quick strokes, he flexed, ensuring she noted the play of muscle beneath his flesh.

Her soft gasp was gratifying, as was her hand pausing over the larger muscles to cup him, stroking downward, slowly now, as though she savored the feel of his flanks.

He widened his legs, bracing his feet as far apart as the tub would allow. "Be sure to scrub in between," he said, suppressing a smile.

Her hand snuck between his legs, a timid foray, just glancing against his balls, and then smoothed back, her cloth-covered palm cupping him.

Roland gritted his teeth. At this slow rate, his balls would be blue and his cock hard enough to drive a pillion through stone.

When her other hand parted his buttocks to allow her access to stroke between, he groaned aloud. The rough cloth glanced against his back entrance, and his cock jerked.

"Oh, did I hurt you?"

"You're damn near making me a eunuch, love," he said between gritted teeth. "Come around the front and be done with it."

As she circled the tub, her expression became more tense, her cheeks fiery. He wondered if that would be her look when he drove into her, stroking her toward ecstasy. "Dispense with the cloth."

Her eyes widened. "Am I finished?"

"My manstaff will be too sensitive to the coarseness of the cloth."

"Then I'm finished?"

Her hopeful expression amused him. Baiting the wench was proving great sport. "Of course not. Use your hands."

Margaret's brows drew together in a fearsome frown for a moment, before she dragged in a deep breath and smoothed her features.

That hint of anger stirred the devil inside him. *Can I stir that flame hotter?* "And be careful not to bring the soap near the head."

"Head?" she asked, her voice sounding strangled.

He reached down and circled the end of his cock with his thumb and forefinger, lifting it to her gaze. "This is the head."

She sniffed. "It looks like a mushroom to me. Why would one call it otherwise?"

The contrast of her prim tone and naked, lush body nearly had him groaning again. "It's called the head because at times it behaves like a man with a will of his own. And this is its eye," he said, stroking his thumb over the tiny hole.

"The eye?"

"Look closely at the tip. See you the narrow hole?"

A milky drop of excitement glistened, obscuring the eye, so he wiped it with his thumb, smearing it over the soft tip. "Do you understand now?" he asked softly.

Her gaze lingered, and Roland's balls drew closer to his body.

She nodded. "No soap in the eye." Then her eyelids dipped. "What would happen if I did…get soap in the eye?"

"The lye would burn me."

Her lips pressed into a determined line, and she dipped her fingers into the soap dish. She worked a thin lather between her palms. Then she stood beside him and grasped him near the root.

Roland closed his eyes and let his head fall back.

Her hands were small, but strong, and stroked and twisted on his shaft as she cleansed him. But these weren't the quick swipes she'd delivered before. She loitered over the task. Was she becoming aroused? Had his ploy to accustom her to his body worked?

He pumped his hips, tunneling his cock between her palms, and her grasp loosened for a moment before encircling him again.

His hands moved restlessly at his sides, his fists clenching and releasing, his cock gliding faster. Until he realized he was nigh to bursting from the drugging motions of her hands.

He turned to face her, just the length of his staff between them, and saw another flare of panic in his wife's eyes.

But he was close now and not caring how he might frighten her. He'd soothe her upset later. He gripped her shoulders, finding her skin just the thing to fill his restless hands, and pumped faster, his gaze falling to her slim fingers as they glided up and down his cock.

She stroked higher up his shaft then back down, tugging him now—and he felt much like a stallion on a lead, not yet broke to harness. His hips bucked, his body straining closer to release.

Then she clasped the head of his cock, and his toes curled into the metal bottom of the tub. His fingers dug into her soft shoulders.

When her fingers caressed the bulb, the "mushroom", a little trickle of lye slipped into his eye.

Roland sucked in a deep breath, his rise halted in one blistering oath as the inside of his cock caught fire. "God's Ballocks!"

Her hands fell away, and she took a step back, her face pale as parchment. "I'm sorry, milord. Have I caused you pain?"

Roland bit his tongue against the litany of curses crowding the back of his throat. But the sight of her wringing her soapy hands and chewing the edge of her lip had him dragging in a deep breath. "I think I'm clean enough, my dear," he choked out, waving her away.

Then he lowered himself back into the tub, gingerly letting his cock submerge to rinse away the last traces of the stinging soap.

While the fire licking the inside of his cock cooled, his ardor waned, and he was able to view her innocent error more clearly and see it as a gift. A woman's first experience with a man's passion ought not to be with his seed striping her face and belly.

"Shall I shave your beard for you now?"

Roland shuddered, a vision of his throat split open like a fish's gullet skittering through his mind. "Bring me a sharp knife. I'll do it myself."

Margaret brought him a steaming-hot towel.

"Thank you, wife." He pressed the towel to his beard to soften the coarse hair and shot her a curious gaze. "Shaved many men?"

She pursed her lips and shook her head. "None. But I watched my mother shave my father."

"And you thought to start with me?"

One fine brow arched in a look that held a hint of challenge. "Why, are you nervous?"

"Petrified." He held his hand out for the knife she brought him, then ran his thumb across the edge to test its sharpness. "Have you a mirror?"

She presented a polished silver mirror and held it up for him while he shaved, dipping his knife into his bathwater to clear the blade between strokes.

When he scraped the last of his bushy beard and mustache away, his wife gasped. He ran his hand over his chin and glanced up at her.

The sacrifice of his fine beard was well worth her look of wonder. Roland grinned. "Do I have a weak chin?"

She shook her head.

"Any deformity that will cause you to lose your supper?"

She grimaced and cast him a glare. "You know well you have a handsome face."

Roland chuckled at her disgruntled tone.

She turned and started toward the brazier again, giving him her back.

"You wanted an ugly husband?"

"I wanted an impediment," she muttered just loud enough for him to hear.

But she must have misspoken. "Well now you may be satisfied." Roland stood and stepped out of the tub. "Bring a cloth to dry me." Then remembering the pretty words, added, "Please."

She sighed and hurried over with a square of linen, her gaze on his wilted staff. Her expression—both relieved and with another emotion he had a harder time defining—was almost comical.

Did she think he'd be unable to make her his wife this night? "Never fear, Margaret," he said, smiling to reassure her. "He will rouse again."

She stumbled as she approached, but kept her eyes downcast. He thought he heard a low curse, but her sweet lips were pressed into a thin line when she looked up.

Roland kept his gaze above her head as she wiped him dry. When she came to the areas that caused her the greatest embarrassment, she looked away and daubed, joggling his cock roughly. "Have a care wife. You've already held him in your hands—can you not look at what you dry?"

"I'm a gently bred lady, milord," she said, her words gusting as though she was out of breath. "Convent-raised. 'Tis a sin for me to see you bare as the day you were born."

"This is no sin when we are wed. 'Tis your duty to obey me—and I command you to be at ease. You may look your fill, woman. Accustom yourself to the sight of me." He gave her a sly sideways glance. "You may also touch whatever you've a mind to."

She gasped and tossed the towel at his head and stomped toward the brazier where she made a great show of warming her hands. "Insufferable ass!" she muttered.

Perhaps she hadn't misspoken before. Roland enjoyed her small display of pique, relieved she proved she held a little fire beneath her pretty, placid face. He had thought a meek, malleable creature would suit him well, but this wench stirred his blood—and his cock, for it unfurled. "Margaret, love?"

She remained faced away.

"I'll warm you soon enough," he said, letting his voice drop to a silky growl. "Come away from the fire. I find I'm impatient now to feel your soft body beneath me."

Her back stiffened, and she peeked over her shoulder. Her glance fell to his manhood. "But I'm frozen through, milord." Her voice sounded as though she strangled.

He strode toward the bed and settled himself on the edge, and then patted the mattress beside him. "Come, my dear. It is too late to pray for intervention. 'Tis time we do this deed."

Margaret hated the little smile that curved his wicked, *well-formed* lips. He patted the bed as though encouraging a pup to jump up beside him.

Margaret was no dog to jump to his bidding—no matter how handsome her master might be. She still felt a little breathless at how well the man had cleaned up. His bushy beard had hidden a broad, square jaw with a cleft at the center of his chin. But he was still a ruffian, and she was very nearly his wife, unless she could find a way to deflect his intent in the next few moments.

Unfortunately, the way his gaze raked over her body told her he wouldn't be easily dissuaded. She had to try. She couldn't surrender her freedom or her will so easily to this oaf. "But I'm ill, milord. I'd not want to give you what I have."

"Ill?"

She nodded quickly. "Fevered."

"As am I," he said, his smile stretching wider. "See how well we suit?"

She very nearly stomped her foot, but suspected her jiggling flesh would only increase his mirth. "Truly, milord. My skin is hot, my breasts ache and my belly feels as though I've swallowed green apples. I think I'm dying."

A guffaw gusted from him, shaking his shoulders. "And I've the remedy," he said, laughing so hard he doubled over with it.

"You mock me!" she hissed.

"No, no," he said, gasping. "Your innocence pleases me, Margaret."

She stomped her foot. "You are pleased I'm ill?" she asked, her voice rising.

"You aren't sickening, love. You're experiencing desire."

"I most certainly am not!"

As she had feared, her anger only increased his merriment. He chuckled and leaned back on the mattress, resting on his elbows—which gave her an alarming view of his broad, hairy chest and the oak branch rising from his groin. The thought fluttered across her mind that the man had muscle on his muscles, so ropey and defined were the ridges that crossed his belly and striped his thighs. Her nipples prickled.

Her husband's dark gaze swept over her nude body. "Your breasts dimple because they reach for my touch."

Margaret's mouth gaped for a moment. Then she snapped her jaw shut. "They most certainly do n—"

"Your skin flushes as your blood rushes to ready the places where our flesh will join." He ignored her sputtered denials. "And your belly tightens, anticipating our joining."

She shook her head, her eyes widening. "I'm a good girl. I do not lust for you, milord."

"Lust is God's way of giving us reward for what we are duty-bound to fulfill."

"You're talking about…the *begetting,*" she said, feeling her lips twist with disgust.

"Yes, it's time to *beget.*" He did it again—*patted the bed beside him!* "Come sit beside me. I promise not to pounce."

But his expression didn't reassure her. His dark eyes glittered, spots of color sat high on his cheekbones and his jaw flexed, the jerking muscle belying his relaxed pose.

She lifted her chin. "Will you touch?"

"Without a doubt." He raised one eyebrow. "But so may you."

Her resolve to escape began to crumble beneath the knowledge that their joining was inevitable. This man was as stubborn as a jackass. "You will not wait until I am more familiar with you?"

Roland shook his head. "By morning, my sweet, we must show proof of our union."

"You mean you must make me bleed." Her voice trembled.

"There will not be a great puddle of it—just a small smear."

"But I will feel pain."

"Only a little—if I do my job well in preparing you to accept me."

He sounded so assured, her suspicion was aroused. "You've deflowered many virgins?"

"Never."

"Then how can you know?"

"I know I don't want to harm or frighten you."

His quiet reassurance calmed the last butterflies fluttering in her belly.

He sat up and lifted one hand, palm up. "Come."

Margaret dragged her feet, walking toward the bed, her heart pounding so loud she was sure the lout could hear it. She turned and slid onto the mattress, taking care not to touch her thigh to his. This close, she felt even more aware of her nudity, and so very small and inconsequential next to his large, powerful frame.

His "limb" grew in proportion as she stared at his lap. *He will split me in two with that great trunk of his!*

He placed his hand on her knee and patted her. "All will be well."

He does think I am a dog! If he asks me to fetch, I'll bite him. But his palm warmed her skin, and his fingers curved around her thigh to slip between her legs.

Margaret stiffened, her breaths coming so fast now she felt lightheaded. Each pant drew in his freshened scent, not as repulsive as it was before, deep into her lungs.

He traced the line where her thighs pressed together to just beneath her sex.

"You may breathe, love," he whispered and slipped his fingers deeper between, scraping his fingertips along the edges of her nether lips.

No, she couldn't breathe—not with his fingers snug against her…woman's part. Then moisture leaked from inside her to wet her curls and his fingers circled, drawing more liquid in an embarrassing quantity. "Stop!" She covered his hand with hers.

He nodded and pulled away, stretching out over the mattress. "If you don't want me to touch, you will touch me."

"But why must we touch? Can't you just…"

"Mount you and rut like an animal?"

Her eyes rounded. "Well, put like that—"

"Believe me, I'm so hard I could hammer a post with my staff, but you are a virgin." His face grew still. "You are, aren't you?"

"Milord! I am convent-raised!"

He snorted. "I've swived a blessed sister or two in my time. Means naught…so, a virgin it is." He sighed. "Let's get on to the touching. You may begin wherever you wish."

Although sitting this close to his rangy frame inspired a fierce curiosity, she remained firm. "I've no desire to touch you. I fear, sirrah, that we are at an impasse."

His gaze swept over her, pausing once more on her curls. "I'll have you before this night is through. I am a patient man when the situation needs, but know this—by morning, you will surrender your virginity and your body to me."

Margaret forced her mouth into a straight line rather than the pout that threatened to pucker her lower lip. She'd tried every tactic she knew to delay this moment.

Perhaps Grania was right. Maybe God had other plans for her.

She closed her eyes tight. "I am ready, milord."

"No, you're not, love."

She opened one eye and peeked down at her husband.

The smile that curved the corners of his lips was at once rueful and pained.

"Well, is there something I must do? I've told you I'm ready."

"Lie back and open your legs, my dear."

Her eyebrows shot up. If she did as he asked, he'd be able to look into a part of her she'd never seen. The tips of her breasts tingled again.

She lay back and spread her legs a few inches, and then held her breath.

He sighed. "Well, that's a start." His hand lifted and settled on the curve of one breast.

Heat surrounded the globe and her nipple puckered.

His thumb rasped over the sensitive tip and Margaret shivered. "Like that, do you?"

"I'm cold," she replied, not willing to let him know how much turmoil his touch stirred in her body.

He shook his head and bent over her, shocking her thoroughly when he took her nipple into his mouth and suckled her like a babe.

She might have laughed at the odd sight if a rush of red-hot heat, like a smithy's poker, hadn't shot from her breast to her belly. She gasped and her hips pulsed upward.

He groaned, the sound vibrating on her breast. Then he drew back and flickered his tongue on her other breast.

So overwhelmed with sensation, she could only squirm and gasp beneath him.

Then one massive thigh slid over her legs, and his knee inserted itself between hers. The crinkly hairs covering his leg tickled the insides of her thighs, and she opened further. He pressed another knee between and she widened again, now not caring that her sex was fully open to the marauder above her—and weeping for his caress.

He moved up her body and smoothed back her hair. Below, the soft mushroom head butted against her overheated flesh. The sound their sexes made as they met was succulent, gasping.

"Margaret?"

Her breath hitched at the thickness pressing at her entrance. "Hmm?"

"You're ready now," he growled.

A trembling started in her lower belly. "I'm certain I'm not."

He pushed inside, stretching her with just the rounded end of his…stump.

"Jesus, Mary…" He withdrew until his flesh barely kissed her furrow.

"That's better," she gasped. "Is it over yet?"

His shoulders shook and he rested his forehead on her shoulder. "Love, we've barely begun."

"Oh." *He means to do that again?* She braced herself.

"You wound me with your lack of enthusiasm."

"Why are you dallying?" she asked, holding herself rigid against the agony she was sure to experience once he rammed the rest of his sex inside her.

"Never have I heard of a virgin so eager to get the deed done."

Forcing unconcern into her voice, she said, "The sooner you finish, the sooner I may bathe."

He lifted his head and his brow furrowed. "You feel unclean? Lord, tell me you're not overzealously religious."

"I'm not overzealous." *Could this slacken his determination?* "Would that be a bad thing?"

"It would spoil your enjoyment—but I'd strive to do my duty by you," he said his tone wryly amused.

She huffed, irritated now with his unwavering resolve. "All this talk of duty. Methinks it's just a man's excuse for frequent coupling."

"True." He grinned down at her. "Do you feel better now?"

She nodded and realized it was true. Their silly conversation had taken the bite out of her fear. "I'm not frightened any longer."

"Thanks be to God." He nudged her again…down there.

Margaret took a deep breath and made herself relax as he tunneled into her, pushing deeper than before, stretching her inner walls to accommodate his intrusion.

"You can hold onto me."

The way he growled his words sent a shiver through her. She met his gaze, questioning.

"Put your arms around me." His voice sounded more strained now. His cheeks were flushed, his jaw tight.

She reached around his broad back and found his skin was soft and stretched over muscle as hard as an iron shield. Her fingers smoothed over him, exploring his texture, enjoying the ripples that rolled beneath her palms as he started to move.

"Yes, sweetheart. Touch me," he whispered.

She reached lower to his amazing buttocks and glided her hands over the rounded muscles. Remembering her first sight of his pale, powerful backside, she could scarce believe she clutched it, her palms curving to bring him closer, her nails digging into his flesh to urge him deeper. The urgent itch growing inside her seemed to assuage with his movement.

Roland grunted and pumped in and out, stroking deeper each time.

Margaret squirmed a bit and discovered that if she tilted her hips, he slid straight and unimpeded. She raised her knees and hugged his hips with her inner thighs.

"That's it. Move with me."

Margaret didn't understand what he asked, but friction built inside her tight channel, tingling hot. This time when liquid flooded her, she sighed her relief, for his movements were aided with the lubrication and the snugness seemed to ease.

He flexed and pulled out, then paused.

She moaned and gripped his waist tight. As close to a complaint as she would allow herself to make.

"I'm going to hurt you love—just this once."

She marveled over the trembling that shook his shoulders as he hovered above her. Never would she believe he strained to support his own weight. Then she remembered what he'd said and her heart lurched. "Hurt me?"

"Your maidenhead."

"Oh!" She met his gaze, not wanting him to see her sudden fear. "I'm ready."

"Good girl." He kissed her lips. "Now, wrap your legs around me."

She did so, slowly and awkwardly, aware that once again the angle of their joining changed. It felt more natural—and cozy. Wrapped tightly together, they were as close as two people could be.

He stroked once, deeper than before, and tapped something inside her that halted his progress. "Damnation!"

She held her breath as he stroked back inside—this time thrusting sharp against the barrier until it tore.

Margaret gasped and jerked her hips backward, trying to escape the pain that burned like fire. But he followed her movement, sliding deeper inside, filling her channel to bursting. "We're finished now?" she asked, a sob hitching her breath.

He nestled his hips closer to hers, prodding deeper still.

Was there no end to him?

He lowered himself on top of her, settling his frame like a blanket over her body.

Margaret was at once warmed, head to toe, and overwhelmed by all that masculine strength surrounding her, filling her. Tears pricked her eyes, and she blinked to clear them.

His hands cupped her cheeks and urged her gaze to his. "I've no experience with virgins, and I know I'm a rough man. But if you tell me you've more pain than you can bear, I'll stop now."

Margaret glanced away from the intensity of his stare. "The deed is done?"

"Yes."

She felt his body tense above hers. He'd fulfilled his *duty*, but didn't want to end their joining. "There's more?"

"If you want it."

She could tell he certainly did by the tension that made his body rigid. "Will it be painful for me?"

"Perhaps a bit at first, but it will ease. You may even come to enjoy it."

That gave her pause. If the itch and heat she'd felt were only a hint of the discomforts she would experience…

But was his eagerness to bed her something she could use as leverage in this one-sided relationship? Something that might give her some small portion of power so that she wouldn't be swallowed whole by his needs and commands.

Margaret stroked her hand down his back and watched his nostrils flare. She licked her lips as she'd often seen the dairymaid do when she sauntered past the knights.

Roland's avid gaze followed the slow swipe of her tongue.

She tightened her legs around his waist and discovered that her inner muscles could clench him tight as well.

Her husband shuddered and his eyes closed.

Perhaps, if God hadn't given her the knight of her dreams, she held the means to mold him into a more suitable husband.

With another feminine squeeze, she whispered into his ear, "Teach me, husband. Teach me how to please you."

Chapter Three

ଞ

Roland congratulated himself. He'd persevered despite her trepidation. He'd been firm, but gentle, with her initiation into the marriage bed. His reward for his patience and consideration manifested in her soft, husky voice and the snug clasp of her legs as she drew him closer into her embrace.

Teach me how to please you.

He'd nearly spilled his seed inside her heated depths then and there. Could a man ask for more than a wife eager to learn her duties? Eager to fulfill his needs?

But they were far from finished, and he still had to prove that her confidence in his ability and his gentleness wasn't misplaced.

Despite the moist warmth that surrounded his cock and the capitulation that shown in her wide, curious eyes, he tamped down the urge to plunge deeply, harshly inside her. Instead, he ground his teeth and pulled away.

"Can you not continue?" she asked, her hands clutching at his back.

He barely concealed his snort and pressed a quick kiss to her pouting lips, determined to draw on his arsenal of sexual knowledge learned in the beds of many women to deliver to his new wife an experience beyond her belief.

Perhaps the way to cement her devotion would be to provide her satisfaction. That his own body clamored for release was an impediment, but he would carry on. And Lord, this first time, he wanted to see delight rather than fear or pain in her expression. Her sweet features would soften and glow with pleasure before he took his own.

"Let go with your legs," he rasped.

Her brows drew together—confusion and impatience warring in her expression. "But—"

"Trust me."

Slowly, she lowered her legs to the bed and her arms fell to her sides, sweeping over the sheets as though looking for a place to brace herself. She must have read the intent in his eyes because her eyes widened.

Was his expression feral, hard-edged? Because he certainly felt like an animal. All of his body was primed to pounce. She brought every low instinct to the fore. Something in her quiet watchfulness—her delicately flaring nose, the downward curve of her pink lips... Lord, was there nothing about her that didn't make him hard?

Her breath hitched—a soft, delicate gasp that only tightened his balls closer to his groin. But he slid down her body and latched onto a rosy, puckered nipple and drew softly. When a hand clasped the back of his head to pull him closer, he obliged and suckled harder, drawing a delicate moan from her sweet lips.

Her legs moved restlessly against him. Her thighs quivered along his flanks. He moved to the other breast and ignored her breathless cry when he nipped the flaring bud and pulled it between his teeth to lavish it with wet strokes from his tongue.

Never had he given more than a passing thought to the delight he could wring from a woman by merely playing with her breasts, but Margaret's excited little gasps kept him there, sucking, biting, lapping at her stems until her thighs splayed wide and her belly trembled and pulsed.

Her innocent invitation didn't go unnoticed, and his groin tightened. Roland drilled his cock into the bedding for relief. When he moved further down her belly, he pressed kisses to her soft skin, tongued her belly button and then glided lower still.

As his lips met the soft, curling hairs at the top of her sex, her hands slid between them and she covered herself. Her thighs clasped his sides tight. "What do you think you're doing?" she asked, her voice high and strained as she tried unsuccessfully to close off access to her femininity.

He bit back a grin, knowing he'd probably shocked her to her toes, and gave his scowling brown mouse a hot glare. "Open your legs for me, love," he said, growling, liking the hectic color that tinted her cheeks and the high, rounded arches of her fine dark eyebrows.

"But you can't—"

"Of course, I can," he purred. "Open your legs and I'll prove it to you."

"Is—" she squeaked, then clamped shut her lips. At his grin, she narrowed her eyes and cleared her throat. "Is this done?" she finally ground out, her hand still firmly cupping herself.

He inserted a finger between hers, sliding to her nether lips, testing the moisture gathered there and finding her body more than ready. "Open your legs," he commanded her once more. He lifted one brow. "Would you deny your husband?"

Her gray eyes blinked. "This will truly please you?"

"Above all things, wife."

She pondered that thought for a long moment, and her jaws and throat worked as though waging an internal argument. Finally, she withdrew her hand and relaxed her legs around him, letting him shift to plant his elbows on the bed between her splayed thighs until he was braced over her sex.

Her succulent sex. Open wide. Glazed with honey. He leaned close and inhaled, holding her wide-eyed gaze.

"That's…" Her nose scrunched as she sputtered. "That's disgusting!" she cried out. "You're sniffing me like a dog. I swear to you, I'm no bitch to your sire."

"Your scent is rich, filled with the sweet perfume of your arousal." He marveled he could manage a coherent sentence. Perhaps there was a minstrel inhabiting his skin. He had a sudden urge to tell her how sweet her rosy nether lips smelled.

But he didn't think she'd appreciate any attempt at prose right now. Wanting to cut short her ability to speak and therefore distract him, he stuck out his tongue and lapped at the moisture clinging to her velvety soft outer lips.

Her gasp was thin, reedy. Her subsequent breaths rasped like a jagged breeze.

He licked again and her mouth opened wide and curved around a deep, guttural groan.

Again…and her belly undulated, lifting her sex to his mouth, pressing hard against his lips.

At her eager invitation, he nestled his mouth between her outer lips and began to lick and suckle the thin, pink inner lips. Her eyes drifted shut and her hands fluttered to the pillows beside her head.

Roland thought he'd never seen a woman more beautiful, more lost in her passion. He felt powerful—more manly than he'd ever felt before.

If this delicate wanton awaited him each night of his wedded life, he'd never stray from the marriage bed.

While her head thrashed on her pillow and her moans soughed between her swollen lips, he plied her body with sensual tortures, tasting her ripening arousal in the silken juices that spilled from inside her. Her responses were completely natural, completely without pretense. She pleased him deeply, filling him with a tender emotion he wasn't willing to acknowledge.

Instead, he plunged his tongue into her, lapping at her inner walls, his lust building as her cunt clasped and opened in greedy gulps in response to his ministrations. *Soon*, he'd take her soon.

His own body trembled with the need to plunge inside her. His skin broke into a sweat, the fever of arousal heating his face and chest. A powerful urgency knotted his groin, overfilling his cock so the skin surrounding his shaft felt ready to split from the pressure.

"*Milord*," she moaned. "*Please!*"

He withdrew his tongue and inhaled deeply. "Roland, wife," he ground out. "Call me Roland."

"I'll call you cruel if you do not end this," she complained. Her fingernails bit into his scalp, tugging his hair hard.

He grinned, enjoying the flame snapping in her gaze. Not so much a mouse now, and not the least bit acquiescent. He pushed a finger into her tight channel, twisting it into her, wriggling it to scrape his knuckles against her inner walls.

Her hips jerked off the mattress. "Please, more. *More.* Come inside me, please."

He pressed another finger inside her and nearly groaned as she spasmed around him, squeezing him tight, her inner muscles milking his fingers.

She was nearly there, nearly ready for the fucking he intended to give his tender bride.

His lips closed around the hard knot at the top of her sex, and he plunged a third finger into her, stroking inside. His little wife keened loud enough to make him wince. When he sucked hard on her love-knot, an unladylike squeal rang in his ears.

"*Roland*, damn you. *Pleeeaase!*" The word stretched into a wail.

He snorted and opened his mouth to give one last suckle to her engorged sex then lunged up her body, covering her before she could catch her startled breath.

Margaret reached eagerly for him, wrapping her legs around his waist, her arms around his neck and pulled him down to her. Her head rushed up to meet his, her lips mashing inexpertly but enthusiastically against his.

Then he was pushing inside her, pressing past swollen lips into her heated cunt. It swallowed him like a greedy mouth, slurping, sucking him inward with writhing spasms. He pushed deeper, pulled out, and then slammed forward to seat himself fully. His thighs bunched as he came up on his knees, his buttocks tightened and flexed. Then he was lost in the furious storm, pumping in and out, faster, harder.

But sweet, sweet Margaret didn't balk or protest against his rough loving.

Her breaths came in soft gusts, her gaze locked with his and then her neck arched back, her head pressing deeply into the pillow. Her mouth opened around a scream.

Below, where their bodies blended and churned, her cunt rippled all along his shaft, squeezing him tight. His balls exploded and cum gushed through his cock with each harsh stroke he delivered. He shouted and pummeled her soft sex, driving as deep as he could until he was spent. Even then, he didn't want to stop. He rocked against her, his movements slowing now, his cock caressing her channel in lazy glides that tunneled and withdrew until his thighs trembled and finally, he stopped.

His chest billowed around his gasps as he tried to regain his breath. His forehead dropped to hers and he kissed whatever he could reach—her cheeks, the end of her pert nose, her lips. So soft, blurred and rosy—they opened and her tongue darted out to mate with his in slow, teasing glides that soothed and fed his need to sustain their sensual connection.

At last, he drew back to gaze down at her.

Her breaths were evening and her gaze slid away.

He knew he should withdraw and give her body ease from his weight and intrusion. Gathering what little was left of his sapped strength, he attempted to move off her, but she tightened her legs around him. "I'm heavy," he whispered. "I'll crush you."

She gave a tiny shake of her head, still not meeting his gaze. "Can we stay like this?"

He might not understand the feminine mind most times, but this once he understood. She wanted to be held. The depth of their passion had likely frightened her.

He was uneasy too with how quickly things had gotten out of hand. She was young and soft and needed his comfort. Another test as a new husband.

Keeping his hips resting snugly between her legs, he raised his chest and rested on his elbows. Then he let his head sink to rest in the curve of her shoulder as he fought to regain his own breath and shattered mind. What had happened? He'd meant to take her gently, but he'd rutted her like a wild boar.

"Will we do this often?" she asked softly.

He felt a smile tug at the corner of his lips. *Often?* As soon as his cock regained its rigor, he intended to do it again. But was she asking because she feared it would be so, or because she wanted it? He lifted his head and studied her face, hoping for some signal he was doing the right things. Roland had never bedded a virgin or a gentlewoman. Had he misread eagerness to serve his needs as passion?

She met his gaze, her expression only curious, her cheeks pink, but from exertion or embarrassment? He wished he knew. But the way she stared steadily back told him the girl had courage.

The longer their gazes locked, the more worried he became. Had he been a bit ham-fisted? Too rough in his handling of her delicate body? Maybe he should leave her alone for now. He didn't want her soured to the marriage bed so soon in their relationship.

So despite her request to remain as they were, he withdrew his cock, sliding slowly from her body.

Disappointment flared in her eyes, and he rolled to his side, pulling her into the curve of his body, his hands turning her to face away so he wouldn't be tempted by the sight of her lovely, apple-shaped breasts—and so that he didn't have to look into her face and wonder anew what her expressions meant. For once, he felt inadequate, unsure of himself. He'd never considered what went on in a woman's mind before and wished he'd paid as much attention to that as he had learning to plant a lance in an opponent's chest.

But he had brought her satisfaction—a swift, glorious explosion if her scream and the scratches on his back were any indication of its intensity. Perhaps he worried for naught. He'd gifted her with release. He'd shown consideration by ending their lovemaking and allowing her rest. Maybe she'd be well enough recovered to take him the next evening. He'd be miserable with unabated arousal until then, but he'd persevere one more time for the sake of his tender bride.

His wayward cock nestled the crevice of her buttocks, a hellish temptation he ground his teeth against. "Sleep," he said, wincing at his rough tone.

Her sigh sounded suspiciously like a huff.

Margaret lay in the circle of her husband's strong arms with his hairy chest against her back. Now that curious heat that overtook her mind was past, she worried that she might have lost footing in their relationship.

Shouldn't he have been more eager than she to continue? If she were honest with herself, she hadn't wanted it to end quite so soon—however hot and sore her nether parts were.

His transformation into the man she deserved had already begun, and with surprising results.

She'd married a handsome man. That fact still amazed her. All that hair had hidden a man who rivaled Lancelot in masculine beauty.

She'd married a man whose touch lit a firestorm of passion inside her. One with a sense of humor that when properly directed would provide her a great deal of amusement. He was intelligent, therefore teachable—she'd work on his manners. But how could she shore up her position in his life?

She wanted to be more than his bedmate. She wanted his ear concerning matters that affected both their lives. She wanted his respect.

And yes, his affection. She thought she might have a mighty craving for his affection.

What did he see when his steady gaze landed on her? She was plain. Her hair was mud brown. Her eyes weren't crystal blue or warm brown, but an indeterminate gray.

She was a mouse. He, with his fire-streaked dark hair, handsome face and powerful body, was a lion.

If she didn't get a measure of respect from him, he'd swallow her whole. But what skills did she have? She didn't have a glib tongue, couldn't tease as handily as the dairy maid. Hadn't a body that men couldn't resist following with their gazes.

Perhaps her form wasn't the enticement, but what she did with it might be.

If the key to a man's happiness lay in the satisfaction of his appetites, well, wouldn't his sensual appetites be a weapon she could use? Had she the courage to entice him or attempt to enslave him in that way?

The thought of bringing him to his knees with passion ignited a curl of flame inside her own belly. She rubbed her buttocks against him to see whether he was still awake and felt the prod of his rigid staff. Encouraged, she nestled closer and opened her legs to allow his sex to slip between her thighs and held her breath. Would he understand her invitation?

Roland tightened his arm around his little wife's waist. He'd read her invitation all right and smiled at how well things were progressing between them. His rough play hadn't frightened her at all. Now, he had hopes he could mold her into the wife he wanted. He'd make a lusty wench of her yet.

She rolled within the circle of his arms and met his gaze, hers shyly sliding away. Her hand crept over his chest and her fingers slid into his hair to pluck.

He waited for her to give him a signal of what she wanted now. His arousal grew as her legs snuggled closer and her belly rubbed his lengthening cock.

"Husband?" she began, her voice a barely audible whisper.

"Yes, wife?"

"What you did before..." She bit her lips and her gaze darted to his then away again.

His lips began a slow upward curve. "When I pleasured you with my mouth?"

She nodded and tucked her chin low as her cheeks grew pink. "Um...would that also please you?"

Roland's chest billowed with his sharp inward breath. Did she mean...? "More than anything," he said, surprised he could speak past the growl threatening to rumble from his chest.

Her soft hands slid down his chest, and she leaned slightly away to make room to slide lower, past his belly which tightened at her slight touch. When she reached his cock, his eyes closed and he held his breath, waiting for her to touch him there.

Her hand trembled as her fingers glided over his length. "Teach me what brings you pleasure, milord."

Sweet Jesus! *She* pleased him—more than he could say. His jaw clenched when her warm palm encircled his shaft and suddenly she was scooting down the bed, her hot breath washing over his belly until her mouth was poised over him.

She waited there. Roland took a deep breath and reached down to grasp the crown of his sex. "Your lips...here," was all he could manage to say.

She needed no further instruction. Her hot mouth engulfed the head, robbing him of coherent thought. His hips bucked, and she gripped his staff hard with her hands and continued to suckle him, her tongue gliding around him, taking his breath and his mind.

So sweet. God, she was perfect. He thrust his fingers into her hair and guided her as gently as he could, showing her with little surges of his hips that she could take his cock deeper into her mouth. She murmured eagerly, the sound vibrating on his sex.

He wrapped a hand around both of hers where they gripped him, and together they stroked up and down his shaft until she got the idea and pushed his hand away. Beneath her wicked mouth and firm hands, his cock filled to bursting. If he didn't end it soon, she'd be in for another surprise.

But she drew away and stared, holding him straight up with one hand grasping him near the root. "I can't believe my body accommodates you." She stuck out her tongue and licked the silvery bead oozing from his eye.

"Does it want to accommodate me now?" he gritted out.

Her face was taut, her desire plain in her heated gaze. "Please?"

Roland had a fleeting thought that he'd succeeded beyond his wildest fantasy in molding her into the wanton wife of his dreams. Feeling very pleased with himself and filled with a warm affection he'd never known for a woman, he smiled and extended his hand.

That green-apple ache was back in Margaret's belly again and silken fluids seeped to wet her woman's furrow. Now, she recognized both as desire—her body's open invitation to her husband.

Staring at his hand, she swept out her tongue to rim her lips. His nostrils flared, and his gaze dropped to watch. Still, his fingers curled in invitation. She knew that if she wanted to keep the upper hand she should make him wait, but she suddenly realized she didn't want him bound to her will, at least not here.

She lifted her hand and slid it inside his rough palm and let him pull her up his body until she rested over him. The view from on top was heady and made her tremble with want. His body was hers to take. However she wanted. Beneath his dark gaze, she stared down at him, marveling at the muscle that flexed at the side of his jaw, at the broad chest that spanned hers and beyond, at the thickly corded thighs that bunched as he held himself in check.

In their bed, she wanted to be overwhelmed...even frightened...by his need. He thrilled her beyond her imaginings.

She leaned over him, her mouth an inch above his. "Take me, husband," she whispered. "Please."

His chest rose and a large, rough hand cupped her shoulder and squeezed, then he rolled over her, gently tucking her body beneath his until he covered her from head to toe.

This time he hovered over her. His sweet breath washing over her cheek and lips. "*Margaret.* How you please me."

She smiled, her lips trembling. He'd give her power if she wanted it. She gladly gave him the acquiescence he needed.

"Come into me, husband."

Their bodies blended, his cock gliding easily into her moist depths. He hooked his elbows beneath her knees and raised them, pushing them upward to tilt her hips to take him deeper still.

A growling rumble erupted from his chest, and she knew he was quickly becoming lost in their passion as he stroked into her, again and again. His eyes darkened and his jaw tightened. Her heart skipped a beat at the ferocity of his expression and her palms bracketed his cheeks and urged him down for a kiss.

When their lips met, she sighed, and he drew her breath into his mouth. When he drew back his head, he speared her with a look. "I won't be gentle."

A grin tugged at her lips. "Think you I'm a mouse?"

He gave a short, fierce shake of his head, clearly beyond words.

"Take me. I'm yours."

Thus released, his thrusts were fast, furious, ravaging. They strained together, his body pummeling hers as her hands raked his back, urging him on. When at last they both erupted in lusty shouts, they shared laughter that reflected their triumph over each other—but they knew they had both won a prize beyond measure.

* * * * *

Grania took a deep breath, bracing herself for the worst, expecting her young charge to be hastily gathering her belongings for a quick escape. Without knocking, she pushed open the door and entered a bedchamber alight with the morning sun.

The sight that met her aged eyes had her grinning. The young couple lay naked, a sprawl of tangled limbs, their bodies obviously still joined as they slept.

The face of Margaret's new master was a wonder—as handsome as any knight in a fairytale. Margaret's slackened mouth held the curve of a satisfied smile as her face peeked from beneath one bronzed shoulder.

Grania quietly shut the door, pleased her plan had worked so well. The bath had eased Margaret's tension enough for her to shed her maidenly fears. For what young woman could resist such a finely made man?

With visions of russet-haired little hellions scampering around the keep, she decided to wake the kitchen staff to prepare food to break the couple's fast. They'd need strength to continue their lusty battle for supremacy.

Also by Delilah Devlin

✿

About the Author

☙

Delilah Devlin dated a Samoan, a Venezuelan, a Turk, a Cuban, and was engaged to a Greek before marrying her Irishman. She's lived in Saudi Arabia, Germany, and Ireland, but calls Texas home for now. Ever a risk taker, she lived in the Saudi Peninsula during the Gulf War, thwarted an attempted abduction by white slave traders, and survived her children's juvenile delinquency.

Creating alter egos for herself in the pages of her books enables her to live new adventures. Since discovering the sinful pleasure of erotica, she writes to satisfy her need for variety--it keeps her from running away with the Indian working in the cubicle beside her!

In addition to writing erotica, she enjoys creating romantic comedies and suspense novels.

Delilah welcomes comments from readers. You can find her website and email address on her author bio page at www.ellorascave.com.

Tell Us What You Think

We appreciate hearing reader opinions about our books. You can email us at Comments@EllorasCave.com.

DANCE OF THE PLAIN JANE

Lillian Feisty

ഇ

Chapter One

📖

"You gotta see this chick, man. She is so fucking hot!"

Michael grunted and took a bite of his Tandoori Chicken. He hardly tasted it. Indian wasn't his favorite type of food, but when his Navy pals dragged him to the Bombay Cafe after a ten-mile swim in a very choppy San Diego Bay, he had been too tired to argue. Now he simply needed to put something in his grumbling gut and he didn't much care what it was.

"You ain't kidding. If her hips don't lie then I want the truth, the whole truth and nothing but the fucking truth!"

His friends weren't here for the food, either, it seemed. They kept talking about some belly dancer who'd given them all hard-ons for the entire weekend following the previous Friday night's performance.

"Why do they have a belly dancer in an Indian restaurant, anyway?" Michael took a deep swill from his beer bottle.

"Who the fuck cares? She's got great tits!" Bubba shoved a large piece of Naan bread into his mouth, then held his hands twelve inches in front of his chest to illustrate just how large the tits in question actually were.

Michael polished his black-rimmed glasses. "Bubba, when was your last girlfriend?"

Still chewing, Bubba closed his eyes and considered the question. "Can't remember."

Michael placed his glasses into his jacket pocket. "I rest my case."

"Hey, I like tits. I'm not going to deny it."

Jackson, a farm-raised boy from Nebraska, neatly scooped into his Dal. "No one's asking you to deny it, Bubba. Maybe just start referring to them as breasts instead of tits."

"Whatever."

Michael grinned and downed the last of his beer. Supposedly impressive cleavage aside, he was anxious to get home and bury his nose in a book. Lately he had been more interested in novels than women and that was just fine with him. Life was a hell of a lot easier that way.

He threw a twenty onto the table. "Boys, it's been a pleasure but I'm gonna hit it."

"What? Man, you can't leave. The show's about to start." As if to emphasize Jackson's words, the lights dimmed and the sultry drumming sounds of a Middle Eastern song floated through the room.

The guys had picked a table in the back, apparently prime seating for viewing the "show". While that might be true, it would also make it pretty conspicuous when Michael made his exit through the hushed crowd.

Oh well. Tolstoy was waiting.

"See you at oh-five-hundred sharp," he murmured as he pushed his chair back and stood.

Generally his fellow teammates were some of the sharpest men in Special Ops, but at that moment a bomb could have gone off in the place and they wouldn't have batted an eye. They stared, hypnotized, enthralled by the exotic music and the promise of a glimpse of a voluptuous dancer's skin.

He shook his head and turned to leave.

The dancer emerged from the side hallway. It became clear that in a moment she was going to be right in his path, blocking his exit. He held back, waiting for the least noticeable moment to make his escape—by nature he was a man who kept to the sidelines. He gave the woman a quick scan to see what had his teammates in such a state of sexual excitement.

She wore a bra that clasped behind her neck, its cups decorated in coins that dangled and swayed with her slightest movement, the tinkling sound floating across the room. Michael conceded she had nice breasts, high and shapely, but not too big a handful. Unless a guy had small hands, which he didn't.

She was barefoot. How did she glide like that? She seemed constantly on the balls of her feet, and they never ceased moving. Her red toenails whirled beneath her full blue skirt, giving him peekaboo glimpses.

The drumbeat sped up a little and her hips moved with the rhythm. Her arms floated beside her in a serpentine way as she moved into the center of the room.

Nope. Not his type. He liked his women blonde and lean — skinny, even — like his last girlfriend. Of course, Trixie thought those little pink sweetener packets made up their own food group, which probably meant she was killing herself to stay thin, but that didn't change the fact that she looked just like every other woman he'd dated.

His type of women.

This belly dancer, though — she definitely had a belly. It shook gently as she did some shaky thing that could only be described as a belly roll. Okay, it was an impressive move. But this whole thing was about the belly, wasn't it? Hers was a little pooch that contrasted against her narrow waist. It shouldn't have been sexy. So why was his cock suddenly stirring? Something so womanly, so beautiful and feminine…it symbolized all the things he had eliminated from his life.

A rose vine tattoo climbed across her abdomen. The bright red and green ink started beyond his view beneath a coin-covered sash tied low on her hips, and wound its way up, above her hip bone, climbing around her lower back. He'd give anything to see where that rose vine began. The thought made him wonder what her pussy looked like, what she smelled like.

The Middle Eastern music climbed toward its crescendo. She faced away from him now, and he noticed a businessman leering at the dancer's chest. Michael drew in a sudden breath. He wanted to dash across the room and smash the man's face against his fist.

Where the fuck had that thought come from? Despite his chosen profession, he wasn't generally a violent man.

But it wasn't just the businessman watching her, was it? She had every customer hypnotized as she began to lean back, further and further, until her long brown hair brushed the ground. He conceded that in order to make such a pose seem effortless the woman must possess amazing control of her body.

His cock jumped. He was so fucking hard. He couldn't remember when he'd last been this hard, and he thanked God for the dimmed lights—his team didn't need to see the effect this woman was having on him.

Then she looked at him, speared him with her overly made-up eyes from her upside down position, and he almost yanked her by her hair right out of that room. He didn't want others looking at her anymore. His.

The music stopped. The room erupted in applause, but the belly dancer jumped directly into the next song. When she broke eye contact, Michael felt as if he had been released—but released from what?

He shook his head. He had to go. Now. All eyes were on the dancer as she waved a large piece of sheer blue fabric over her head and began spinning in circles.

He could leave now without anyone noticing.

He almost made it. But he couldn't keep his eyes off her, and she caught him staring. He froze. It was like an electric current connected their gazes and he couldn't look away. Was it his imagination, or did she smirk at him?

She began dancing in his direction.

* * * * *

It was *him*.

Even bent over backward she had suspected. But now, watching him try to escape, she was positive. Jane recognized him, but he wouldn't be hard to mistake, would he? Way over six feet tall with broad, swimmer's shoulders, a flat-as-a-board stomach and arms that looked strong enough to lift her with one hand.

Or fuck her against a wall without breaking a sweat.

She had seen him so many times and not once had he noticed her. He lived in her neighborhood. She didn't know exactly where, but somewhere close. She occasionally saw him running, his long, strong legs sure and steady as they carried him away from her. He never caught her watching him.

He noticed her now. She was satisfied to see him glued to where she had nailed him with her stare. For a second her step faltered—after all, this was the guy she had spent many nights dreaming about, pretending her vibrator was his cock. Pinching her nipples as she pretended it was his mouth biting her. Rubbing her clit as she imagined what his tongue would feel like.

Fantasizing about binding him to her bed. Or even better, having him bind *her* to the bed.

They'd had coffee together several times. Well, not actually together, but in the same local coffee shop, at the same time. She'd spent many hours formulating exactly what to say to him the next time she saw him there. Then he'd disappear for weeks on end and she'd lose her nerve.

But now she was in her element, and she wasn't going to chicken out tonight.

The slow sitar sounds wafted across the room, forming a direct connection with her core. The song started slowly. Jane began to move.

She knew she was seductive. That's why she'd started dancing ten years ago. It gave her another identity, something so different than the plain-Jane engineer she turned into at nine o'clock each morning. But at night…

The drum pulled her hips forward in a figure eight, slowly at first, but building momentum.

His gaze drifted lower, to her belly, to her hips. *No, I'm not like that skinny bitch you used to go running with.*

The song continued to increase its tempo, the beat of the exotic drum pulling her hips from side to side, forward and back. She raised her hands above her head and crossed her wrists, as if they were tied above her. Her bare feet moved her forward as she slid her neck from side to side, never once releasing him from her stare. He watched her, still as a statue.

She danced around his rigid body in a twist-walk until she was behind him. Very subtly, she intruded into his personal space—he probably didn't even realize that she was nudging him into the center of the room. But then there he was.

The music sped up again. She loved this song. It gave her extra confidence, made her feel even more alluring. She shimmied her shoulders and discovered the movement caused a tightening sensation in her breasts as her nipples rubbed the inside of her heavy bra. This was like a fantasy come true, dancing for this man. Not only did she fantasize about him while she masturbated, she fantasized about him when she danced by herself.

And during the day, dressed in her usual tank top and jeans, with no makeup, she'd see him at the coffee shop and be too shy to say hello.

She still hadn't. But now, as she danced, his dark brown gaze fixated on her as she circled him, she knew him. Knew for certain that he wanted to fuck her. Knew that he was leashing his desire for her.

Her.

She danced with her back to him, but every few beats Jane looked over her shoulder and nailed him again, just so he knew she was still in control.

The crowd watched, mesmerized, as though observing a sacrifice.

In a way they weren't wrong.

This man of her fantasies—she thought of him as Michael—was about to become hers. This was her world now, and she was the Goddess.

* * * * *

He was going to fuck her. The question was, was he going to do it in front of all these people or wait until her performance was over? His cock was ravenous for her, just as his stomach had been starving for food earlier. He didn't care where he had his dinner, just as long as he got his fill.

God knew, at some point tonight, this dark-haired, pale-skinned beauty was going to get her fill of him. And Michael's patience was wearing very thin.

In fact, it was about to snap.

With her back to him once again, her waist-length hair swayed just a few inches away, and he inhaled its aroma, as if the scents of cinnamon and spices would be some kind of substitute for what he wanted to do—lick her and see for himself if her skin tasted the way she smelled.

That would have to wait until later. Right now he clenched his fists at his sides, using the deepest part of his self-restraint to keep from grabbing her, jerking her curvy body against his and burying himself in her softness.

Her hips swayed, circling back and forth, until she touched him. His hardness must have surprised her because when she bumped her sweet ass against his cock her timing faltered. But she didn't jump away. Instead, she kept dancing, her hips jerking up and down, up and down, to the music.

He couldn't take it any longer. As if she sensed that he lifted his arm, ready to drag her away, she bounced forward and spun slowly around until she faced him. This close he could see the details of her face. Her heavy makeup didn't hide the deep green of her eyes, the freckles across her nose, or the slight smile on her red lips as she took her veil and ever-so-slowly raised it above his head. The sheer fabric whispered over his dry lips, caressed his arms, wrists and hands, then landed softly on the floor.

She was sinking, too. Her elegant hands fluttered in the air as her knees bent, and then she was on the floor next to the blue veil, sitting back on her heels.

The frantic drumbeat accompanied her as she tossed her head from side to side, her brown hair following her movements, flying through the air in a graceful arc. He could see each muscle of her abdomen working to sustain her dance and support her body as she leaned even further back.

Then the music ended and, except for the fading tinkle from the coins of her costume, silence filled the room.

She was on the floor, on her knees, but when she looked up there was no mistaking the challenge in her eyes. She breathed heavily, her chest heaving as she took in air. Sweat beaded between her breasts.

That's when Michael's patience snapped.

* * * * *

When he swooped down and yanked her off the ground Jane was glad for it. Tonight she had put everything into her performance and now she was exhausted, spent. She was probably too weak to walk. And even if none of her fantasies came true it had been worth it just to be carried away in his arms.

Now she knew why that always happened in romance novels — once in a while it was nice to be rescued.

With one arm underneath her legs and another supporting her back, she felt his strength. He lifted her weight as if it were nothing — and she knew that certainly wasn't the case. His chest was solid against her body, and he smelled like beer and the sea. She was dying to lick his neck and see if he tasted like saltwater.

The chiming noise of her costume was the only sound in the restaurant. He carried her across the room and just as they were about to disappear into the hallway she heard a lady ask, "Does she give lessons?"

Jane smiled against his chest.

When they entered the hallway she waved her hand in the direction of the storeroom. With seemingly no effort at all, he managed to open the door and close it behind them without ever shifting her position.

Except for an old desk and a few stacks of boxes, they were alone. He reached over to flick on the light, but Jane grabbed his arm, stopping him. She wasn't ready for fluorescent reality yet, and the moonlight coming through the storeroom window provided enough illumination for them to see their way around.

"What the fuck was that?"

She looked up at him. "I hate the lighting in this room."

"I mean, what were you doing out there? That dance?"

"Michael, I—"

"What did you call me?"

"Um, Michael."

"How did you know my name?"

She looked directly into his dark brown eyes. "I guessed."

"You guessed." He took a few steps and sat her on the desk. "You guessed."

She shrugged. "I do that sometimes."

He began pacing the room. "We'll discuss that later. Right now we need to deal with what went on during your performance."

"We do?"

"Yes. You were working me out there. You had me so fucking hard I almost lost control in front of a roomful of strangers, not to mention my team."

Jane smiled to herself. "I'm sorry."

"No you're not." He stopped pacing and placed himself directly in front of her. "But you're gonna be."

With a hand on each knee he opened her up and stepped between her legs. "What's your name, anyway?"

"Jane."

Slowly, he lowered his mouth to hers. She waited for a forceful kiss, but instead he brushed his warm lips against hers, and when she leaned forward, frustrated and needing something more, he pulled back.

"Well, Jane," he said with just a hint of a smile. "It's time you got a dose of your own medicine."

Chapter Two

ജ

Jane gulped. "Um, can I have some water first?"

"No."

"Okay."

"Jane, lean back a little and put your hands on the desk."

She leaned back.

"Do you get horny when you're dancing?"

Only when you're involved. "Sometimes."

"I think you did tonight. I think you wanted me."

Staring. She was only capable of staring at him as he lifted one of her legs, then the other, and placed each of her bare feet on the front edge of the desk. "Tell me you wanted me."

Boy, did she. She'd had a crush on him for over a year, but until this night they had never exchanged a word—and now this virtual stranger wanted her to expose herself, even more than she already had, and admit something so intimate?

She took a deep breath. "I wanted you."

He pushed her skirt over her knees, knees that had begun to tremble, and let the fabric rest on the top of her thighs. "How much?"

Jane felt her legs part just a little more. "A bit," she lied.

He stepped back. "Just a bit?" The side of his mouth tugged up in a semi-grin, and that slight action said so much. It was the confident gesture of a man used to having women want him, a man used to having control.

Ah, but who had been the one in control during her dance? That had been her.

Jane. Plain Jane.

And she wanted some of that power back.

She let one of her knees fall lower. "Maybe I wanted you more than just a little."

He crossed his arms over his chest. "Show me."

When she looked between her knees Jane saw a stranger, a strong man who could easily overpower her. Oddly, the thought didn't scare her but instead made her pulse jump and her pussy throb. For some reason she trusted him, but she hoped it wasn't because her secret crush had given her brain a false sense of security.

Was she really going to go through with it? This was the moment of truth, and she knew that if she didn't put an end to things now, she probably wouldn't be able to do so later.

She took a deep breath. "What do you want to see?"

* * * * *

For a second Michael thought she was going to back down and that would have disappointed him. Not because he would have missed having sex with a gorgeous woman who was currently doing a damn fine job of convincing him to find a new type, but because he sensed some deep part of her wanted to do this and he didn't want to see her let herself down.

Jane licked her lips.

"Lift up your skirt."

She tugged the fabric until it pooled across her stomach. She went to pull down a bra strap, but Michael stopped her.

"Did I say you could take off you bra?"

Her hand froze. "No, but—"

"You had your fun out there but now I'm calling the shots. Do you have a problem with that?"

She raised her brows at him but argued no further. "Well, what do you want me to do then?"

"Open your legs all the way. I want to see your panties."

She paused only a second before she spread for him.

"Blue panties, to match your skirt I assume."

"Mmm," she managed.

Michael was happy to see her green eyes darken at his words. "And I see a little damp spot on them, so I'm guessing you like to be ordered around a little."

"I do not." But she reclined just that much more on the desk.

"I want you to touch that damp spot, Jane."

She closed her eyes, and then her hand fluttered over her abdomen before landing between her legs. She touched herself, lightly at first, then soon finding her rhythm, lifting her hips in a manner not unlike one of her dance moves, raising her pelvis up and down as she rubbed against her own hand.

Then her ass was scooting down on the desk, and she was making little sounds from her throat...

His cock hurt from it.

Maybe it was the costume, but he wanted to fuck her until she was *his*, tie her to a bed, own her, make it impossible for her to ever do this for any other. He never wanted another man to see her naked or exposed. Ever.

She gripped the desk behind her head with her free hand, and with the other she used two fingers to rub one particular area—her clit. Michael knew what that meant.

He walked to the side of the desk. "Don't come."

Her eyes fluttered open, unfocused and glittery in the moonlight.

"Not even if you say please."

"Please?"

"No." He reached down and lifted one breast out of her bra. When he pinched her nipple she gasped, and with white knuckles she gripped the edges of the desk.

He didn't want to touch her, wanted to save that pleasure for later, but he couldn't help himself. Ethereally, she lay before him, as if some ancient God had placed her on the table just for him, with her legs spread wide, her belly soft and her breasts pale and round.

And she was waiting.

Michael leaned forward and took her nipple into his mouth. He wasn't gentle, he sucked hard, pulling the areola deep across his tongue until she grasped his head with her hands. He smelled the scent of her pussy on her fingers.

Her panties were sopping wet against his palm, and it was easy to pull the damp fabric aside and plunge a finger into her. She met him, coaxing his finger deeper, and when he inserted a second, and then a third he felt her stomach begin to quiver.

"I said, don't come," he said.

"Fuck off!"

"Later."

"Please get on top of me, Michael."

With a great deal of regret, he slid his hand out of her pussy and stood. "I thought I made it clear that I was the one in control in here."

She pushed herself up and tossed some hair out of her eyes. "I said *please*," she ground out.

"I believe that came after you said 'fuck off'."

"Fine. If you don't want to finish this, then I'm outta here." She shoved her breast back into her bra and jumped off the table.

He reached out and grabbed her arm. "Did I say I didn't want to finish?"

"But...you..."

"What I said was, 'don't come'."

She narrowed her eyes at him.

"I see no need to hurry."

After a moment, she looked to the side. "I couldn't help it."

He should be fucking her instead of arguing about why they should drag it out. In his mind, this thing started the minute she shimmied her way through the doorway back in the restaurant, so, by his estimation, he'd been denying himself for over an hour.

Enough foreplay.

Suddenly Michael found himself once again wondering who had command of the situation.

He was done playing games.

"Okay, Jane. I want you to turn around and bend over."

Chapter Three

80

Jane whipped her gaze up to meet his. Was he serious? What was he going to do to her if she carried out his request — no, his order?

"Do you trust me?"

She did. For some crazy reason she did.

"I want you to turn around, bend over and grab the far edge of the desk."

The desk was large, so the position automatically thrust her ass up and out, pointing at him, and although her skirt covered her backside, she felt totally exposed as she assumed the naughty pose.

"Now turn your head and rest your cheek on the desk. And close your eyes."

Once her eyes were closed all her other senses came to life. The feel of the wood against her naked abdomen, the incense-like scent of the storeroom, the chiming lilt from the coins on her costume as they fell to rest on the desk — what would it feel like when he actually entered her? She might die from sensory overload.

She waited to see what he was going to do. Was he going to spank her? She had never done anything so racy before, had never really thought about it, but at that moment Jane was so excited, she knew Michael could ask her to be his sex slave and she would have happily handed him a leash and collar.

She practically jumped off the desk when she felt the firm caress of his hand on her ass. It wasn't a spanking, but it felt nice, and she couldn't help moving back against him a little. He lifted her skirt.

"Did you cast a spell on me?" he wondered aloud.

With her eyes still closed, Jane grinned. Had she cast a spell on him? Myra, her belly dance instructor, was indeed known for her ability to seduce men. But Jane doubted very seriously that that particular trait had been passed on to her.

Then he wasn't touching her anymore, and she heard some shuffling around. Was he getting something to spank her with? She didn't think she could be any more turned on, but the thought of Michael slapping her ass with some long, hard implement caused her to squirm where she stood bent over the desk.

He must have known she was about to look up because he barked, "Keep your eyes closed."

"They are."

"Good."

He murmured something she didn't quite understand. "What?"

The sound of a cell phone slapping closed slammed through the room. "I have some bad news."

Had he taken a phone call?

Aparrently so.

It was official. Even with her ass in the air waiting for a spanking—or something—she was Plain Jane. She squeezed her eyelids shut because no—she would not cry.

"Really?" she managed to reply.

"Fuck. I have to go."

She was going to have blisters from gripping the desk so hard. But she couldn't stand up and face him, not now. It was humiliating enough to be ditched in this position, but to actually face him would be so much worse.

"You're *leaving*?"

"I have to go."

"Now? What could possibly be so important?" That sounded pathetic so she added, "Never mind. I don't want to know."

"That was my boss. Work, you know…work."

"Right. Work."

There it was again, the soft, warm feel of his hand on her skin, this time firm on the small of her back. "Get up."

"No."

"Yes." A gentle yank on her hair punctuated his command. "Yes."

She didn't have much of a choice, what with his pulling on her hair and all, so she stood up, turned and looked him in the eye. God, why did he have to be so solid, so strong? And why was he suddenly in such a hurry to leave her?

"I'll call you," he said.

"Don't bother."

He took her chin in his hand and tilted her head up. "You don't have a boyfriend, do you?"

Oh, how she wanted to lie. "No," she muttered instead.

"Good."

She moved her chin out of his grip. "Do you?"

"Nope. No boyfriend."

"You *know* what I meant."

"I'll call you as soon as I return, and I'll explain."

"Return from where?"

"I don't know. And I don't know when I'll be back, either."

She rolled her eyes. "Good answer."

He lowered his head until his lips were just a breath away from her own. "Do you promise?"

"P-promise what?"

His fingers, long and strong and tender, lightly traced the outline of her bra. "That you'll wait?"

She shook back her hair and leaned forward. "No." she said.

And then Jane grabbed his shoulders, yanked him to her, and kissed him with every ounce of seduction she possessed.

* * * * *

Twenty minutes — that was all he had.

With Jane — sweet Jane — kissing him like this it was almost impossible to remember why he had to go, and when she wrapped those long, strong legs around his waist he had no choice but to press his cock against that soft, damp place between her thighs. It became apparent he wasn't going anywhere just then. The chief could wait five extra minutes. Saving some diplomat who got himself in trouble — again — could wait five minutes.

She made a little noise of protest when he set her down, but when he ripped her panties away from her body she gasped, then smiled, and when he unbuttoned his jeans and removed his cock her eyes widened and, subconsciously he was sure, she spread her legs a tad wider.

"It's huge!"

He smiled at that. "And it's impatient." He picked her up and, like a good girl, she rewrapped her legs around him. "Hold on."

Her wavy hair spilled over his shoulders as she grasped his head between her palms and kissed him. He took a moment to taste her, savored the scent of her hair filling his nostrils, but he needed more. He needed to feel himself inside of her. Needed to feel her surrounding his cock.

Never letting her go, he turned and crossed the room. He could feel her pussy, slick and warm, on the length of his dick. He could have come right then, just from the friction of walking three steps with his cock against her cunt.

Instead, he backed her against the door and drove right into her willing cunt.

"Oh my God." She gasped in his ear and repeated her earlier exclamation. "It's… You… God! You're big!"

"Should I stop?"

"No! God, no. Do it again."

He did. He kissed her and fucked her, and each time he drove into her the coins on her bra swung back in a rhythmic chime.

"Michael?"

"Yeah?"

"Oh my God!"

"I know, baby. Just let go."

"You feel—I mean—would you please kiss my breast?"

He leaned down and pulled her nipple into his mouth, sucking just hard enough to give her a sting. Already, he was beginning to know her taste. Already he was beginning to know *her*.

"Yes. Don't fucking stop."

There was no way in hell he could have. Instead he picked up his rhythm, worrying for a minute that he was driving too hard—but no. She was moaning so loudly he was sure the entire restaurant could hear her.

Good. Let them know she was *his* now.

The thought of possessing her drove him closer to the edge, and she was so goddamn tight, but he wanted—no, needed—to experience this with her, together, so he reached between their bodies and teased her clit, knowing the little action would invite her orgasm.

It worked. She tossed back her head, reached up and grabbed the doorframe above her. Pressing her pelvis forward, she ground against him, fucked him back.

Through it all, she watched him. He had never made love to a woman while staring her in the eye, and the sensation felt odd, but he couldn't look away. A strange, overpowering connection locked their gazes, similar to when she had caught him staring earlier.

He felt her everywhere—surrounding his cock, wrapping around his hips, pressing against his chest...and somewhere else, too. Somewhere inside, a place he couldn't quite pinpoint...

He came hard. His grip on her hips would leave bruises, but at that moment he didn't care. Michael lifted her, slid her one final time onto his cock. Clamping her ankles to his buttocks, she screamed his name in her own release.

Afterwards she collapsed against him in a sweaty, panting lump.

For a few moments he held her, stroking her hair. "I know, baby."

"Mmm. Tired."

"I'll put you to bed."

"That sounds nice. I'll get my—"

"Fuck."

She looked up, startled. "What?"

"I gotta go."

"No, we just... *No*." She shook her head

He shifted to put her down, but she clamped her legs and arms tightly around him. "You are not really going to run away after what just happened."

Fuck. Taking this woman home and making love to her until she couldn't walk sounded like heaven. Instead, there was a good chance that within twenty-four hours he'd be skulking through some humid jungle with a seventy-five-pound pack on his back, miles away from his girl.

The hardest thing he'd ever done was slide out of Jane's body. For the first time in fifteen years, Michael regretted his choice of career. A CPA would never run into this problem.

But he wasn't a CPA. Duty called and Michael was already late.

He buttoned up his jeans, deliberately averting his gaze from her. He was afraid that if he laid eyes on her tousled hair, saw her hurt expression, he'd lose control and go AWOL.

"Oh, Michael?"

The simple sound of her voice snapped his gaze to where she stood.

Or to where she was bent over, to be more accurate.

Chapter Four

ა

It wasn't enough. *She* wasn't enough.

As she drove home, humiliation scorched her cheeks. She was pathetic. Fucking her against a wall hadn't persuaded him to stay, so why should a sexy pose have done the trick? Her ass wasn't even her best asset! At least he hadn't laughed — she couldn't have handled that. But was the alternative any better?

Instead of laughing, Michael kissed her senseless, yanked her against his chest, pressed his rock-hard erection against her hip, and just when Jane thought he was going to succumb to her seduction and whisk her home, his cell phone vibrated against her thigh from inside his pocket.

He took the call, kissed her one more time, ignoring her mortification, and then he was gone.

Just after he snapped one last command at her. "Wait for me."

As if.

Obviously the gods felt sorry for her. She had been prepared to drive around her block for hours, like she usually did, searching for nonexistent parking spots, when she saw an opening directly in front of her walkway.

"You're not off the hook," she told the gods aloud. "You think a parking spot is going to make up for what happened tonight? Only a bottomless bottle of vodka is going to do that."

"Jane? Are you talking to yourself in there?"

She started and looked out the driver's side window. Her neighbor, Abby Rogue peered through the glass, her perfectly drawn auburn brows furrowed in concern.

Jane would have preferred to stay in her car for the rest of the night, listening to sad Eighties love songs and crying into her steering wheel, but she knew her neighbor would never allow such behavior.

Abby would, however, allow cocktails and even perhaps the depressing music, so Jane grabbed her bag, opened the door and stepped out of the car.

Just looking at Abby made Jane want to turn on the waterworks. Things like this never happened to her best friend. The woman was like a movie star, with her glamorous red haircut, spunky personality and cool, retro clothes. No man in the world would leave Abby ass up in the air, waiting for some risqué action.

Nope. That little experience was reserved solely for the Plain Janes of the world. When Abby was in a room, everyone knew it. Unlike Jane, who could only keep a man's interest when she piled on the makeup and shimmied her breasts in a guy's face.

"Oh, sweetie, what happened?"

Jane's eyes began to burn.

"Another obnoxious jerk at the restaurant?"

She sniffed. "Yes."

Abby put an arm around her shoulder. "Come upstairs, tell me what happened and I'll fix you a drink. Have you eaten?"

Jane smiled. For all Abby's bombshell looks she was really an Italian mama at heart, and twenty minutes later Jane was seated at Abby's pink kitchen table, drinking Cosmopolitans and eating leftover lasagna.

"Can you please tell me what's wrong with me?" Jane whined after she had relayed the story to Abby. Well, most of it, anyway.

She refilled Jane's glass. "Nothing is wrong with you."

"We were just about to have sex and then he takes a phone call!"

"That is slightly strange."

"Oh my God!" Jane slammed her glass onto the table. "I know!"

"You know what?"

"I know why he took off."

"You do?"

"It was my ass!"

"Your ass."

"Yes. He had me bent over the table, with my butt in the air and when he saw how fat it is he booked it right out of there."

Abby held up her hand. "Whoa, sister. You had your ass in the air?"

Jane traced a line on the table. "Mmm."

"You naughty thing! Was he going to spank you?"

She took another healthy gulp of her cocktail. "I'll never know, will I?"

Abby sighed. "Jane. I'm sure he had an important reason for leaving."

"It certainly was an *immense* reason."

"It was?"

"Yes. My ass."

"Oh, enough already! For heaven's sake, this was one guy. One. It means nothing, and you have an amazing ass."

"Oh, it's easy for you to say."

"What's that supposed to mean?"

"You're tiny and cute and have, like, ten boyfriends at a time."

"I do not!"

"You do. And the only way I can get a guy interested in me is to glue chimes onto my bra, put on a ton of makeup and shimmy around a roomful of people."

"That is not true."

"And the minute the lights come on, poof!" She snapped her fingers. "The seduction ends." Again, Jane felt the tears burning. "I thought he liked me."

"Oh, sweetie. I'm sorry this happened to you."

"Me, too." Jane took another huge bite of lasagna.

By the time she fell into bed two hours later the night's humiliation had been nicely numbed by vodka and carbs.

Still, in her dreams, when she danced, it was Michael who watched her.

* * * * *

Jane dragged herself through the rest of the week, and on Friday night she arrived home after work with the sole intent of moping her way through the weekend.

Abby had other plans.

For some crazy reason Jane had given her friend a key, so around eight o'clock that night Abby let herself into the apartment wearing a black dress and high-heeled shoes.

"Get off the sofa."

Jane looked up from the carton of rocky road ice cream she was working her way through. "Excuse me?"

"Up. We're going out. It's Friday night and your pity party has just ended." From the depths of her bag Abby produced a silver cocktail shaker and a plastic cup, which she proceeded to fill with clear liquid. "I made you a Corpse Reviver. Drink up and then I'm getting you dressed."

It took three cocktails and a lot of persuasion, but somehow, two hours later, Jane found herself also wearing a dress and leaving the safety of her apartment.

"You look so fucking hot!" Abby exclaimed for the zillionth time as they walked the two blocks to The Lounge, their local bar.

She grinned to herself. *Abby's right — I do look hot.*

Abby had dressed Jane up in a pink vintage slip, and over that she wore a black lace, short-sleeved dress.

A low whistle greeted them as they walked through the door of The Lounge. "Abs, you look gorgeous as usual. Who's your beautiful friend?"

"This is Jane."

"Jane? You sure don't look like a Jane."

No doubt the bartender was playing it up, but she didn't care. As far as she was concerned the night was off to a proper start—cocktails and compliments—and that was a lovely kick off.

Pretty soon she'd stop thinking about Michael and wishing he were the one giving her compliments. She knew he lived somewhere in the neighborhood, so she couldn't stop her glance from zipping around the room, searching for him. She breathed a sigh of relief—and disappointment, if truth be known—when she didn't see him.

After two or three rounds they were more than ready to hit a dance club. They walked the few blocks to The Warehouse, and a pounding drumbeat of loud music greeted them. It was one of Jane's favorites from the Eighties—*Take On Me*—so she grabbed Abby's arm and dragged her directly onto the dance floor.

Jane had forgotten how much she enjoyed dancing for herself. Usually it was either for an audience, or for some fantasy involving Michael. But that night she immediately lost herself in the music, and had a blast acting silly on the dance floor with her girlfriend, especially during the remix of *Girls Just Want to Have Fun.*

The men found them in no time at all. At first it seemed strange dancing with a partner instead of alone, but she quickly overcame the sentiment. Besides, this tall blond guy with the chiseled jaw wasn't exactly hard on the eyes. And the way he was pressing up against her backside proved he was interested.

It felt nice.

Maybe she did want a dance partner. Or two. The night was young.

She inhaled a familiar scent and her heart stopped. Turning her head, she looked to the side, her breath suddenly hard in her throat.

The man was tall and cute and…

Not Michael.

Disappointment slammed through her gut.

Jane turned and pressed back into the blond guy. Maybe she'd take this one home tonight—she needed a positive sexual experience to get *him* out of her head. His belly felt a little soft against her back, but that didn't really matter. He was there and he danced just fine and God, he smelled a lot like Michael. Such a unique scent, too, like saltwater and motorcycles and—

Must stop thinking about the bastard.

So this wasn't *him*, she still liked it when he ran his hands up over her arms, and she didn't mind at all when he pulled her a little closer against his hard abdomen and his even harder—

"Hey!"

She spun around to face a tall, brown-eyed, brown-haired man who at that moment was grinning like the devil at her.

"Hello, Jane. I'm back."

Chapter Five

හ

It was *him*.

Again. What had he done with the blond guy? A quick glance and she found him standing at the edge of crowd, rubbing his jaw as if he were in pain.

As if someone had just decked him.

She whipped her gaze back to *him*. "We were dancing. You can't just go hitting people whenever you want."

"I told you to wait."

At least a head taller than any other man in the club, Michael stood before her, rigid, his long, strong arms crossed over his broad chest. The sight of him caused Jane's pulse to speed up and her stomach to lurch.

Kind of like scallops. She was allergic to scallops.

He reached out, grabbed her arm and tugged her away from the dance floor.

"Hey!" Abby placed herself directly in his path. "Let go of my friend!"

"It's all right, Abby. This is *him*."

"Him?"

"*Him*."

She pulled Jane to her side. "Leave her *alone*."

Michael took a step towards Abby. "Who the hell are you?"

"I'm her best friend, and that means I won't let you hurt her again."

"What are you talking about?"

"Don't be an idiot! You think you can just get my friend all fired up for the first time in years—"

"Abby!" Jane interrupted.

Abby ignored her. "Bang her against a wall and leave her bent over a table while you flitter off to your next appointment?"

"Wait a minute—" Jane took a step towards her friend.

"No! I'll kick his ass myself before I let him touch you again!"

By this time Abby had marched herself right up into Michael's face. He looked a foot down at the petite redhead and shook his head.

"Before you kick my ass, may I ask you one question?"

"No."

"Can I have one dance with your friend?"

"Hell no!"

"Yes!" Jane gave her friend a narrow-eyed look. "Yes. Let him have one dance."

"What? Why?"

"One dance."

Abby remained silent until she seemed to comprehend that Jane had something up her sleeve. "Fine. But one wrong move out of you and you're toast!"

Abby was about the size of Michael's thigh, but he nodded and clasped his hands behind his back. "Fine."

"I'm watching you."

"Noted."

"I'm glad you both worked that out." Jane stepped forward, took Michael's hand and tried to ignore the warm touch of his fingers taking her breath away. "Now, let's go."

Jane led him by the hand through the crowd, but as soon as they reached their destination she released his hand, turned, and faced him. "Wait here."

"No."

She nodded her head to where Abby stood, arms crossed over her chest, staring at them. Michael rolled his eyes, but remained where he stood.

Jane backed onto the dance floor, allowing herself to be swallowed by the bodies moving around her. She smiled when she heard the DJ expertly meld the current drumbeat with that of the next song…could it be? Could she get so lucky?

She could.

Prince's *Darling Nikki* blared through the speakers, the erotic lyrics making her smile, and she worked the music, her hands on her stomach, her hips gyrating—exaggerated and sexy. She loved this song, but had never danced to it before. Why hadn't she? It was provocative, erotic, but it would have meant dancing for herself.

She had stopped doing that long ago.

Not anymore. This song was exactly what she needed to show Michael that she was a dancer. An artist. And if he thought she was going to wait around patiently until he knocked on her door for a booty call he was in for a nice little surprise.

Her eyes drifted closed as she moved to the music, taking the part about grinding quite literally, and when she reopened her eyes she discovered her plan was working. A cute guy—and his friend—had spotted her grooving and were currently making their way toward where she danced. Perfect. She stole a glance at Michael and saw that he remained in his spot, his hands clasped behind his back and his black boots anchored to the ground.

Once again, Jane closed her eyes and thought about her favorite fantasy, the one where she was a harem girl, tied to a silk-covered bed, spread-eagle, while two men sucked hard on her nipples and another licked her clit. And there was one more man, entering her pussy with his long, hard cock. She thought about what it would feel like to have four men touching her, sucking her, fucking her…

Her fantasy was coming to life. The cute guy and his friend were grinding right along with her, and two more boys were saddling up behind her as well. She stole a glance at Michael and was very satisfied to see a vein pulsing along his jaw line. But he hadn't moved. Not yet.

Five of them now, surrounding her—behind her, pressing against her ass as she rubbed against a foreign body—at her side, fondling her arm, breathing on her neck. Her skin burned, sweat beaded between her breasts, and she became warmer as the men engulfed her. She lifted her arms above her head as she played out the song, grinding her hips, and when the blond guy stepped up and positioned his leg in just the right spot for her to ride him that's exactly what she did.

Just when her crotch made contact, it ended. The boys were gone, scattered into the crowd like so much confetti, and Michael stood in their place, looking pissed off and dangerous.

"You should really stop throwing people around like that. It's not nice."

In response he grabbed her arm and dragged her along as he weaved their way off the dance floor. Abby looked ready to pounce, but Jane stopped her with a meaningful look. She wanted to deal with this herself.

She ran to keep up with him, down a graffiti-covered hallway until they reached a door that he kicked open and pulled her through. They landed in a back alley, their only company a dim streetlight.

She looked up into his narrowed eyes, noticed the deep frown of his mouth, the severe lock of his jaw.

When he stepped closer, lowered his head toward hers, backed her right up against the cement-block wall, Jane sucked in her breath. He looked menacing, dangerous... She should have booked it right out of there.

Instead she waited for his lips to touch hers.

He went deeper to trace her collarbone with hot, whispery kisses.

His hands gripped her arms, steadying her shaking body as he moved lower, softly kissed her breast through the lace of her dress, then her stomach, and when his head was level with her pussy she pushed forward, silently begging him to press his mouth to her there.

Instead he pressed a kiss at her hipbone and Jane discovered an entirely new erotic zone. She sighed, wishing that he hadn't hurt her like he had. It would have been so nice to take him home, to fuck him, to sleep next to him.

To go for coffee with him the morning after.

He was on his knees now, kissing her thigh. "You're so goddamn beautiful."

"Shut up. I'm not sleeping with you."

"I always thought you were cute."

"What do you mean, always?"

"At the coffee shop. I always tried to get a look at your face, but you were constantly bent over some book, with your hair in your eyes."

"You knew that was me?"

"I figured it out after I left the other night."

The reminder of what happened snapped Jane back to reality. She tried to push away, but his grip was tight on her hips. "Let me go."

"Not yet." He raised her dress, the air cool against her naked thighs. "From the moment I saw you dancing in that restaurant I haven't been the same. Can't stop thinking about you."

"Stop. Someone might see." She looked around the alleyway but there was no sign of life.

"Don't care," he said, lifting her dress until he exposed her fully to his gaze.

"I see you have on black panties tonight." He grinned, looking up at her. "To match your dress, I assume?"

She nodded.

"I've been wanting to do this all week."

She believed him. With one quick jerk he ripped off her panties, then immediately began teasing her exposed clit with his tongue. She leaned back against the cement wall, angled herself against his mouth, lifting her leg until one knee rested on his shoulder.

Already turned on from her erotic dancing, she closed her eyes, savoring the pleasure of him as he spread her lips wide between his fingers, licking her pussy with long, sure strokes. He did this a few times, avoiding her clit until she whimpered for him to pay attention to the sensitive nub.

She felt his fingers teasing her, sliding beyond her passage to her anus, where he applied a light pressure that sent her right over the edge. She rocked her pelvis against his mouth one final time, and he held her steady as the alley tilted and her knees buckled and she heard his name screamed from somewhere deep inside her throat.

After a moment she drifted back to reality and realized he continued to softly lap at her a moment longer.

"Your pussy — it's amazing."

She smiled. "Thank you."

"I bought you a present. On my trip."

Jane rolled her eyes. "Oh, it was a trip now, was it? I thought it was just work."

"Often, my job requires me to travel."

"Let me guess. You usually get called away right after sex."

Still on his knees, he pulled her dress back down, and then reached into his jacket pocket. "Sometimes. But we can talk about that later."

Michael stood and held out a little red box. He flipped the lid open to reveal the most unique ring Jane had ever seen — intricately carved gold surrounding a brilliant, sparkling emerald.

He grinned at her a little sheepishly. "I found this in Colombia—would it be too cheesy for me say the stone reminded me of your eyes?"

Her gaze jerked from the ring to his serious brown eyes and back down again.

"Um, Michael?"

"Yes?

"What the fuck is that?"

Chapter Six

છ

Michael looked at the box in his hand. "It's a ring."

"Are you insane? Let's see if I have this correct. You fuck me, ditch me, then show up out of nowhere and expect to just pick up where we left off? Because you bought me a…a…*souvenir*?"

He shrugged. "It's not a souvenir. It's a gift. It made me think of you."

She stared at him as if he had grown a second head.

"Hey, I'm not asking you to marry me or something. Think of it more like a token of my affection."

"You really are insane."

"Look. Once before you said you trusted me. Do you still?"

She shook her head and looked away. "Yes. I don't know why, but yes. I trust you."

He breathed again. "Then let me have one night."

She narrowed her gaze back at him. "Why?"

"To persuade you to give me another chance. And to make love to you like you've never been made love to before."

He knew she wanted to say yes, at least to that last part, but she needed just a little more persuading.

Before she realized what he was about, he dropped the box back into his pocket and seized her arms. He then brought them behind her back, encircling both of her wrists in one of his hands. Immobilizing her, he lowered his mouth and kissed her.

To his satisfaction she kissed him back, meeting him full force, making little mewling sounds against him, obviously frustrated because her arms were restrained. Instead of loosening his grip, he tugged her wrists back further, enjoyed the feeling of her breasts pushing against him.

How he wanted her. But this time he wouldn't take her against a wall. This time he wanted her tied up, helpless as he pleasured her, convincing her to trust him, not just tonight but forever.

"So," he finally said against her wet mouth, "Are you going home with me?"

"No."

"What do you mean, no?" he demanded.

She looked up, grinning. "Let's go to my place instead."

That was all the invitation he needed.

* * * * *

"You know, I brought this ring back all the way from Colombia."

Jane shut her apartment door and turned her gaze to the crazy man she had just let into her home. "So?"

"Don't you want to at least try it on?"

"No."

He leaned down and kissed her. "You sure?"

"Yes." With her heart pounding, she walked away. Too bad he was crazy because she had to admit it wouldn't be all that horrible to be kissed like that every now and again. Still, she hadn't taken him home because of some piece of jewelry—no matter how gorgeous. She had taken him home because of a little promise he had made about giving her the best sex of her life. And even if the guy was loopy, she was willing to take him up on his offer.

Yup. She was that desperate.

"So." She didn't quite know what to do. It wasn't every day she had the man of her fantasies promising her an amazing night of passion, and she wondered if she was supposed to make small talk, or perhaps offer him a beverage.

"Can I get you something to drink?"

"You got beer?"

"No."

"Tequila?"

She shook her head. "Uh-uh."

"Where's your bedroom?"

Okay. So that was it for the small talk. She led him down the hall into her bedroom.

"Holy shit."

She looked around. "What?"

He shrugged off his jacket and threw it onto a chair. "It's like an opium den in here."

For a minute they both stood staring at her bed.

It took up the majority of the room, with a red silk quilt covering the mattress along with piles of pillows in deep purples, greens and black. A slatted iron canopy draped in jewel-toned silky fabrics enclosed the space, giving it the feel of a private den or an Arabian tent.

"Get on the bed."

She turned to him. "In my clothes?"

"Take them off." Michael tugged one of the red silk veils off the canopy and trailed it over his fingers.

With shaking hands, she lifted her dress up over her head and tossed it onto the floor. She hesitated for a moment, but one look at his unyielding expression and she flung the bra aside, too. Kneeling on the bed before him, naked, she felt naughty, very like the harem girl she fantasized about being. She didn't know what he was going to do, and her pussy throbbed in anticipation.

Michael slipped his t-shirt over his head, exposing his sinewy torso to her gaze. Sucking in a breath, she tried not to come right then, watching each of his muscles flex with his slightest motion.

He settled beside her on the bed. "Give me your hands, Jane."

She held out her hands, let him wrap her wrists in silk while she stared at his body, momentarily failing to notice him lean back, or his grin of wicked intent. She nearly fell flat on her face when he gave the fabric a tug. Only a swift lurch forward kept her upright.

"What the hell?" She yanked her wrists but it quickly became obvious that she couldn't wiggle free. He was completely in control.

"I've had ten years of SEAL training, so trust me, I tie a secure knot."

Then, in one motion, he elevated her arms above her head and pulled the veil over one slat of the canopy.

"What the fuck are you doing?"

In response he tugged the veil until she was forced to elongate her back into a stretch. "Torturing you." Then he tied her to the bed.

Also on his knees, he took a moment to look over his bound prisoner. "Fuck. I think that's the most stunning thing I've ever seen."

"You're crazy." So why was it, then, now that he had her restrained and on her knees, her arms bound tightly over her head, that she could feel the juice from her pussy dripping onto her inner thigh? She had never been tied up before, but heck, she was up for the new experience.

Heart pounding, she waited as he unlaced his boots and kicked them off. When he unbuttoned his jeans and kicked them off too, she nearly died from the visual pleasure of *him* — all six foot plus of him — in *her* bedroom.

He wore boxers, and Jane closed her eyes and licked her lips as he shrugged them down his hips and threw them onto the floor.

"Jane?"

She opened her eyes and nearly died. He had his cock in his hand, his dick looked rock-hard in his fist as he began pumping his hand up and down the impressive length. "I've been thinking about you nonstop for seven days. And then when I found you, you were surrounded by a bunch of assholes."

She had no response, mesmerized as she was by the sight of him masturbating before her. God, he was gorgeous.

His face was impassive, but the little drop of pre-come leaking out of his dick suggested he was as turned on as she was. She shuddered. Oh how she wanted to take that cock in her mouth, suck that glistening tip until he ejaculated his creamy seed deep into her throat.

She yanked on her ties, but they didn't budge.

"Seven days in the middle of nowhere, rescuing some fucking diplomat who got himself kidnapped." He leaned forward and kissed her lower stomach, just at the start of her rose vine tattoo. The pumping motion of his arm told her that he still had his hand on his cock. Lucky hand. "And the entire time I wanted to know where this flower began. And I wanted to taste your pussy."

Her nipples hardened at his words.

Next to her now, he looked her in the eye. "I wanted to kill those fuckers who were touching you at the club. Especially when I saw that you were liking it."

He took a nipple between his fingers and pinched. "No one but me ever again."

She closed her eyes. "Yes, Michael."

He moved away then, and she saw he was digging for something in her nightstand. Shaking, she waited.

"You're a naughty girl, aren't you, Jane? I knew it would be here somewhere."

She closed her eyes, knowing what it was he had discovered. When the buzzing sound filled the room her cunt began throbbing for it.

He returned to her side and tucked a lock of hair behind her ear. "If one cock's not enough for you I'm happy to oblige. As long as the other cock requires batteries, that is."

She waited as he dragged the tip of her silver vibrator across her dry lips, her chin, over her chest until he paused at her breast to press the throbbing toy against a nipple.

And he kissed her. Kissed her with a surprising tenderness that melted her heart.

Her wrists strained against the silk as she kissed him back. The bondage heightened her sensitivity and frustrated her at the same time — she had no control over her pleasure.

"Please," she heard herself begging for the second time that night.

Her body trembled as he used the toy to skim her body, across her ribcage, tracing her tattoo, over her pubic hair. And when she felt it humming against her clit she looked him in the eye and begged. "Fuck me, Michael. Please. With the vibrator."

"Spread your knees wider."

She inched open as far as she could, her pussy so sensitive now that the air against her wet sex felt like an erotic caress.

"Beautiful."

Her pussy dripped, and the creamy juice allowed the dildo to slide easily across her slick flesh. She bucked forward as he played with her, paying attention to her clit, then her inner lips, outer lips — he was doing a thorough job of it but, "Inside," she rasped. "I want it inside."

"Like this?" he murmured, teasing the mouth of her pussy.

"All the way in!"

He leaned forward to take a nipple in his mouth, and as she felt the sharp bite from his teeth as he — at last — pushed the vibrator deep into her body.

She tensed, then moaned in pleasure as he found a rhythm… But if he would just push it a little harder, fuck her a little deeper, she was right there…

Instead he withdrew.

He moved behind her and she closed her eyes, let her head fall back against his shoulder, taking pleasure in the way his hot, solid body cradled hers.

He touched her everywhere—his hands on her breasts, caressing her stomach, her ribcage, his mouth hot against her ear. With a long, strong finger he stroked her pussy from anus to clit and back again, continuing the slow torture until she was moaning incomprehensibly.

Then he brought his hand to her lips, and she could smell her arousal on his skin. "See how wet you are?"

When he slid his finger into her mouth, she closed her eyes and sucked him deep, wanting so badly for it to be his cock instead.

And then he was spreading her pussy wide, tapping her clit with the pulsing vibrator, as he breathed into her ear, "Go on now, baby. Come for me."

She did. Her orgasm came fast and hard, in shattering, unstoppable waves.

He gave her no chance to recover. He must have released her wrists because the next instant she felt the firm grip of his hand on the back of her neck, pressing her forward until her head rested on a silk pillow.

With her bottom in the air, she felt a moment of embarrassment. If it was true that he didn't think that part of her was attractive, there was no hiding it from his gaze now.

"You have the most beautiful ass."

Whether he spoke the truth or not, she smiled. The fact was he made her feel beautiful and, she realized, that was all she needed for the moment.

He reached between her thighs, smoothed a hand over her pussy, still slick and sensitive from her orgasm.

"You're perfect." His fingers toyed with her, moved from her cunt to her ass in lazy possession. The first slick circle caught her by surprise, had her gasping, catching a moan with a bite of her lower lip.

She heard a squirting sound followed by the touch of his hands, slick with lubricant as they massaged her skin. He must have discovered the bottle of lube along with her vibrator. Her body trembled with anticipation—she knew what he intended to do.

Then his fingers were spreading her ass and there was no mistaking the hard tip of his cock pushing at her, and when he broke through, his entrance eased by her own pussy juice mingled with lube, the moan escaped. And then the world became that one point of flesh right there, sliding home. Deep, slow and steady, so fucking hot she couldn't breathe. She tensed at first, but then surprised herself by tossing her head back in pleasure, pushing back into him until his cock was deep and she was full.

"Baby, I've been wanting this all week."

"Is this what you were going to do that night, before you got called away?" She had to know.

"Yes."

He began to move, and she cried out as an exquisite pain filled her. Could she do this? But the next instant she felt a heavenly vibration filling her cunt. A strained wimper came from low in her throat.

"When you were dancing with those fuckers at the club, is this what you wanted? To have both your holes filled at once?"

"Yes," she admitted, shocked at her answer.

He pushed deeper still, and as he did so she ground herself against the purring vibrator inside her pussy. The dual penetration filled her completely, resulting in an overwhelming pleasure that seemed almost gluttonous.

And then he began to fuck her ass, slowly at first, but soon meeting her rhythm as she thrust back into him. She alternated between fucking the vibrator and fucking him, her body sinking lower until she was grinding her pelvis against the bed, her clit rubbing her palm as she used the tips of her fingers to push her toy deeper and deeper.

With his arms on the bed supporting his weight, he sank with her until the length of his body covered hers. She turned her head to the side, desperate to feel his breath on her face, and he lowered his mouth to her ear. "Do you like me fucking you like this?"

"Yes."

"Good. Because you're mine now, and I can do this to you whenever I want."

"Oh God. Yes." His possessive words excited her as much as his cock did, and her climax tore through her body with an intensity that brought tears to her eyes.

The next moment she felt his entire body tense, and then his hot liquid filling that virgin part of her body.

Panting, he collapsed beside her, pulling her with him. "I wasn't kidding," he whispered against her ear.

She nestled her back against him. "Hmm?"

"You're mine now."

Some feminist part of her said she should argue his macho words. But he felt so good, and would it really be so bad to be his?

What if he belonged to her, too?

* * * * *

The next morning, while she slept, Michael slipped away.

Falling for Jane was like jumping out of a helicopter without a parachute. The impact slammed through his entire body, stunning him, and he wasn't sure if he was strong enough to survive.

After their lovemaking, Michael had tucked Jane into her bed, holding her tight as he explained the details of his job. She didn't say much about it, just listened until she fell asleep to the murmur of his voice.

He, on the other hand, had lain awake all night, holding her and thinking about the fact that he couldn't live without her. He had been right that first night—she had cast a spell on him, a spell that had pushed him head over heels for her.

Finally, around five-thirty that morning, while she was still dead to the world, he had decided to clear his head with a walk to the coffee shop

Settling into an overstuffed chair toward the back, he sipped his double espresso and stared into space. *You are such an idiot–a complete moron.*

He took off his glasses absently cleaned them. How many times had he seen her here in this very place? Probably hundreds, each time ignoring the plain Jane at the corner table.

An image of her naked body, bound to her opulent bed like a harem girl, flashed through his head. Plain Jane? Ha! He didn't fucking deserve her, but that wasn't going to stop him from getting her.

It would just take some time.

Michael was gazing out the window, contemplating how long he'd like to keep Jane tied to her bed, when the coffee shop door was flung open. She was gorgeous even now, dressed in her pajamas and panting as if she had just sprinted the four blocks from her apartment. Barefoot.

He pushed back his chair with a clatter and stood. "Jane? What's wrong?"

"You can't do that!"

He walked towards her. "What? What can't I do?"

"Leave me with no explanation. Again."

He took another step closer. "I just went for coffee."

"I trust you, Michael." She lifted up on her tippy-toes and kissed him. "I know your job requires me to be understanding—and I'll get used to that. But you can't just disappear—you can't."

He took a deep breath. "I know."

"Do you promise never to do that again?"

"Yes." *Anything.* "Yes. I do."

Green eyes sparkling, she held up her hand.

Michael's heart jumped when he saw the shining emerald ring on her finger.

"Good." She smiled and kissed him once again. "Now. It's time to fulfill another one of my fantasies."

Grinning, he leaned down and kissed her ear. "I'd be more than happy to oblige."

"Great." She plopped down into an overstuffed chair. "I'll have a skinny double latte."

He stared down at her. "That's it?"

"Oh! And a bagel with cream cheese."

"Wait. This is your fantasy? Coffee and bagels?"

"Yes." Her smile was brilliant. "Coffee, bagels and you. What more could a girl want?"

About the Author

ରୋ

Despite a lingering fascination with Aqua Net and Camaros, Lillian Feisty has finally outgrown her wild youth and settled down to do what she has always dreamed of doing: writing romance novels.

Why romance novels, you ask? Well, it all started when she was 14 and discovered Jane Austen. After reading Pride and Prejudice in one day, Lillian promptly decided each book she read thereafter would include a version of Mr. Darcy. She soon realized that the only place in the library where she was likely to find such a thing, was the section with well-worn paperbacks featuring beefy heroes and half-naked ladies displaying Eighties hairdos and 19th century costumes. She read these "trashy books", as her grandmother used to call them, with an insatiable appetite. Once she had plowed through the library's collection, Lilli began writing her own romances. Her first story featured a hero with a striking resemblance to Jon Bon Jovi; of course, he drove a Camaro.

Although she spent the majority of her twenties working just long enough to pay for extended trips to Europe, Lilli also managed to earn a degree in Creative Arts and snag her very own hero. Although she continued to write, it was only when she turned 30 that Lilli realized she wasn't getting any younger, and it was time to get to work on that dream of writing romance novels for a living.

Lillian welcomes comments from readers. You can find her website and email address on her author bio page at www.ellorascave.com.

CLUB VAMP

Allyson James

ജ

Chapter One

ဆာ

Closing time.

Another night come and gone, another day without an answer.

Adam Chase locked the doors of the club, the padlocks clicking with empty finality. Kenelm had already retreated downstairs, and Adam had to go to him and tell him they'd failed yet one more night.

He walked through the dark club, catching a glimpse of himself in the mirrored wall, a tall man with a mane of blond hair hanging in a tail against his black suit. His hard, square face held a grim expression, his dark blue eyes empty.

A door in the back of the club led to the private quarters, a staircase leading to the bowels of the place—Kenelm's sumptuous home spread under the Manhattan club, hidden, unseen, secret.

Lord Kenelm awaited him in the living room, which was decorated in black silk and crammed with priceless objets d'art Kenelm had collected through the ages. This morning he sat on a gilded sofa studying an Egyptian scarab, solid gold with a sapphire on its back.

His full name was Ghislain Avent Brennan, Lord Kenelm, but he didn't make anyone say all that, not even his blood slaves. He went by Kenelm, a title he'd held since the eighteenth century.

He'd long since abandoned eighteenth-century garb for more modern dress of jeans and boots and black leather. Black haired and black eyed, he fit the vampire stereotype just fine. His dark eyes could suck you to your doom and frequently did.

Adam had first seen his eyes in Paris, the year 1848, when a mob had begun another revolution and the city reverted to madness. Adam, an Englishman in the wrong place, had been stabbed and lay slowly dying. Kenelm lifted him out of the muck and took him home.

His magic had saved Adam and allowed him to live for the next century and a half without aging. Adam wasn't a blood slave, he was Kenelm's best friend and partner in crime. And what crimes...

Kenelm didn't look up from studying the scarab, which they'd found in Egypt the year Petrie had begun his excavations. "Such a beautiful thing," he said absently, turning it in his fingers to catch the light. "A beetle, an insignificant insect, recreated to be a revered and valuable object. On the one hand, the Egyptians were the most boring and practical people on earth, and on the other — incurable romantics."

"She didn't come," Adam said.

"I know." Kenelm looked up, eyes burning Adam all the way across the room. "If she had, I'd have felt her."

Adam crossed the room to the bar on the other side, pouring himself a glass of malt whiskey. He lifted the glass, questioning whether Kenelm wanted any, but the man shook his head.

Adam knew what he wanted and needed. They'd better find this woman soon, or Kenelm wouldn't be able to leave the compound, even at night.

Adam drained his whiskey glass, swallowed the soothing liquid and removed his jacket. Underneath he wore a white silk shirt, which he also removed while Kenelm ignored him. He made his way to the sofa and knelt just as Kenelm returned the scarab to its place on the end table.

"The man said she'd be in Manhattan," Adam said, trying to sound reassuring. "We'll find her."

Kenelm gave him a deprecating look. "Do you know how many people live in New York City?"

"Not at last count, no."

"Many." Kenelm thumped his feet to the floor and rested his arms on his knees. "The phone book is about three feet thick. I'm ready to find this woman, kick some ass and take her back home."

"You and me both."

Kenelm lifted Adam's wrist and ran his tongue across it. "You drank way too much Scotch tonight."

"I was depressed."

"I hate Scotch." Kenelm's mouth heated Adam's arm as he licked his way up to the bend of his elbow. "Ready?"

Adam nodded once. His pulse was beating fast, his cock stiffening. Kenelm leaned down and sank his fangs into Adam's wrist. Adam hissed a breath through his teeth at the first suckling, then moved his body in rhythm with Kenelm's mouth. He stroked the jet black hair that flowed across Kenelm's shoulders.

He was lucky, he knew. He'd have been dead long ago, but Kenelm had chosen him for this mission, which guaranteed him long life and protection. All Adam had to do was keep Kenelm alive, a difficult task but one he gladly performed.

Kenelm gave one final suck and raised his head, wiping blood from his mouth.

"Better?" Adam asked.

"Better."

He wasn't completely sated, and Adam knew it, but Kenelm would never say so.

"Ready to hit it?" Kenelm asked. "It's what, eight in the morning?"

Since all the clocks had struck the hour, there was no denying it. Kenelm rose, his energy restored for now.

He was a big man, tall and wide-shouldered, black hair falling in a thick swath. He was a pure vampire, one of the last of his kind, a man who could put a human into a trance at five paces and leave him there until he was done. He could be gentle when he remembered to be, but most of his lovers were perfectly happy to have it rough.

He snaked his arm around Adam's neck and kissed the side of his mouth. "Thank you."

Kenelm always said *thank you* — in a deep velvet voice with a hint of gravel. It was a survival trait of vampires to be irresistible, and Kenelm had that trait in spades.

They went to the bedroom where Adam stripped off while Kenelm leaned on the doorframe and watched. "Do you have *any* ideas?"

Adam paused in the act of pulling off his briefs, deciding to tell the truth. "No. Not a one." He kicked off the underwear and faced him, nude. "I haven't been much help, have I?"

Kenelm flicked his gaze over Adam's body. "You compensate."

Adam's balls tightened and lifted, responding to the powerful need of Kenelm's gaze. Without word, he walked to the bed. The covers had already been removed, the sheets cool and inviting. Adam lay down on his back and laced his hands behind his head.

Kenelm wanted the oil tonight. He rummaged in a drawer for the glass bottle then removed his clothes with deliberate slowness, while Adam's skin prickled in anticipation.

Kenelm was a being made for sex and blood. Hunger and lust, trapped and mixed up inside a hard male body. Standing over the bed, Kenelm poured oil across Adam, letting the fragrant liquid stream across his skin before sitting beside him and working in the oil with his hands.

Adam basked in warmth. Kenelm had just fed, which made him strong and flush with heat, his skin almost glowing. It made him dangerous, sometimes gentle, sometimes letting loose his full strength. Adam was never sure what he would do.

Tonight his dark gaze was intense as he rubbed the oil around Adam's areolas and slid hands to his navel. Then down to his cock, where he took Adam in both fists and began to work him.

It was going to be one of the wild nights. Kenelm's fingers clicked against his palms as he slid fingers on and off Adam's cock, his grip tight and designed to bring Adam off very fast.

Adam tried to will himself to hold back, telling his body to lie still and enjoy as long as he could. He clenched his fists at his sides, trying to keep his hips from leaving the bed as Kenelm's hands stroked and pulled, stroked and pulled.

Kenelm watched him with fathoms-deep dark eyes, liking the challenge but still wanting to win. There was no way he couldn't win, and when Adam came it would be explosive, but for now the game was to see how long Adam could last.

"Damn you," Adam said, and Kenelm gave him the smile, ruthless and arrogant.

Fire flowed up and down Adam's body, shooting tendrils of excitement that elongated his cock even more, daring Kenelm to enclose all of it at once. Kenelm closed his grip so tight it was like fucking almost, except the slippery friction of his fingers was a little different from that of a quim.

"A hundred and fifty years," Adam murmured. A hundred and fifty years since he'd started playing this game with Kenelm, and Adam had still not tired of it.

"A hundred and forty-six," Kenelm corrected. "It took you a while before you let me touch you."

"I was ignorant."

"You were a man of your time. But I have lived and seen— so much more."

He fell silent, and Adam knew what was coming. Kenelm cranked him harder and harder, and Adam's self-control stretched to the breaking point. All of the sudden it was no use, he had to let go. He envisioned his come leaking all over Kenelm's hands, Kenelm leaning down to take it in his mouth, and his climax washed over him. He moaned…

And Kenelm let him go, cold air flooding Adam's cock just at the point of explosion. The fire died enough to keep Adam from releasing, and his body raged.

"Fuck."

Kenelm laughed, that deep, dark laughter that said the rest of Adam's day would be interesting. Kenelm was on the bed before Adam drew another breath, hard hands lifting Adam's hips and opening his thighs, so Kenelm could get on his knees and fit right between Adam's buttocks.

He'd lubed his cock with the oil so all he had to do was ring Adam a little with his finger and then enter. Adam's wanting body drew the cock all the way inside.

"It's nice to have friends," Kenelm said as he started his slow, in-and-out seduction, "for a hundred and forty-six years."

Adam's reply was incoherent and obscene. His mind was a blank of sexual ecstasy and built-up tension, Kenelm deep, *so goddamn deep,* inside him, and his own cock standing up hard and heavy.

Just when he couldn't stand it any more, Kenelm closed his fist over Adam's cock and squeezed. Adam released in screaming joy, lifting his hips to let Kenelm fuck him for as long as the man wanted. Today, it was for a long, long time.

* * * * *

Adam lay on his side later that afternoon, drifting in and out of sleep, a sheet draped half over his body. Kenelm lay behind him, not bothering with the sheet. He clicked the remote over Adam's hip to flip through channels on his wall-mounted television.

Adam could care less what was on the news and drowsed, seeking sleep so he wouldn't be too exhausted tonight. The club opened at nine, and Kenelm might feel well enough to make an appearance.

Kenelm ran his fingers absently through Adam's hair, his touch gentle, far from what it had been earlier. Whenever they shared a woman, Kenelm could be almost tender, but when he was in a mood, he knew Adam could take his rougher side. Adam could, and enjoyed it.

Because it was Manhattan, there was always news, most of it gloomy—gloom drew more viewers than gladness. A suicide on a bridge. A fire at an apartment on the Lower East Side. A subway stuck in a tunnel for two hours, and when tempers started to fray, a woman had shared out the cake she'd bought for an office party and led a sing-along. Well, that news had turned happy.

Needing more grit, the news channel turned back to the fire. A young woman stood in front of the apartment building, microphone in her face, speaking in the earnest tone of journalists everywhere.

"The fire began at eleven a.m. and no one yet knows the cause of the blaze," she said. "Neighbors smelled the smoke and reported it. Apparently no one was home in the apartment when it started, and the owner had no pets." It seemed important to add the line about the pets. People worried about pets.

She had short brown hair, curls buffeted by cold October wind, and wide, very earnest blue eyes. Red lips, full and lush and made for kissing. A neck a vampire would love to bite. In short, a savory woman, much too good to stand shivering in front of a burning building with soot on her face.

She had a European cast to her features, high cheekbones and pointed chin that indicated Russian or eastern European ancestry. Her accent was American, her attitude American, so he concluded she'd been born here.

Kenelm had a different reaction. He hurriedly clicked buttons of the remote and zoomed in on the woman.

Adam saw it. At the base of her neck, in the curve of her collarbone was a tiny tattoo, a stylized ankh. The sign of Osiris.

Kenelm leaned over Adam like he'd go right through the screen.

"It's her." His eyes held dark rage, and beneath it, hope. "Go get her."

Chapter Two

ℬ

Helena Girard stood her ground, the flames behind her making even the cold day roasting. Soot and smoke and ash coated her throat, rendering her voice raw. Her first assignment, and it was a brutal one. Well, they wanted to see what she was made of.

She swigged water the cameraman Josh handed her and wiped her mouth. "Ready?" she croaked.

Josh shouldered the camera, adjusted one or two things, and gave her a signal. Helena lifted her microphone.

"Two hours ago, this street was business as usual. Witnesses say the front windows on the second floor blew out and the fire spread quickly. Those exiting the building had no idea what caused the blaze. Fire crews are working furiously, and the mayor wants answers, now."

From her earpiece, the voice of her co-worker back at the station said laconically. "Okay, that's enough. Thanks."

Easy for him to say. Helena gazed earnestly into the wide camera lens. "This is Helena Girard, WLB News."

Josh lowered the camera and rolled his shoulders to relax them. Josh was an old pro and his presence had helped her get over her first-day-on-the-job jitters. Nothing seemed to rattle him.

Passersby who'd stopped to watch her began to drift away. Even fires got boring after a while.

One man remained. He had stood for thirty minutes on the sidewalk opposite her, immovable despite the crowd flowing around him. *Good looking,* she thought as she pretended not to notice him. Blond hair, tall, handsome body, eyes that could have you ripping off your clothes before you knew what hit you. Seductive.

While I'm here with wind-whipped hair and soot all over my face. Not that I could have anything with him anyway. I can't risk that I wouldn't kill him, and killing him would be a damn shame.

"How long do they want us here?" Josh asked her, setting the camera carefully on the ground.

"Until the bulldozers come, I guess." Fire crackled behind her, coupled with the steady rush of water of hoses. Blue-Eyes still watched her.

"Want me to grab some coffee?" Josh offered.

"That would be fantastic."

Josh moved off while Helena tucked her mic under her arm and backed out of the way of the frantic firemen.

"Helena Girard?"

Even Blue-Eyes' voice was seductive, warm and gravelly, making her think of hot baths and oil massaged all over her body, a firm cock pressing between her legs. *I wish.*

"Yes?"

"Can I interest you?"

Oh, yes you can, you hunk of a sex god. "Interest me in what?"

The man held out a card. It was black, glossy, with a scarlet logo that read *Club Vamp.*

"It is invitation only," the man said. "I would like to invite you."

He had a slight accent. English, she thought. It made him all the more delicious.

She took the card but shook her head. "I can't interview you. Interviews have to be cleared with the features department. You'll have to contact them."

"You misunderstand," he went on in that adorable voice. "I want to invite *you*, not your television people. It is a private invitation. I saw you this afternoon and decided you would be the perfect guest."

She blinked. "Why?"

He brushed back a wisp of her hair, smiling a little. "You just are."

She went still in shock. She never let men touch her, because it was much too dangerous—for them—but she loved the way his fingertips feathered over her skin, the flushed warmth in her body.

"My name is Adam Chase," he said. "The doorman is instructed to admit you. We open at nine."

She knew what Club Vamp was. A place you could be with a vampire—oh, yes, they were real—and take no hurt from it. They needed sex and blood, not necessarily in that order, and you could wallow in ecstasy and emerge again like nothing had ever happened to you.

The vampires admitted only those they chose and gave their guests their ultimate fantasy. The rich and famous vied to get in, but it was for members only and the vampires were very selective about who became members.

Helena had never tried to find out what it took to become a member. She didn't know if she could hurt vampires if she had sex with them, but she didn't really want to find out.

It was brilliantly sunny today, proving Adam wasn't a vampire himself. What was he, then? A barker for the club? Someone who recruited members? If she went to the club, a vampire would choose her, not the gorgeous Adam. What good would that be?

She tried to hand the card back to him. "No thanks. I don't like vampires."

"Keep it." He smiled again and backed a step. "I will look for you tonight."

Without another word, he turned and walked away, showing her a tantalizing backside in tight leather pants before he disappeared.

Oh, he was beautiful. It was tempting to show up at Club Vamp just to feast her eyes on him again. She could sit in the corner with a virgin cocktail and drink him in. *We'd be perfect for each other. Except for my curse.*

She knew she'd go home, curl up on her bed, and try to forget about blue-eyed Adam. Watch *Buffy* reruns or something. No dressing up and going to Club Vamp, not even to satisfy her curiosity.

So she never understood why, eight hours later, she stood at the black-painted door of Club Vamp on Forty-Eighth Street, handing the card to the doorman and telling him Adam had sent her.

* * * * *

Helena walked in, keeping her reporter's eyes open. If coming here turned out to be a big mistake, she could at least do a story on the club and earn some brownie points with her boss. Reporters weren't allowed in, which was why she'd finally decided to come tonight. Or so she told herself.

The club seemed normal enough. Dark room, loud music, large bar, three bartenders mixing drinks with lightning speed. Mirrors on one wall—to prove vampires cast no reflection? Muffled black velvet walls and lots of drapes.

She found a table far from the dance floor and ordered a martini from a waitress in skimpy black vinyl. Helena sipped it, watching people dance. None of them seemed to be vampires, not that she thought she could spot one, unless that was what the mirrors were for. From what she understood, the biting here went on in back rooms.

After she'd sipped the last of the martini, she threw the cocktail stick back into the glass, disgusted with herself. She admitted the truth—she'd come here specifically to see Adam, liking the way he'd smiled at her, thinking maybe they could get to know each other better, even if it could go no further than that.

He was nowhere in sight. Likely he was only a man who drummed up business for the club, no matter how seductive he had to be to do it. In spite of his smiles and his touch he had no real interest in her.

She stood up, snatched up the beaded silk shawl she'd dragged out for this special occasion, threw a tip on the table, and turned to march out.

Someone touched her elbow. "Do not leave yet."

The velvety, erotic voice, the warmth, the tall presence— yes, it was Adam.

He wore black leather pants, black shirt, black suit jacket, his blond hair pulled back into a ponytail. A diamond stud glinted on his earlobe matching the diamond stickpin in his lapel. Against all this black his eyes blazed blue.

"Hi," she said.

He gave her a slow smile. "Hi." The word sounded strange on his lips as though he was unused to the idiom. "Kenelm wants to meet you. He's due out any minute."

"Kenelm?"

"Lord Kenelm. He owns this club."

Helena suppressed more disappointment. Beautiful Adam was a pimp for his vampire, and Helena had no wish to be a vampire's whore. "Is he really a lord?" she asked skeptically. "Or is that a title he takes to impress customers?"

"First Earl Kenelm. He was awarded the title by George the Second of England for services to the realm. Including a pile of money and a huge estate."

Hmm. She could stay and interview Vampire Lord Kenelm and ask him what it was like to dance the minuet, or she could go before Adam handed her to him as a tasty snack.

"Well, thanks for the invite, but I have things to do…"

"Here he is now." Adam gestured to the rear of the club, planting himself next to her in such a way that she'd have to climb over a chair to get around him.

From the shadows in the back of the club stepped the vampire that must be Lord Kenelm. She expected a fanfare, an announcement, a herald, maybe his adoring blood slaves raising him on their shoulders. No, he simply walked out into the club and stopped. The patrons, intent on dancing, didn't even notice him.

Helena didn't understand how they could *not* notice him. Black hair, eyes like a gateway to night, tall body, wide, wide shoulders and strength that blew her away even across the room. He wore black—what else?—a silk suit similar to Adam's with a ruby stickpin in his tie. He turned his head, not so much scanning the room as honing in on Adam and Helena next to him.

As though moved by invisible strings, he floated across the club directly for them, his feet an inch from the floor. People melted out of his way, most as though they hadn't even seen him.

What, he can't walk twenty feet like everyone else?

She remained rooted to the floor, lips parted, as the large, powerful man with sin-dark eyes drifted to a halt in front of her. The sin-dark eyes pinned her in place as one hand came up and touched her cheek, the gold band on his finger cool.

"Helena Girard." Not a question, delivered in a to-die-for voice while callused fingers caressed her skin. A decadent man, but not soft.

"Yes." She didn't ask how he knew her name—Adam had seen her broadcasting, and the WLB News website listed her picture and bio.

Kenelm's fingers moved from her cheek, silkily traced her throat, and came to rest on the red tube-like dress she'd donned to come here. He pulled the fabric down a fraction to touch her collarbone.

"You bear the mark."

He meant the ankh tattoo that she'd gotten when too little to remember. As her body had grown, the tattoo had stayed in the same place and same shape and size, which she'd been told was unusual.

"Yes."

"Then you know you do not need to fight. We will not hurt you."

His eyes grew darker and wider. Vampires could entrance with their eyes, and Helena hurriedly shifted her gaze to Adam.

She found Adam one step closer, hemming her in on her right as Kenelm blocked her way forward. She also became aware that both men were highly aroused. Not only did their gazes lock to her, but Adam stood close enough that her forearm brushed the large bulge in his leather pants.

Going to bed with someone like Adam was one of her wildest fantasies. The man had the aura of one who could please, who would smile and let his blue eyes shine as he took her in.

But she'd never dreamed of having sex with a man like Kenelm. He was too much, too high, too far. He would devour her, never mind the pleasure of it, though she had the feeling she'd die in ecstasy.

"I have to warn you that if I have sex with either one of you," she said in a steady voice, "I might kill you."

Kenelm's brows quirked the slightest bit, and if anything he looked more interested. "You do not need to threaten us, daughter of Osiris." He slid his fingers through hers and raised her wrist to his lips.

Osiris? She had the insane urge to babble, "My father's name was Bob," but she actually had no idea what her father's name had been. Helena was an orphan, raised by a charitable institution after she was found abandoned with no clue to her identity. *Helena Girard* was a name picked out at random.

"I meant, I can't be intimate with a man," she said. "I'll hurt him if I do."

Kenelm did not answer. He feathered a kiss to her wrist, lips warm.

Warm. Did that mean he'd just fed?

Her quim tightened as Kenelm ever so lightly stroked the inside of her wrist with his tongue. "I can control it under normal circumstances," she said. "But during sex, if I let go…" She drew a breath. "Let's just say men avoid me."

Another lick, another draw of fire. "When you orgasm, you cannot contain yourself, you mean?"

"Yes. That's what I mean." She could orgasm right here and now with his tongue on her wrist.

"With me," he said softly, breath on her skin. "It will not be a problem."

"Because you're a vampire?" she squeaked. "I don't know, I might still fry you. Believe me, celibacy is better than risking manslaughter. Or vampire-slaughter."

Kenelm gently released her. "Will you show me what you do? On Adam, if you're afraid of frying me, as you say."

Helena darted a gaze at Adam, landing in blue, blue eyes that held vast interest in her. Sexual interest.

"I don't want to hurt you," she told him. "Even though you tricked me into coming here you don't deserve that. Me walking out in a huff, yes, you having a heart attack or dropping dead, no."

"You said you could control it," Adam replied in his *come into my bedroom* voice. "Show me carefully."

"He'll come to no harm," Kenelm said. "I will not let him."

Helena didn't have much doubt that Kenelm could make things happen to his liking, but still she hesitated. Years of experience showed her the terrible things her power could do.

Kenelm's smile deepened, and he looked at Adam. "She does not want to hurt you. She's sweet."

"I see that." Adam laced one large hand under Helena's hair. "You can touch without danger, obviously," he said softly, leaning down to her. "And kiss?"

He brushed her lips to hers, much the same way Kenelm had trickled his kiss to her wrist. Fire stirred in her belly. Usually her strange power didn't manifest until she came, but Adam's lips were powerful, mastering, and he tasted as delectable as he looked.

He slid his tongue into her mouth, a bite of spice, and Helena lost it. Electricity sizzled and danced from her fingertips and bit deep into Adam, engulfing him in a wild sparking nimbus.

Chapter Three

ဆာ

Helena gasped and jerked herself away from him. Adam's eyes were wide, his body shaking with the charge that snaked over him in glowing waves.

Kenelm never blinked. He stepped behind Adam, placed his large hands on Adam's upper arms and closed his eyes. The electricity seeped from Adam into Kenelm and dissipated harmlessly.

Helena gaped. "Are you all right?"

Adam opened his eyes, languid and heavy. "Mmm, what a ride. Men *avoid* having sex with you?"

"I just electrocuted you! You could have died."

Kenelm slid his hands to Adam's waist. "Not with me behind him. You see? As long as I am there to absorb the energy when you have sex, he'll be fine."

A vision flashed into Helena's head of Adam, naked and delectable, riding her on a sumptuous bed, while Kenelm, equally naked, knelt beside them and ran his hands all over Adam's body.

Why didn't that alarm her? It should alarm her.

But it didn't, it made her horny as hell. A lifetime of toys and photos of the hunk of the month couldn't possibly compare with basking in the arms of a man. Or two.

The temptation tantalized her. She could have Adam, whom she'd wanted since she first set eyes on him. Kenelm would let her.

"Why?" she asked. "Why would you offer this to me?"

Adam smiled a slow and promising smile. "For the joy of it, my dear." He covered one of Kenelm's hands with his own, a gesture that made her stomach flutter.

"But he's a vampire." She felt safer looking into Adam's blue eyes than Kenelm's very dark ones. "Vampires never do anything without demanding a price."

"That is true," Kenelm said. "But we can give you a night and a day of the most exquisite ecstasy you will ever know."

The flutter moved to her heart which pounded hard and fast. A night and a day of pure ecstasy with these two men. Adam with his blue eyes and faintly accented voice, Kenelm with a touch like sin.

He was offering to let her have a man inside her, making love to her, while he siphoned off the killing electricity. Two men, bringing her to orgasm, Adam touching her, Kenelm watching with his night-dark eyes.

She put her hands to her face. "You are both tempting me all to hell. Please don't do this to me."

Kenelm reached across Adam and touched her ankh tattoo. "But I must ask you, daughter of Osiris. I need you."

"And what's with the *daughter of Osiris* thing? I'm not Egyptian."

Kenelm's secret smile returned to his mouth as his finger brushed the hollow between her breasts. "We will explain. You must decide quickly and come with us. There isn't much time."

"Why not? Why isn't there time?"

A sudden explosion filled the entrance of the club. The music halted, the bartenders dropped bottles and people screamed. Smoke and a whiff of sulfur drifted on the air.

"That is why not," Adam said, his expression bleak. "They've come for you."

* * * * *

The Guardians existed outside time and space, in limbo and darkness, without thought. Whenever a true vampire found a daughter of Osiris and tried to unite with her, then the Guardians were fated to act.

The Guardians had been created by Ammut, the crocodile-headed goddess who ate the hearts of the damned. She raised the Guardians to keep pure-blood vampires, who could mate only with the female descendents of Osiris, from strengthening and spreading.

The lightning of Osiris had settled in the daughter called Helena Girard, and she could restore her vampire to his full strength. Which must be stopped.

Both Ammut and Osiris had long ago ceased to be worshiped or even thought about except by a few pagan sects. But the Guardians lived on, in stasis and forgotten, ready to perform the one task for which they were created.

Now they burst into Club Vamp, armed in bronze, seeking to slay the daughter of Osiris and her foul vampire lover.

* * * * *

"They're the *what?*" Helena shouted.

She was beautiful and Adam wanted her. She was Kenelm's, fated for him but the kiss had sparked deep need for her. She tasted like honey and oranges, and reminded him of a woman he'd lost long ago.

"Guardians," he repeated. "They've come for you."

Four huge men wearing little but bronze greaves and breastplates and holding enormous bronze swords started across the room. Patrons of the club screamed and fled, but the warriors didn't hurt them. They honed in on Helena with deadly intensity.

"Get her below," Kenelm snapped. "I'll clear the club."

Adam wanted to argue—*No, you get her below, I'll clear the club*—but he spotted the fury in Kenelm's eyes and decided to obey him. He took the bewildered Helena's arm. "Let's do it."

"What are we doing exactly?" she protested as he began shoving her toward the door in the back of the room.

Behind them, Kenelm raised his hands. His vampire magic rolled over the club, the power of his mind soothing, quieting. The men and women who'd come to the club for the titillation of vampires began to relax and smile. Calmly they walked out to the street, blank looks on their faces. The doors swung shut behind them and the locks clicked.

The Guardians now had a clear field of attack. Adam hustled Helena through the door and down the stairs toward Kenelm's compound. She went willingly, less afraid of him than of the four determined warriors with sharp swords.

At the bottom Adam shoved her through another door and raced back upstairs to help Kenelm. He found Kenelm still standing in the middle of the floor, his powers raising a shield between himself and the bronze-clad warriors. Adam knew the shield would not hold. Kenelm had lost too much strength.

"Is she safe?" Kenelm asked without turning around.

"Yes. Now let me get *you* safe."

Kenelm lowered his hands. In that moment, the Guardians attacked.

Adam grabbed Kenelm around the middle just as swords came hacking down on him and dragged him from the club. He banged the door to the compound shut and flipped the many locks closed. He didn't have Kenelm's powers, but a good dead bolt or seven helped.

On the other side of the door, the warriors rammed it, banging the smooth, seamless door with sword hilts and fists. Kenelm pressed his hands against the door and willed it to hold.

When he backed away, his face was gray and weary, lines deep around his eyes and mouth. Blood oozed from under the ripped sleeve of his jacket, and he sagged when Adam put his arm around him.

"Thank the gods they're from the Bronze Age," he muttered as Adam helped him down the stairs. "They haven't figured out guns. Or nuclear weapons."

"Don't give them ideas," Adam answered.

They found Helena in the black-silk living room. She looked up when they walked in, her blue eyes round with astonishment. "You own all this?" she asked, waving her hand at the artwork.

Kenelm shrugged, sliding his ruined jacket from his body. "Trinkets I've picked up through the years."

"Trinkets?" She lifted a gold statuette of a cat that had come from the tomb of Tutankhamun.

Kenelm's lips quirked. He slid off his tie and let it drape across a gilded Regency chair. "We need to make love, daughter of Osiris. I tend to be—rough—so Adam will keep me from overdoing it."

In shirtsleeves, his collar unbuttoned to reveal a V of dark skin, he moved to Helena and cupped her face in his hands. Whatever wound he had sustained had already closed, though his shirt bore a red hole under the sleeve. "Like you, I sometimes lose control."

She reacted to him. A woman couldn't help *not* reacting to Kenelm. "You want me to have sex with you?" Her voice had softened, dipping to the sultry range. "With four armed men banging on the door upstairs?"

Kenelm made a negligent gesture with his fingers, and the sound of swords on the door went away. The warriors were still there, but he'd muffled the noise.

"My magic can hold them for a while. By the time they break in, we'll be ready to face them."

"We might be naked when they break in."

Again Kenelm almost smiled. "We must be quick, but that does not mean we will not enjoy it."

Her eyes grew more languid. "You promised me a night and a day of pure ecstasy."

"And you will have it." He smoothed her hair from her forehead. "Would you like Adam first? To get you used to it?"

Adam chuckled, though his heart beat rapidly. "The warm-up act. What a compliment."

"You are gentler than I am."

"She has an electric touch." Adam ran fingertips through Helena's hair, brushing Kenelm's hand along the way. The idea of sharing this beautiful woman with his lover made him pounding hard.

She looked from one to the other, her eyes like a dusky sky. "Are you both crazy? Or maybe I am. I'm the one down here with you."

She didn't look as alarmed as she could have been, but that was Kenelm's effect. He dampened fear and heightened joy, and Adam had firsthand knowledge of how much joy Kenelm could heighten.

Kenelm spoke as slowly and calmly as though they had all night. "I won't force you, daughter of Osiris. The magic won't work if I do. It must be your choice."

"Will you *please* tell me what the hell is going on? I can't make a choice if I don't know what my choice is."

For answer, Kenelm lifted her into his arms and sat down with her on the black velvet sofa. She crossed her long legs over his lap and settled in, looking happy to be there.

Adam took a chair across from them, leaning forward with elbows on knees. He enjoyed studying these two people — one he loved and one he was falling in love with.

"Once upon a time," Kenelm said, "there was a daughter of Osiris who saved a vampire."

"When was this?" Helena asked, the natural curiosity of the journalist springing to her eyes.

"Right now." Kenelm's velvet voice caressed, the vampire charm high. "When a daughter of Osiris mates with an ancient vampire, he will both save himself and create offspring. A child to raise."

Her eyes widened. "A child?"

Adam saw longing flicker across her face. A woman who could not safely have sex with a man would believe she could never hold her own child in her arms.

"That is what I can give you," Kenelm said. "And the twenty-four hours of ecstasy. I haven't forgotten about that."

"And in return?" A skeptical look crossed her face, along with pain. "I give you the child to raise?"

"No. You raise her with me. You stay with me as my life-mate."

"You'd keep me here? What about my own life, my career?"

"Have your career. I don't mind staying at home and looking after the children."

Adam hid a smile. The idea of a dark sex lord like Kenelm being a stay-at-home dad amused him. And yet he knew Kenelm had a deep capacity for love, which Adam had been lucky enough to touch.

Helena twined her arms around Kenelm's neck, already aroused and scented with desire. "Let me get this straight. You want me to have sex with you and have your children? But you want your friend to have sex with me first to loosen me up? Then what does he do? Go home?"

"Adam lives here," Kenelm said. "He is my lover. He is watching us, hard as a rock, wanting to be your lover, too."

Her blue eyes flicked to Adam again, even as she snuggled against Kenelm's broad shoulder. "You two are gay? Or bi, I guess you'd be."

"Adam has had no male lovers but me. I have had only one other, long, long ago when I first became a vampire. I had no intention of taking another male lover until I met him." He glanced at Adam. "You can understand why."

"Yes." She was purring now. "He's absolutely beautiful."

"He is." Kenelm's dark eyes held fire, and Adam's cock hardened still more. There wasn't much Kenelm wouldn't do, and he'd done it all to Adam.

"Shall we suck him?" Kenelm asked Helena. "I think he'd like that."

"You're absolutely right," Adam answered.

"Then let us see you," Kenelm said.

Happily. Adam fumbled with his buttons, hands shaking, and stood up to peel the leather pants down his legs. He sat on the chair again, the upholstery tickling his backside.

He spread his legs to let them see how huge and ready his cock was, knowing exactly what Kenelm liked him to do. He pulled his hard balls forward then ran his fingers all the way up the length of his cock, swallowing a groan.

"Hurry," he said, his words slurring. "Before I come. I want to come on you. Both of you."

Chapter Four

෨

Helena's heart thumped as she stared at Adam's cock, bared for her. Kenelm's eyes darkened as he riveted his gaze on his friend, his throat moving with a swallow.

She wondered about their relationship—Adam was not a vampire, nor did he bear the servile attitude she'd seen in people who had chosen to be blood slaves. Kenelm was obviously massively wealthy, scarily powerful and sexy as hell, but Adam was his own man.

These speculations danced in the back of her mind, but the front of her mind spun with excitement. Adam was beautiful, and Kenelm's magic almost made her forget the four ferocious men upstairs who wanted to kill her.

Kenelm put his hand on her arm and guided her to kneel on the soft carpet. "Have him," he said. "Enjoy him."

Helena's position on the floor let her examine Adam's cock up close, dark and long, thick and ready. Adam stroked it lightly with his fingers. "Please, Helena," he murmured. "You won't hurt me."

It had been so long since Helena had attempted to find pleasure with a man that she'd almost forgotten what to do. College dates had quickly dried up once she discovered she couldn't control the electricity in her fingers. Well, not entirely—some men hinted they wanted to be shocked possibly to death by her, but such men were too creepy to contemplate.

Kenelm knelt next to her, his long black hair spilling over Adam's bare thigh. His broad hand rested on Adam's waist, his eyes on Helena. Helena leaned down and licked Adam's tip, which tasted warm and salty and good.

His cock moved, beckoning her touch. She explored him with her fingers, his velvety shaft, the coarse hair at his balls, the smooth tip, the enticing lip of the flange.

"Mmm." Adam spread his legs a little more, shifting his hips forward.

Kenelm's black gaze took in everything she did. She knew he watched to stop her electricity if it flickered out of her, but she could tell he enjoyed seeing what she did to Adam, and he enjoyed Adam's reaction.

Adam enjoyed it too. He unashamedly splayed his legs open, groaning aloud as Helena licked her way up and down his cock. She slid her fingers around the stem, amazed at how large he was.

She had a feeling that Kenelm would be even larger. She darted a glance at Kenelm's groin as she drew her tongue around Adam's flange, her mind quivering with possibilities.

Adam lolled his head against Kenelm's shoulder, his blond hair mixing with Kenelm's dark strands. "She's so sweet. Thank you, my friend."

For answer Kenelm kissed him, catching Adam's moans of delight on his tongue. Helena watched, mesmerized by the two strong mouths taking each other in a practiced way. What would it be like to watch these two men making love?

Her fantasies made her quim squeeze and liquid dampen her underwear. It never occurred to her that watching two men kiss would be a turn-on, but then, she'd never met Adam and Kenelm.

She lowered her mouth over Adam's cock, wishing she were more practiced, because Adam was obviously used to skilled pleasure. She did her best, licking and nibbling and suckling. The taste of cock in her mouth plus the sight of Adam and Kenelm was enough to trigger an orgasm if she let it.

Adam must have thought so too. He rocked his hips, sending his eager cock into her mouth, his balls hard and standing firm beneath his base. She loved the dark golden hair there, loved the way he lifted his ass as though begging her to stroke it.

Daringly she eased her fingers into the warm place between his cheeks and wriggled her finger until she found his anal star.

"Oh, yes," he whispered. "I'm going to come."

Yes, come for me. Helena's heart pounded in excitement. To taste his come, what would that be like? Heaven on her tongue. His cock moved in her mouth, and any minute now...

Kenelm lifted Helena away, ripping her from Adam's lovely, lovely hardness. She made a noise of disappointment.

"No, make him wait for it," Kenelm said, his voice raw like he too was on the point of explosion. "You will ride him now, and let him get you ready for me."

Adam looked up at him, eyes clouded with frustration. "Bastard. Some day you'll let me finish."

"Maybe. Imagine how good that will feel."

"Damn you," Adam said, but he laughed, as though he and Kenelm had this argument all the time.

Kenelm fetched a bottle made of thick blue crystal, a work of art itself. The oil inside smelled like a work of art too, all spicy and warm.

Kenelm set down the bottle and unbuttoned his shirt. Helena got lost in looking at him, his incredible hard body shadowed by the placket, the dark hair on his chest that beckoned her fingers. Would she find a heart beating under her touch or silence?

Kenelm dribbled oil over his fingers, droplets spilling to the carpet unheeded. He smoothed his hand up Adam's cock, making it glistening and slick. Adam's head dropped back, then he moaned as Kenelm leaned down and a brushed light kiss to Adam's tip.

"Soon, my friend," he promised.

Adam gave Helena a half-smile. "Are you going to take off your clothes, love? It would be nice with clothes, too, but I want to see you."

Kenelm turned a dark gaze to her, waiting.

Helena put her hand to the back of her dress and began to unzip. It was exhilarating, and unnerving, to have these two men watching her with undivided attention, waiting for fabric to fall from her flesh.

The room was slightly colder than what she was used to, she discovered as she stood in nothing but strapless bra, panties, and thigh-high stockings.

Adam smiled at her. "By the gods, you're beautiful."

Her skin heated, and she remembered her dignity enough to not stammer thanks. She decided to pretend she had no worries about undressing in front of two men who looked like they wanted to devour her, and unsnapped her bra.

Definitely colder than she was used to. Her nipples rose to firm peaks and seemed to reach toward Adam and Kenelm. Before she lost her nerve, she slid her panties off, hoping she looked incredibly sexy and not as shaking and clumsy as she felt.

Both men fell silent, and she glanced up at them.

Kenelm had sat back, his face quiet, while Adam's smile made him unbelievably gorgeous. His jutting cock didn't hurt, either.

She walked to Adam and placed her hands shyly on his thighs. "I'm ready," she said.

"Almost," Kenelm answered for him. He rose and slid his hands, still slick with oil, across her waist, over her breasts, fingers plucking the tight buds. He dipped his slick hand to her quim, brushing it once. "Go to him," he whispered.

Adam reached for her. She placed her hands on his shoulders and straddled his thighs. He stroked the petals of her quim, opening her, nearly sending her to orgasm with his very touch.

"You're very wet."

"Can't imagine why," she said shakily.

"She likes us." Adam's smile grew brilliant, and he eased her down onto the tip of his waiting cock.

* * * * *

She felt so nice. Adam lifted his hips, liking how the folds of her quim eased around his cock. Sweet woman who smelled so good. He leaned forward and licked a trickle of sweat from between her breasts.

"Adam," she murmured.

He tried to go slow, getting her used to having a man inside her. He felt her tightness, then her slight gasp as she opened like a flower. Yes, Kenelm was wise to let Adam have her first, and so generous. Adam was the first one in her, the *first*.

The fire in Helena's fingers began. Faint lightning crackled through her hands as her thighs rocked against his, tight and fine.

Kenelm moved to stand behind him, strong hands drifting to Adam's shoulders. Adam leaned his head against his lover's chest as the lightning entered Adam's body and flowed into Kenelm's.

Kenelm made a noise in his throat that became a purr. "Lovely."

Adam thought so. Her fire tingled through his body, not hurting him because Kenelm drew it from him, in much the same way he drew Adam's blood into his body when he fed.

Adam had never had a woman like this. She was tight, tight, squeezing him hard like Kenelm's fist. Her lightning shivered faster, snaking through Adam's body in waves. Kenelm calmly drew it out, never letting it burn.

He loved Kenelm's hands delving inside his shirt, pulling it down to bare his shoulders. Kenelm slid his fingers between

Adam's body and Helena's, pulling on Adam's tightened nipples, cupping the globe of Helena's breast in his hand.

Helena's eyes widened. "I'm going to come," she panted.

"Not yet," Kenelm murmured, his voice driving Adam to the edge. "Ride a little longer. Enjoy yourselves, my friends."

Adam's fingers bit into Helena's hips, pulling her harder onto him. Behind him, Kenelm moved Adam's hair out of the way, baring his neck.

"Yes," Adam moaned. "Please."

He held back a cry as Kenelm's fangs sank into his neck. The faint pain, masked as usual by Kenelm's magic, coupled with Helena's pressure, released him. He pumped upward into Helena, loving the feel of her around him, of Kenelm's hands, of his mouth, his teeth holding Adam fast.

Helena screamed. Her hips moved with her climax, her walls clenching his cock in heavy pulses, the electricity from her fingers covering his body. The lightning went through him like no orgasm ever had, to be absorbed into Kenelm's mouth.

Adam felt his seed shoot into her, their joining complete. Helena rocked and danced on him, her nipples hard little points. Kenelm continued to drink, feeding on sex and electricity as much as he did Adam's blood.

Finally as Helena began to calm, the fires died. Helena drooped in happy exhaustion and Adam gathered her into his arms, letting her head rest on his shoulder. Kenelm eased away from Adam's neck, fingers touching the wound to close it.

"Stronger," Kenelm said. "Already I am stronger."

He sounded stronger, the wicked glint in his eye deeper and more gleeful than Adam had seen it in a long time. A playful Kenelm was a dangerous one, and Adam's cock stirred as he wondered just how dangerous Kenelm was going to be.

Adam touched Helena's hair. Her eyes were closed, breathing even, the lightning gone. "She's fallen asleep."

Kenelm pressed a kiss to Adam's neck and unfolded to his feet. "Carry her to the bedroom. I will finish while she is relaxed from you. I have no wish to hurt her."

Adam stroked his hand up Helena's limp form, a protectiveness welling inside him. He knew Kenelm needed to join with her to save himself and her, but he would be there to make certain Kenelm remained gentle.

"Come on, love," he said, lifting her into his arms, but Helena slept on.

* * * * *

She woke with Kenelm inside her.

She nearly screamed in shock. *Kenelm. Inside her.*

He was huge. He spread her like nothing ever had, his large body wedged between her legs, fists taking his weight, muscles cording with strength as he held himself over her. He was stark naked and so was she, both of them lying on a soft bed hung with black silk.

"Helena, look at me."

Helena bit back another cry and stared into eyes black as a moonless night. As soon as their gazes connected, she felt lassitude, a relaxing of her muscles, fear and worry ebbing.

"I'll not hurt you," Kenelm said, his voice a near whisper. "But you have to believe me. Can you do that for me?"

"Adam?" she gasped.

"I am here."

She turned her head to see him stretched out at her side, also naked, his honed body like a work of art. Blue eyes regarded her steadily.

"Look at me, Helena," Kenelm commanded.

Reluctantly she turned back to Kenelm and was caught again by his fathomless eyes.

Making love to him was different from making love to Adam. Adam had smiled and held her with warm hands and made her want to laugh in delight. Kenelm demanded her to focus on him and nothing else. His body dominated hers, wanted hers, would have hers.

His cock was so damn big. It spread her wide, and only by lifting her hips could she accommodate it. He stayed still in her, his arms shaking a little as he held himself back.

"Are you all right?" he asked.

Adam skimmed his hand across her shoulder, but she couldn't look at him. Kenelm's eyes held her, bringing her in, in, in. A lock of hair fell over his dark face, a few wisps catching in the shadow of whiskers on his jaw.

He waited for her answer. She gave a tentative nod, then groaned out loud when he pushed even farther inside her.

She'd thought him big before, *this* she'd never be able to take. She gulped a breath to scream, but Kenelm's touch on her face calmed her. "Shhh. I will make it easy for you."

Adam moved closer to her, his presence comforting. "I won't let him hurt you."

Kenelm did not look at him. His entire focus was for Helena.

Slowly he eased himself out and just as slowly came back in. He'd been right—she'd never have been able to endure this had Adam not taken her first. She felt faint surprise that she wasn't sore, but Kenelm's mesmerizing magic had likely taken care of that.

Another slow stroke, and another. Tentatively she squeezed the huge thing inside her and was rewarded by Kenelm's eyes growing heavy.

"Adam, you are right, she is sweet." Kenelm's voice grated.

He was filling her so full. Her entire body flushed and tightened with the wonderful pressure.

"More?" he asked her.

She nodded against the cool pillows. "Yes. More. Please."

"She likes you," Adam said. He smoothed her hair. "Doesn't his cock feel good? So damn big you don't think you can take it, but then he makes you able to take it."

The fantasies his words spun through her mind made her writhe with delight. Adam on his knees looking back at Kenelm, smiling as Kenelm thrust his hard, slicked cock straight into him.

The fires began. When she'd made love to Adam, Kenelm had dispersed the electricity, but there was no one to do it for him. It snaked all over his body, ropes of light on his naked skin. Any other man would scream with so much power streaking through him, but Kenelm laughed and drew it into himself.

"Beautiful," he said. "You are beautiful, my Helena, inside and out."

His words triggered her release. More sparks snaked from her hands and body as she lifted her hips to him. He stroked into her, her body pliant now, over and over until she couldn't see. Wonderful darkness swamped her until she realized he was coming too.

His seed scalded into her, her body wanting it, knowing she belonged to him. The joining was nothing like her joining with Adam, which had been pure pleasure. This was something deeper, more basic, a whispering through her body that this was *right*.

"Love you," she whispered.

Kenelm groaned. He pumped into her, faster and harder, and she could take it because she was his mate. His. Forever.

She was also aware of Adam next to her, his lips at her temple, his fingers on her hair. Her two lovers. She wanted to laugh. Yesterday she'd had no lovers, today *two*.

Kenelm gave one last thrust and sank down to her waiting body. "Thank you," he whispered, his body heavy on hers, his breath hot in her ear. "Thank you."

They lay together for a while, calming, then Kenelm withdrew, inch by slow inch, until he eased out, still hard. Helena felt momentarily bereft until Adam kissed her.

The kiss went on and on, his tongue tasting the corners of her mouth, for all the world like he had just made love to her instead of Kenelm. Kenelm rolled to her other side, his body warm against her.

When Adam eased away, she found Kenelm's gaze fixed on them both, his smile feral. "You have restored me, daughter of Osiris. And fed me your fires."

He sat up and with the stroke of one arm made every candle in the cavernous room explode into light. A hot wind blew the bed hangings, and the candle flames danced.

"Damn, I haven't felt this good in years." He quirked his black gaze to Adam. "Are you ready for me?"

Adam laughed, a dark eager laugh. "I was born ready for you."

With a growl, Kenelm was on him.

Chapter Five

ဆ

Kenelm astonished him. Adam had lived with the man for a hundred and fifty years, as his lover for all but four of those years. He thought he'd learned everything Kenelm could do, but he realized now he'd never been in bed with Kenelm at full strength.

Good thing Adam liked it hard, he decided. Kenelm had him flat on his back, Adam's feet curled around his head, Kenelm holding him while he slicked Adam down and entered him. The best, the best. Kenelm drove in mercilessly, and Adam loved every second of it.

Helena lay beside them, propped on her arm, watching them with round eyes. She appreciated watching them, if the little smile on her face indicated anything.

After a long time Kenelm came, his face twisted in ecstasy, and Adam was not far behind. Kenelm withdrew, kneeling back on the bed, breathing hard. "I need more."

"Insatiable," Adam chuckled, his body relaxing. "As usual."

Kenelm's hungry gaze flicked to Helena. "Can you?" he asked her.

She wet her lips, considering, but Kenelm was hard to resist. In the end, she held out her arms.

Kenelm made love to her, deep and fast, and after she climaxed, Kenelm withdrew and returned to Adam. He went back and forth between them, his mate and his lover, until Adam and Helena were sleepy with satisfaction.

Adam imagined the future between the three of them, when they'd teach Helena to take them both at once—Kenelm in her quim and Adam in her ass—how fine that would be. She was nowhere near ready yet, but they would teach her.

Adam fell asleep while Kenelm rode Helena one more time, dreaming of glorious things to come.

* * * * *

Helena lifted her head and sleepily brushed her hair from her face. Adam slept soundly next to her, Kenelm tangled on his other side, one brown arm slung across Adam's bare hip.

The room was quiet, the wind gone, the candles guttering or already burned out. She had no idea how long she'd slept, time being hard to gauge in this room. A few minutes? Hours? Days?

She really should give a thought to getting up and going to work. Kenelm needed an alarm clock in here—any clock. She sat up, wondering where the shower was, and then she remembered why they'd scurried down here so quickly and hid themselves behind bolted doors.

The Guardians. She heard nothing from upstairs, but Kenelm had dampened the sound. They could still be there.

As though he sensed her movement, Kenelm flicked open his eyes. He showed no indication he'd been asleep. Unlike herself and Adam, who'd fallen exhausted onto the bed at the end of the last round of lovemaking, Kenelm looked alert and ready to play.

"Um," Helena ventured, "weren't there four armed warriors upstairs wanting to kill me?"

"They are waiting for us." Kenelm's voice was low and silky. "Shall we go fight them?"

"We?" She stared at him. "Who's this *we?*"

"You and I, daughter of Osiris." He reached for her hand. "You and I now have the strength of gods."

Between them, Adam shifted in his sleep, and Helena got lost looking at him. She thought he'd wake, but he only made a faint noise, drew a long breath and drifted deeper into sleep.

"Explain how we now have the strength of the gods," she said, keeping her voice low. "Because I had sex with the two of you?"

"Because you had sex with *me*. Sex with Adam was just for fun."

And what fun. The man knew some techniques.

"Go on," she prompted.

"The daughters of Osiris were made to breed with vampires. The gift of Osiris to us. A curse too, because if we cannot find a daughter of Osiris, then we fade and die. Daughters of Osiris can mate with none but vampires. Which is why you fry everyone but me."

"But my parents weren't…" She broke off. She'd never met her parents, knew nothing about them. How did she know they weren't a vampire and a descendent of a god?

"It took me a long time to trace you," Kenelm said, giving her an understanding look. "I knew you'd come to Manhattan, but from there I had no leads. Your parents died when you were young, didn't they?"

"When I was a baby. I don't remember them at all."

He traced her cheek, his touch holding fire. "Your mother was a daughter of Osiris, your father a vampire. He was a lesser vampire, not as strong as I am, and so couldn't save your mother when the Guardians found them. An eye witness I finally tracked down said your father died in the daylight trying to protect her. That was in Russia. Your mother came to New York and hid you before the Guardians caught up to her. The Guardians never found you."

Tears stung her eyes. "The charity has no record of her. I was Baby X. They didn't even know my name."

"They chose a beautiful one. Helena." The backs of his fingers grazed her cheek. "But the new name did make you difficult to find. For the Guardians, and for me."

"And now you expect us to go kick the Guardians' collective butts? The same guys who killed my parents?" Sudden rage swept her, and she sat up. "Wait a minute—the same guys who killed my parents? I've changed my mind. I say we go kick some ass."

* * * * *

Adam woke to an empty bed. The warmth and scent of both Kenelm and Helena clung to the sheets and tried to draw him back to sleep, but he sat up, forcing himself awake.

The Guardians. *Shit.* He knew that Kenelm, cocky with his power, and Helena, likely stoked on a sexual high, had both gone to fight them.

He threw off the sheets and rolled out of bed, reaching for his pants. Bloody hell, this wasn't a game.

Adam dressed quickly, throwing a shirt on over his naked chest, then opened a cabinet hidden in the wall and removed a pistol. The bullets nestled inside were silver, good for stray werewolves or vampires who lost control in the club. Now to see if they worked on Guardians.

Adam shoved his feet into shoes and left the room, jogging through the deserted living room and back up the stairs toward the club. He heard the battle long before he swung the door open, the clang of swords, Kenelm's laughter, Helena's screams.

He banged into the club and found chaos.

Kenelm battled three Guardians himself, laughing as he cut and parried with a broadsword he'd kept since the Middle Ages. The Guardians had him backed into a corner, chopping at him with swords of edged bronze. Iron might be harder, but a bronze sword slicing off Kenelm's head could still kill him.

Helena grappled with another, lightning snaking from her hands to the warrior. The Guardian flinched and growled as the electricity engulfed him, but he was a magical creature and could fight through it.

"Helena," Adam yelled. "Get down."

Helena saw him. Her eyes widened but she instantly dropped. *Good for her.* Adam fired once, twice.

Silver bullets seemed to work fine against Guardians. The one fighting Helena jerked as Adam's shots entered his body, the bullets searing right through his breastplate.

Blood stained the bronze, and the Guardian toppled to the ground. After a few seconds, his body disintegrated with a hiss and a waft of noisome smoke. Helena clamped her hand over her nose at the smell of decay.

Adam spent a moment feeling triumph then aimed at one of the Guardians surrounding Kenelm. If Kenelm would get out of the way, Adam could fire.

Kenelm fought on, paying no attention. The vampire was having *fun*. Adam sighted over the gun trying to find an opening.

Sudden pain seared through his middle. He looked down in surprise to see a bronze blade pushing itself out from his own stomach, shoved into him by a *fifth* Guardian who stood directly behind him.

Damn, I should have checked to see if they sent for backup.

As if in a dream, Adam saw his own blood spurt over his clean shirt and puddle on the floor, before the pistol fell from his useless grip and everything went dark.

* * * * *

Helena screamed. The fifth Guardian had come out of nowhere—perhaps hiding himself until Kenelm thought he'd won? Helena ran to Adam and dropped to her knees beside him just as the Guardian yanked the sword out of Adam's body.

Adam's blood streaked the blade. Helena looked up at the grim-faced warrior, his eyes filled with more reason and life than the others'. He must be their leader, the one who gave the orders, the man responsible for killing her parents. He'd killed her father and her mother and now he'd killed her lover Adam.

She snatched up the pistol Adam had dropped and shot the warrior full in the face. He jerked back, blood all over the place, but he didn't stop. His sword came up, ready to slice Helena in two.

"His heart," Adam rasped. "Aim for his heart."

He was still alive. Swallowing tears of relief, Helena obeyed. She aimed and sent the last three bullets into the Guardian's heart. This time he fell, his sword clattering to the ground just before his body fell on top of it. Like the other, he evaporated with a hiss and a stink.

Kenelm threw the warriors fighting him away from him. They scattered, seeming dazed without their leader. Kenelm raised his hand and sent a blast of darkness at them that felled them all.

Helena watched him step over their disintegrating bodies, his face dark and savage, like the deadly night creature he was. She wiped tears from her eyes. "Could you have killed them at any time?"

"Yes." He spat the word in anger and sank to his knees beside Adam. "I was enjoying myself fighting. Idiot, why didn't you stay in bed?"

"Had to help Helena," Adam whispered.

"Damn it." He put his hand on Adam's stomach, blood smeared everywhere. "I was playing—I was so damn happy to have my powers back."

"He saved me," Helena told him. "I don't know if I could have held off the Guardian on my own."

"I know." Kenelm's eyes were full of self-loathing. "My arrogance has almost killed the two people I love best in the world."

Adam smiled, his face stark white. "You love me best in the world? Me and Helena? Aw, that's sweet."

"Shut up," Kenelm growled. He placed his hands over the wound, his eyes closing. Helena sensed vast power in him, far greater than that of the Guardians, far greater than it had been when she'd first seen him.

Adam felt it too. He clenched his teeth as though staving off pain. "I love you too, sweetheart."

Kenelm said nothing, lost in whatever magic he poured into Adam's body.

Helena smoothed Adam's pale hair. "Shh," she whispered, and kissed his forehead.

Kenelm saved his life. Whatever magic Helena had given him, whatever strength she leant, he saved Adam. Near the end, Kenelm turned to her, his dark eyes burning.

"Put your hands on mine," he instructed. "I need your power."

She obeyed. Placing her hands on top of Kenelm's large warm ones, she let out her power little by little, amazed she could control it so well.

They closed his wound, her power lacing with Kenelm's as Adam lay still beneath them, watching with his blue eyes. As the lines of pain eased from his face and he relaxed, he murmured, "I really do love you, you know."

"I know," Kenelm said, his voice like silk, his hands powerful under Helena's. "That's why I put up with you."

Adam smiled, and his eyes slid closed.

* * * * *

"An explosion early this morning at Club Vamp destroyed half the club and injured Adam Chase, the club manager."

Helena stood tall, the microphone at her mouth, her professional reporter voice at full strength. The wind whipped her hair as she stood on the street in front of the club, the afternoon sun shining through patchy clouds.

"Chase was taken to the hospital for minor injuries and released late this morning. He announced that Club Vamp will be closed until further notice."

Kenelm reached across Adam on the bed, cranking up the volume so he could listen to Helena. He'd never tire of listening to her.

"I didn't need to go to the hospital, you know," Adam rumbled beneath him. "You and Helena healed me."

"I wanted to be sure." Kenelm didn't think he'd ever forgive himself for almost getting Adam killed. Power like he'd never felt had surged through him, and he'd let himself wallow in it. *Like an idiot.*

Adam would have come running to his and Helena's rescue no matter what. Adam was just that way. At least Kenelm's newfound strength had allowed him to heal Adam. He'd not had to pay for his arrogance by losing the man he loved.

Kenelm let his hand slide down Adam's torso to his cock. Adam half rolled over and looked sleepily up at Kenelm.

"Mmm. Completing my cure?"

"Something like that."

Kenelm leaned down to kiss him, taking his eager lips. Adam made a noise in his throat and snaked his hand to Kenelm's naked back, fingers sliding toward his ass.

Kenelm broke the kiss. "I don't want to hurt you."

"Fuck you," Adam said, smiling. "I'm fine. Fuck *me.*"

Kenelm returned the smile, his power stirring. He needed it rough right now, and Adam, damn he loved him, was giving him his *come on, I can take it* look.

"Suck me, and I just might," Kenelm growled.

"Any time, lover boy." Adam slid down the bed, away from Kenelm's grasp and rolled over to take Kenelm's giant cock in his mouth.

"Oh, perfect," Kenelm crooned.

Adam was talented with his lips and tongue, knowing exactly how Kenelm liked it. He splayed his hands across Kenelm's thighs, teasing his rock-hard balls. Kenelm lifted his hips, letting Adam get his thumb against Kenelm's anal star and ever so slowly work his way in.

Kenelm fisted Adam's long hair in his hands, moving his thighs apart so Adam could have better access. He loved this man who'd stuck by him through the long years, searching for the daughter of Osiris. Now that he'd found the daughter of Osiris, she loved Adam too. Life was good.

"Hey, wait for me."

Helena's voice sounded in the bedroom doorway and both men looked up at her. She'd shucked her microphone and cameraman, and now grinned at the two of them who were so obviously screwing on the bed.

"Get your clothes off and come on then," Adam called, then he went back to doing wonderful things to Kenelm's cock and ass.

Only a few minutes later, Helena was naked next to Adam, who moved over a little to let her join him licking and nibbling and suckling Kenelm. Kenelm sucked in his breath and swore and loved it.

"So you'll be coming with us?" he asked through his rising orgasm.

"Mmm hmm," Helena replied, her mouth busy.

Earlier that morning Kenelm had cupped her shoulders and told her he wanted her to be his wife, his mate, for life. He had a magnificent palace of a house in England where the three of them could live. Helena could have the life she chose—petted love toy or sharp girl reporter, whatever she liked.

She'd made her choice to join them. Kenelm rejoiced. "I'm falling in love with you," she'd whispered as she kissed him, "and Adam."

He came now, holding tight the two people who meant the most to him. They laughed, happily lapping his cock.

Kenelm rose up on his knees, not sated at all. They'd just made him come before he was ready for it, and that deed could not go unpunished. Adam's eyes darkened as he realized that Kenelm was in one of his moods, guaranteed to further arouse him.

Kenelm took Adam first, entering him in wild plunges, feeling Adam squeeze him tight. Adam writhed and groaned, enjoying every second of it.

Kenelm had hoped to calm himself down on Adam, but it didn't work. His cock was just as hard and pounding even after he'd come and Adam had collapsed on the bed, breathing hard.

Smiling, Helena offered herself to him. She proved, with lightning fire, that she was learning to like it just as rough as Adam did.

Also by Allyson James

≈

Christmas Cowboy

Double Trouble

Ellora's Cavemen: Dreams of the Oasis I (*anthology*)

Tales of the Shareem: Aiden and Ky

Tales of the Shareem: Maia and Rylan

Tales of the Shareem: Rees

Tales of the Shareem: Rio

About the Author

≈

Allyson James is yet one more name for a woman who has racked up four pseudonyms in the first two years of her career. She often cannot remember what her real name is and has to be tapped on the shoulder when spoken to.

Allyson began writing at age eight (a five-page story that actually contained goal, motivation, and conflict). She learned the trick of standing her math book up on her desk so she could write stories behind it. She wrote love stories before she knew what romances were, dreaming of the day when her books would appear at libraries and bookstores. At age thirty, she decided to stop dreaming and do it for real. She published the first short story she ever submitted in a national print magazine, which gave her the false illusion that getting published was easy.

After a long struggle and inevitable rejections, she at last sold a romance novel, then to her surprise several mystery novels, more romances, and erotic romances to Ellora's Cave, and became a bestselling author. She writes under several pseudonyms, has been nominated for and won Romantic Times Reviewer's Choice awards, and has had starred reviews in Booklist and Top Pick reviews in Romantic Times.

Allyson met her soulmate in fencing class (the kind with swords, not posts-and-rails). She looked down the length of his long, throbbing rapier and fell madly in love.

Allyson welcomes comments from readers. You can find her website and email address on her author bio page at www.ellorascave.com.

Tell Us What You Think

We appreciate hearing reader opinions about our books. You can email us at Comments@EllorasCave.com.

CHOOSING MADISON

Sherrill Quinn

ഔ

Chapter One

ഏ

Through the wide view screen at the front of the ship's bridge, Gaelen Brecca stared at the planet his space vessel currently orbited. "I'll teleport down, grab the woman, and we'll be out of here before anyone knows what happened. Stay out of range of their satellites, Chardon. And be ready," he cautioned his communications officer, who also manned the teleportation controls. "There have been reports of Raiders in this area, and you know how much they'd love to get their hands on a royal princess. The ransom they'd get for her would fund their weapons deals for years."

"I'll be on guard, my lord." The blond man didn't look up from his control panel. "Sensors indicate there is another woman with Supreme Lord Travven's betrothed. You may want to take a pacifier, sir."

"Thank you, Chardon." Gaelen moved into the maglift. "Have Commander Ilan meet me at the teleport pad."

The maglift whisked Gaelen to deck fifteen, where he stopped at the med bay to pick up a tranquilizer pistol. He snorted as he remembered what Chardon had called it. A *pacifier*.

Doctor Braden Tabari stepped out of his small office. "What can I do for you, my lord?"

Gaelen scowled. "With every last person on this ship 'my lording' me, Bray, I'd hoped I wouldn't hear it from you, too."

"You are now the First Province of Drace, my lord," the doctor replied, seemingly unperturbed by his captain's burst of ill temper. By the mischief sparking in his dark eyes, Tabari actually seemed to be enjoying it. "It would be inappropriate for us to address you as anything other than 'my lord'. Or would you prefer 'Lord Brecca'? Or perhaps 'Brecca, Bearer of the Most Sacred—'"

"Oh, for the love of Mystros," Gaelen muttered. "I'd *prefer* that you call me Gaelen. We're friends, remember?"

Smiling faintly, Tabari clasped him on the shoulder and squeezed. He dropped his hand and asked again, "What can I do for you, my lord?"

"*Kotka njall.*" After growling the curse, Gaelen raked his hand through his hair. If he'd known that becoming First Province of Drace would put such formality between him and his friends, he'd have told his cousin Rafe to retrieve his own damned woman. Or better still, to go fuck himself. He just might yet, after this fool's mission. He was governor of the largest province on Reivas and the captain of the fleet's flagship. His last mission shouldn't be as some goddamned babysitter for the runaway bride of the Supreme Lord.

Family could be a real pain in the ass sometimes.

With a shake of his head, he brought his thoughts back to the matter at hand. "I need a tranquilizer pistol, just in case the princess refuses to cooperate."

Tabari's eyebrows rose. "That'll go over well with the Talarians. You tranquing their princess and all." The doctor opened a cabinet and withdrew a small, silver gun. "Obviously you've located her."

Gaelen grunted. "After four months of following her trail and stopping by three other planets, yes, we've finally found her." He nodded toward the tranq gun. "I'll only use it if she leaves me no other choice. Make sure you load it with enough for two."

"What, you're planning on bringing a female back for yourself?"

"No." Gaelen didn't appreciate the humor and sent Tabari a dark look. "I want it in case I need to tranq the woman with Juliska if she gives me any trouble."

"What woman with Juliska?" Tabari pushed two vials into the chamber and primed the barrel.

Gaelen shrugged. "A friend, perhaps? We'll be teleporting directly into the house where they are. I doubt she's seen people appear out of thin air before. I want to be prepared for trouble."

* * * * *

Madison Marquette pulled her legs underneath her and settled more comfortably on the plush sofa. She flicked a piece of lint off the skirt of her flirty yellow sundress—her favorite one with flowers—then grabbed her bowl of ice cream. "I'm getting ready to hit the play button, Julie," she called. "Hurry up."

"I'm coming, I'm coming." Her friend, Julie Grant, hurried into the room, carrying a cup of freshly brewed coffee. Even with her honey-blonde hair pulled back into a casual topknot, she still managed to look elegant. She set the cup on the table between the sofa and recliner and dropped down into the easy chair. Clicking the footrest out, she stretched her long legs and sighed. "Don't get your panties in a fist."

"Panties in a twist," Madison automatically corrected. In the two years she'd known Julie, the woman consistently used mixed-up idioms. But Madison considered her to be her closest friend, even if she did claim to be from another planet. She was ditzy but not dangerous.

"So, you never did answer my question." Julie raised an eyebrow. "Since we're getting ready to watch *While You Were Sleeping*, I wanna know. What do you look for in a man?"

She'd asked the question at the video store and again in the car on the way home. Madison knew her friend would keep after her until she answered. "Well, I'm not that different from most women, I suppose," she said, thinking aloud. "I want a man who's strong, who's capable, but who doesn't try to control me. He needs to know and trust that I can take care of myself. I want someone who's stable, dependable. Safe."

She thought about what she'd just said and felt a deep pang of loneliness that was almost a physical hurt. Her last serious relationship had ended over three years ago, after she'd found her fiancé in bed with another woman. What a cliché, but it seemed to be the way her life ran. After the break-up, she'd decided to swear off men for a while, never dreaming the dry spell would last so long.

What she'd told Julie was true. While she wanted someone dependable, she didn't need a man to provide for her. Partially because of Julie's incredible imagination, Madison had turned the stories her friend dreamed up about life on other planets into bestselling steamy futuristic romance novels. She was doing very well for herself. Her sixth novel in two years was due out in a couple of months and she was fast approaching the deadline for her seventh. Her career was right where she wanted it. Her personal life was another matter entirely.

What she needed, what she *craved*, was intimacy. Not just sex, although it had been so long since she'd made love with a man she almost forgot what it felt like. She missed curling up on the couch in a man's strong arms and watching a movie together, or holding hands while taking a walk. Simple stuff.

And, since she was being honest with herself, she missed sex. She loved being with a man, smelling his unique scent, feeling the sweat gathering on his skin, seeing the pleasure steal over his face when he came. She missed a man's cock surging inside of her, rippling over the muscles of her pussy.

Battery operated boyfriends just weren't the same.

"There's no such thing as a safe man." Julie's dry tones broke into her thoughts. "What's this fantasy man look like?"

Madison pushed aside her sadness. "I've always liked 'em tall, dark and handsome, of course. Broad shoulders, nice collarbone, a muscular chest with a smattering of hair. You know, just enough to have a nice trail that leads down to more interesting places. Not that I've gotten anything remotely close to that." Her fiancé had been rather short, with a bald spot and a tendency to spit when he talked.

"I know what you mean." Julie picked up her coffee cup. "Next question. What's your secret sexual fantasy?"

Just as Madison opened her mouth to tell her friend it was none of her business—some things were private, even among best friends, that'd be why they were called *secrets*—there was a flash so bright she closed her eyes against the glare. When she opened them again, two tall men in formfitting black uniforms stood in front of her.

Madison yelled. She slammed her bowl of ice cream onto the end table and jumped over the back of the couch, putting the bulky weight of it between her and the two men. They looked at her and she caught a flare of sexual interest in their eyes before they turned their attention to Julie.

The one on her left was very tall, well over six feet, with shoulder-length black hair and penetrating glass-green eyes. Those eyes had heavy brows drawn over them in a scowl, the same frown that curved his sensual lips. A deep cleft bisected his sexy chin.

The other man was just as tall, just as muscular, with long, dark reddish-brown hair and deep, chocolate-brown eyes. A thin, jagged scar ran the length of his jaw line on the right side of his face. It in no way detracted from his scrumptious good looks. Rather, it took what otherwise would have been a face almost too pretty and turned it into something lethally handsome.

"*Tighinn ne, Juliska Argante tan Talar,*" the green-eyed man said to Julie, his voice a low growl.

The sound rumbled through Madison's body and lit all her nerve endings on fire. Especially the ones between her legs. *For crying out loud…* She really needed to get laid if she could get turned on at the same time she was being scared spitless.

Julie calmly brought the recliner to an upright position and rose gracefully to her feet. "I knew it was too good to last." Her voice held resignation rather than the fear or even shock that Madison expected.

Madison looked at her in disbelief. "Julie?"

Her friend gave an apologetic shrug. "I've been telling you all about me, Maddie. For two years now."

Madison looked back at the two men and couldn't keep her gaze from tracking down their lean frames. Muscles strained the material at biceps, shoulders and thighs. She blinked as the already impressive bulges at their groins grew while she watched. Her nipples saluted a happy response. A strangled sound left her throat, something between a sob of fear and a groan of arousal. "B-but...I thought you were making it all up," she whispered.

Julie lifted her shoulders in another shrug. To the two men she said something in a language Madison didn't understand. The darker-haired one took a step forward, shaking his head. He spoke, and Madison had the same carnal reaction to his husky tone as before. Julie gave him a short retort and held up one hand, palm forward. Then she beckoned to Madison. "Come into the kitchen with me for a minute."

When Madison hesitated, glancing at the men, Julie came to her and put an arm around her shoulders. "It's okay, hon. Come on. I need to talk to you."

Once in the kitchen, Madison paced from the doorway to the counter and back again. "This is so bizarre. I didn't believe you. How could I?" She glanced at Julie. "I thought you were just..."

"Crazy?"

"Eccentric." Madison tried to wrap her head around the situation. She stared accusingly at her friend. "You told me you were from Indiana."

"That's what I told you when we first met. But I told you the truth later." Julie's sigh ruffled her bangs. "My father is the Monarch of Talar, a planet in a solar system near this one. I ran away from an arranged marriage with the sovereign of the planet Reivas. And he's finally sent someone to retrieve me. I always knew I'd have to fulfill my obligations," she said, her voice soft and sad. "Rafe's not a bad man. I just... I wanted to

166

have at least one grand adventure before I had to settle down and become the stodgy, proper Supreme Lady." She reached out and took Madison's hands. "Come back with me, Maddie."

"What?" Madison stared at her friend. "Could you repeat that? I think I hallucinated for a minute."

"I want you to come back with me. You have no idea how much your friendship has meant to me, being so far from home. I have to marry Rafe and I want my best friend to witness the ceremony."

Madison blinked. And blinked again. She caught herself just as she started to look for hidden cameras, halfway expecting some TV reality show host to pop out of the pantry. The friend she'd thought was a bit on the odd side but harmless enough was really a princess from another planet, a princess pledged to marry the ruler of yet another planet in order to maintain the peace between their people.

Oy. It was enough to make her head spin. *I wonder if everything else she's told me is true.* "I can't go to another planet. I have a deadline. And a hair appointment on Wednesday."

"Maddie. Please." Julie tightened her grip on Madison's fingers. "At least come for the wedding. Three days there, a couple of days on Reivas and then three days back. Gaelen can have you back home in two weeks, tops."

"Gaelen?"

"One of the men out there. The one with black hair. He's my fiancé's cousin." Julie gestured toward the living room. "Gaelen's not a very patient man, by the way. I'm actually surprised he hasn't barged in here yet." She took Madison's hands again. "Please say you'll come with me, Maddie. You need at least one grand adventure in *your* life, too."

Madison couldn't believe she was actually considering it. She, who rarely left Chicago or even the state, let alone the country. She hadn't talked to her brother Kendall in almost two weeks, and her father… A muscle flexed in her jaw. Retired Marine gunnery sergeant William Marquette wasn't exactly thrilled with her choice of career. As far as he was concerned, the romance novels she wrote were little better than porn and she was going to burn in hell for them.

Maybe she should just make sure she lived a little before she headed off to her fiery fate.

She drew in a deep breath. For once in her life, she was going to be as brave and adventurous as the rest of her family. "Let me call Dad and my agent," she said to Julie. She grinned at the look of shocked happiness that crossed her friend's face. "What kind of clothes should I pack?"

Chapter Two

ഇ

When the two women came out of the other room, Gaelen put his hands behind his back and stood in a formal military stance. The Earth female went down a hallway toward the back of the house. "We must go, Your Highness." He dragged his attention away from the curvaceous alien woman as the Talarian princess approached him.

Juliska gave a regal nod of her head. Even in the native garb she wore — a form-fitting short sleeved top and blue leggings of some sort — she was every inch a royal personage. Her blonde hair was scraped away from her heart-shaped face and held at the back of her head in a haphazard fashion. Her face was devoid of makeup, showing the natural purity of her skin. No wonder Rafe was anxious to make this alliance. Princess Juliska Argante of Talar was beautiful.

"Yes, I know, Gaelen. As soon as Madison has gathered a few things together, we can leave."

He took a step forward and scowled. "We're not taking additional passengers, Princess." She was deranged if she thought she could treat him and his crew like some sort of galaxy-class taxi service.

Crossing her arms, she assumed a stubborn expression. "If Madison doesn't go, I don't go."

Gaelen rested his hand on the tranq pistol he had tucked into his utility belt. With an inward curse, he knew he could use it only as a last resort. The royal bonding was to keep the peace between the peoples of Reivas and Talar. Should he in essence kidnap the princess and take her back to his cousin against her will… Well, wars had been started for less grievous offenses.

He could faintly hear the voice of the Earth woman in the other room. Because of the translation device all Reivans had implanted, he knew she spoke to her father, her voice strained as she called him "Dad". It would be best if they left before she rejoined them. "Princess Juliska—"

"Do this one thing for me, Lord Brecca, and I will go quietly." Juliska's voice remained soft, serene. "Happily, even. Bring my friend along so she can attend my wedding, then bring her back home again." The knowledge that she had him ass-up over a barrel was in her tranquil gaze. "It's a simple enough request."

"It's not that much of a burden, Gaelen." His second-in-command and bond-brother, Leax Ilan, stepped to his side. "The Earth woman would be good company for the princess."

And would, therefore, keep Juliska out from under their feet. But it rankled, having his actions dictated to him, especially by a spoiled princess. He started to respond but was interrupted by a beep from his communicator. He pressed the comm pip on his collar. "Brecca."

"Lord Brecca, we've just picked up another ship coming into range fast." Chardon's voice was tight, telling Gaelen without words this was no ordinary ship. "They're out of hyper speed and will be at your location in approximately three minutes." He paused. When he continued, he spoke quickly. "Looks like Raiders, my lord."

"Raiders." Leax's voice held the same urgency as Chardon's. "Gaelen, we need to go. Now."

"Oh no." Eyes wide, the princess put one hand to her mouth.

They had run out of time and choices. If they left the Earth woman behind, the Raiders would take out their anger at missing the princess on her. "All right." He looked at Juliska. "Go get your friend."

She nodded and ran down the hallway. Within a few seconds, she was dragging her friend—Madison—back into the open living area. "But I haven't had a chance to pack anything," the woman protested. "And I need to change. At least let me put on some shoes."

Gaelen's gaze tracked over her bare feet with their toenails painted a bright pink, up long, long legs hidden from view at mid-thigh by the skirt of her flowered sundress. She looked more than fine to him. She looked...beautiful. He was about to tell Juliska they had to hurry when she spoke.

"We'll get you something to wear on the ship. There's no time," Juliska said as the woman started to argue. The princess's voice was tight with worry and fear. "These Raiders are not the kind of people we want to wait around for."

Gaelen heard the thud of boots outside. With a scowl, he pulled his weapon and saw Leax do the same. "Too late, Princess. Get your friend behind there," he said, pointing to the sofa, "and stay down." To his bond-brother he said, "Set your weapon on maximum stun."

He and Leax took position on either side of the front door. The door burst open and the first three Raiders inside the house were quickly stunned into unconsciousness. Then Gaelen and his bond-brother had to duck for cover.

Weapons fire lit up the room for several minutes. Gaelen concentrated on trying to take out two Raiders to his left, and from his peripheral vision saw Leax firing toward the back of the house. *Kotka njall.* They'd come in from behind as well.

The princess screamed and he glanced around to see her wrapped in a Raider's brawny arms. Pinned in place by well-aimed shots, Gaelen kept firing at the bastards. The princess kicked wildly, connecting with her captor's shins and making him wince, but otherwise having very little effect. Madison stood up, a long and rounded wooden stick in her hands. She swung at the Raider's head, grunting with the effort. The crack of wood connecting with bone was loud. The man slumped to the floor and lay still.

The two women dropped down behind the sofa. Blinking back his astonishment—and admiration—at the Earth woman's courage, Gaelen turned his full attention back to the Raiders, firing at them in rapid succession. The remaining invaders fell to the floor, stunned to unconsciousness. He waited a few seconds and, once he was sure they were staying put, he jumped to his feet. "Let's go! Before they send reinforcements."

The two women came from around the sofa. Juliska's friend still had her hold on the wooden stick. He looked at her with a raised eyebrow.

She blushed and glanced at the princess. "We Marquettes are fighters." When Juliska laughed and hugged her, a relieved grin covered Madison's face and she mumbled, "*Semper fi* and all that shit."

* * * * *

Madison dropped the baseball bat and looked around her living room. For a blazing battle having just taken place, it still looked remarkably neat. Well, except for the bodies lying around. Looking closely, she saw chests rising and falling with their slow breathing, and she sighed with relief. She hadn't been sure how she'd explain a houseful of dead bodies to the authorities. Or her dad.

Her gaze met that of the auburn-haired man and she swallowed at the heat she saw in his eyes. She looked at the other man, Gaelen, and saw the same raw lust reflected in his gaze. Boy oh boy, these men were hot and making *her* hot. They had been so fierce in their battle, so competent in the way they'd handled their weapons. Plus there was just something about a man in uniform…

Gaelen touched his collar and spoke. He motioned to Julie.

She grabbed Madison's hand and pulled her over to where the two men stood. Gesturing to the men one at a time, she said, "Madison, meet Gaelen Brecca and Leax Ilan. Gaelen and Leax, my friend Madison." She tittered with nervous laughter. "There. Introductions are made. May we please go? Now?"

Madison ended up standing in front of Leax. He wrapped one brawny arm around her waist and pulled her back against him. She glanced over her shoulder and caught his slow wink just as a tingling started in her extremities and quickly spread inward. Her eyes widened and she opened her mouth to cry out at the unfamiliar sensation.

In what seemed like one heartbeat to the next, she went from being in her house to standing in a small, round room. She felt dizzy and a bit flushed. A man stood nearby, a small implement in his hand that looked a lot like a syringe. He started toward her and she tried to back up. When she pressed against Leax's big body, his hands came down on her shoulders and lightly squeezed. His deep voice murmured to her, words indistinguishable but the tones soft and gentle, calming.

She vaguely heard Julie telling her it was all right, that this was a doctor, but all she saw was a stranger heading toward her with a needle in his hand. "No probing!" she yelled.

Julie tried to soothe her. "It's all right, Maddie. He's just going to implant a translation device."

Madison heard every word her friend said, but the one that stuck out was "implant". She shook her head, then swayed as the movement aggravated her already spinning senses. Leax swept her up into his arms and the doctor moved in. Before she could do much more than blink, he'd gently inserted the tip of the syringe into her ear. She felt a small prick and wiggled her jaw against the resulting tickle.

"Do you understand me?" the doctor asked.

She nodded and touched one hand to her ear. She looked up at Leax. "You can put me down now."

"But I enjoy holding you, little one," he said. His voice was deep and soft, bringing to mind tangled limbs on silken sheets. Her nipples hardened and her breathing quickened as he glanced down. His arms briefly tightened, but he released her and let her slide to the floor. He kept one arm around her waist and held her against his body, letting her feel his arousal.

"Lee, why don't you show our guest to her quarters?" Gaelen's intense gaze rested on Madison for a moment before he held out his arm to Julie. "Princess, if you'll allow me to escort you?"

Julie slipped her hand through the crook of his arm. As they stepped out of the room, she looked over her shoulder at Madison and winked. "Don't do anything I wouldn't do," she said with a nod toward Leax.

Madison's face heated and she scowled. She was more tempted by this big man—by both of them—than she cared to admit. There was something of the forbidden in having sex with a stranger, and Madison tried to stay away from things she wasn't supposed to do.

Always being the good little soldier.

She supposed she could consider it research. Even as nervous about this situation as she was, she had to bite back a grin, sure neither man would appreciate her sense of humor at their expense.

Leax held his arm out to her, much the same as Gaelen had done for Julie, though Gaelen's face hadn't held such a wicked grin. Lust rolled off Leax in waves, helping alleviate most of her remaining anxiety. He was sinful temptation she just might not fight. "May I escort you, Madison?"

She tucked her hand in the crook of his arm. Through the soft material of his uniform she could feel the strong muscles of his forearm and barely resisted the urge to stroke him. They left the room and walked down a corridor. She glanced around, looking at the strange texture of the gray-blue walls with their flashing lights at floor level. A small silver ball-thing scooted past her feet and she jumped, clutching at Leax's arm.

"It's just an auto-cleaner," he murmured. "Nothing to worry about."

After taking a right turn into another hallway, he stopped in front of a door and passed his hand over a control panel. The door swooshed open and he motioned her inside. She entered and he followed behind her. She gazed around the room, taking in a small bed against one wall and a metallic table with two chairs that seemed to be built right into the floor.

Leax walked past her to another door. He passed his hand over the control panel there and that door opened. "This is the bathroom."

She eased around the corner and saw a set-up remarkably like any bathroom she'd ever seen. Her eyebrows rose and she muttered, "Guess it's universal."

He grinned, a quick flash of white teeth against tanned flesh. "I can show you how to use the sonic shower, if you'd like."

Madison pursed her lips. She was tempted to take him up on his offer but, nervous, she stalled. "Where's Julie?"

"Princess Juliska is just next door," he responded. He moved behind her, his body towering over hers, blanketing her in heat from her head to her heels. "You're a very beautiful woman." Lips briefly touched under her ear, sending a shiver through her. His strong arms slid around her waist, his hips moved against hers, the hard evidence of his arousal pressing into the small of her back. "Did I mistake your interest in me?" he asked, pulling her even closer.

She placed her hands over his, lacing their fingers together. "No," she whispered.

The feel of his cock against her brought a pool of heat between her thighs. He leaned forward and kissed under her ear and down the side of her neck. With a sigh, she tilted her head to one side and rested her back against his broad chest. When his hands slid from under hers and started moving up her torso, she stiffened.

It's your grand adventure, girl, she reminded herself. *Enjoy it.* She relaxed and closed her eyes. Lifting her arms, she brought them up and over his shoulders, linking her fingers behind his neck.

Cupping her breasts through the bodice of her dress and bra, his thumbs slowly rubbed over the hardening tips. He delicately pinched them, tugging and twisting until the heat in her pussy flared. One big hand slowly gathered the skirt of her sundress up until he could reach under to trace the elastic waist of her panties. He delved beneath the satin barrier and she sucked in her breath.

And when strong fingers parted her folds, finding her slick with desire, that breath left her in a rush.

Chapter Three

ɞ

Leax smelled the sweet, musky scent of Madison's desire, felt it slick and hot on his hand. As he slipped one finger into her heated depths, he heard her groan. His cock hardened further, pulsing almost painfully under the constriction of his uniform. Damn, but he wanted this woman, wanted her with a desire he'd not felt in a very long time. He had seen the same desire on Gaelen's face, seen the same hardness of his bond-brother's body.

Even knowing her for less than an hour, he knew enough to be drawn to her. She had a loveliness of spirit even more enchanting than her physical beauty. She possessed an entrancing wit, was loyal to her friend and remarkably brave, even when she was scared. He grinned, remembering her yell of "no probing" to the doctor.

She rubbed her backside against his erection and lucid thought became more difficult. He added another finger and pressed into her, rubbing his thumb against her engorged clit. "You feel good, dearling."

He looked in the mirror above the sink and continued to ply her nipples with the fingers of his left hand, going from one breast to the other, while his right hand thrust into her wet channel. With her red hair and dark blue eyes, she had an exotic beauty not seen in the women of his planet. Her face was alight with sensuality. Bending his head, he kissed a path along the line of her jaw. "Do you want to take your pleasure, Madison?" he asked, pumping his hips against her buttocks. Gods above, he was ready to come and she had yet to touch him.

Her mouth opened as if she were going to say something, but when he added a third finger and started thrusting into her faster and harder, a throaty moan left her instead. She shifted against his cock, riding it along the cleft of her ass.

"You're so hot, so sweet," Leax groaned. She turned her head and he caught her mouth with his.

Her eyelids dropped and she undulated against his hand. He flicked his thumb over the swollen nub of her clit and she arched against him, then thrust herself onto his plunging fingers.

"Oh God," she cried. Her head fell back against his shoulder. She pumped her hips, her cunt so wet and slick he could barely breathe through the sexual excitement. He slid his thumb back and forth on her clit, quick, hard. Her hips rocked faster and faster against the pressure of his fingers.

He flicked her clit once more and she screamed, her pussy clamping down on his fingers. She shuddered and he held her as she came down from her release.

Her eyes flickered open and met his gaze in their reflection in the mirror. A soft blush spread over her cheeks. He slowly withdrew his hand and brought it to his mouth. Holding her gaze, he licked her cream from his fingers, a low groan of pleasure at the tangy taste of her rumbling from his chest. "Delicious," he murmured. He turned her in his arms and kissed her, letting her taste herself on his lips. Just as he sought to deepen the kiss, his comm unit beeped. He drew back regretfully and touched the pip on his collar. "Ilan here."

"You're wanted on the bridge, sir."

"I'll be right there." Leax brushed her lips with his. "You're adorable, Madison. We'll…talk later, all right?"

She nodded, her gaze flicking down to his erection, which strained against the front of his uniform.

He cupped her chin and brought her gaze back to his. "You can take care of that later, as well." His mouth caught hers again, this time a hard, forceful kiss that staked his claim. Then, with a sigh, he turned and left.

* * * * *

Madison leaned against the wall, her heart racing, her pussy thumping. Empty. Even though she'd just had an explosive climax, she wanted more. Which brought her thoughts around to the stories Julie had told, stories about the customs of her fiancé's people. Customs Madison had thought were make-believe, but now very well might be true.

Two men for every woman, all three people bonded together to live as one family.

One woman, pleasured by her men for the rest of her life.

That woman could be her. With Gaelen and Leax.

Dear God. She had to go find Julie, find out if *that* particular story was true, like all the others.

She walked across the room, straightening her clothing as she went. When she reached the door, it swished open and she stepped out into the corridor. Leax had said Julie was just next door. She looked around. Would that be next door to her left, or to her right? Flipping a mental coin, she chose the one on the right. She passed her hand over the panel, as she'd seen Leax do but, when nothing happened, she rapped on the door with her knuckles. She heard movement from inside, then the door swooshed open to reveal Gaelen, standing before her with a dark blue towel wrapped around his lean hips. When he saw her, his eyes flared with heat.

"Madison." He stepped to one side. "Come in, please."

"I was looking for Julie," she said, hesitating.

"She's in the room on the other side of yours." He held out one big hand. "Come in, I'd like to talk to you." A sinful smile curved his lips and he crooked his fingers. "Come on."

Madison put her hand in his and allowed him to pull her into the room.

"Are you adjusting all right?" he asked.

"I guess so." She stared at his mouth, wondering what his kiss would be like. The old Madison came to the fore, whispering for her to back away, to take her time, to get to know this man before she became intimate with him. But when the door closed behind her and he pulled her into his arms with a low groan, her body made demands of its own and she decided not to fight it. Not now. After all, what was an adventure without a little risk? Her lips parted on a gasp, and he took her mouth with his.

Emboldened by her own determination to be someone different—someone free—and made wild by his touch, she stabbed her tongue between his lips. When his tongue came forward to meet hers, she sucked it into her mouth.

Gaelen groaned again and opened his mouth wider, his tongue dueling with hers. His cock prodded her belly. She trembled and pushed against him, standing on tiptoes to get his erection where it might do her more good. She wanted this man as badly as she wanted Leax.

She slid her hand down his back until she felt the towel. With a quick flick of her wrist, she ripped off the towel and dropped it to the floor. Then she reached between their bodies and wrapped her fingers around his cock. Rubbing a circle over the head with her thumb, she spread the drop of pre-cum pooled in the slit. At his groan, she stroked her hand down the long, rock-hard shaft, squeezing lightly. It had been so long since she'd held a cock in her hand, so long...

He tore his mouth from hers and buried it in the crook of her neck with a muttered, "Mystros!" He pumped against her hand, his own hands coming up to grasp her breasts. Grinding out another curse, he pushed the straps of her sundress down her arms and stared at her lacy bra with glittering eyes. He searched—briefly—for a clasp and, when he didn't find one in the front, he reached in and pulled her breasts up and over the lace cups. Long fingers began pinching and rolling and pulling, and she felt the tug all the way to her creaming pussy.

Gaelen's hands moved around to her ass and he lifted her, whirling toward the narrow bed against the opposite wall. He laid her down more gently than his urgency suggested, coming down over top of her. After a quick lick to one of her nipples, he sucked it into his mouth.

When she reached for his cock, he grabbed her hand and held it above her head, then did the same with her other hand. Transferring her wrists to the strong grip of one hand, he stroked the other one down her body until he reached the hemline of her dress. He shoved the sundress up to her waist, then thrust his hand into her panties and strummed across her slick sex.

"Mystros, you're wet," he muttered against the tip of her breast. "And hot." He slid one long finger into her sheath and back out again, where he circled the opening. When he pressed in once again, she moaned and pushed up to draw him deeper.

She needed more. She wanted to touch him, to taste him. To fuck him and be fucked.

"Gaelen." Madison twisted her wrists in his grasp. "Let me touch you."

"Later," he murmured. Releasing her wrists, he moved down her body until he rested his cheek against her mons. One hand went to her breast and began tugging on her nipple, while his tongue swiped through her folds. His mouth latched onto her clit. He suckled her with the same rhythm as the fingers that pulled on her nipple.

When he thrust two fingers into her needy sheath, her body tightened and splintered. She closed her eyes and cried out, arching against his hand, his mouth. He groaned around her clit but kept suckling her. When she finally settled, she opened her eyes to see him staring down at her. His tongue came out to slowly lick her juices off his lips.

She gulped at the gesture, and remembered Leax doing the same thing with his fingers. Even as she had that thought, Gaelen took her mouth in a deep kiss. His tongue dipped inside, tangling with hers, sharing the tangy-sweet taste of her juices.

He drew back. After another soft, brief kiss, he raised up, bracing himself with one hand flat on the bed. "I wish I could give you a proper loving, sweetling. But…it's not our way."

She licked her lips. If he'd done it any more properly, she might just have expired from pleasure. With a frown, she asked, "What do you mean? It felt pretty proper to me."

He smiled. "We have a certain…practice with lovemaking. Hopefully I'll have the chance to show you." He placed a kiss on the tip of her nose. "You're an extraordinary woman, Madison. So free with your passion."

If only he knew. She'd never been this free before. She was practicing living a life of adventure. "I don't usually…do this with men I've just met."

"Do what?"

Madison made a vague gesture with her hand, indicating their two bodies. "This."

A quick grin tilted his lips. "It wouldn't matter, as long as from now on you only do this with me."

She felt her stomach drop—in disappointment, in dread. What would he think if he knew she'd just been pleasured by his friend?

"And Leax," he added with a wink. After another kiss, he got off the bed and walked into an adjoining room. The bathroom, she supposed. His voice carried easily to her. "We're something of a matched set, Lee and I."

OhGodohGodohGod. She had to get out of here. She had to think, figure things out. She couldn't do that with him so near. And because she didn't know what to say, and was apparently a coward to boot, she slipped out while he was still in the other room.

As the door closed behind her, she heard him say, "I wish we had time to do more, but I need to be on the bridge, so…"

Madison ran. Down the corridor, past her room until she reached the next door, where she pounded against the metal. As soon as it swished open, she shouldered her way past Julie.

"Maddie, what is it?"

Madison started pacing the length of the room. Unsure of where to begin, she paused and stared at Julie, then paced some more.

"Maddie!"

"That story you told me, the one about the, um, mating practices of… What did you call Gaelen's people?"

"The Reivans."

Madison nodded. "The Reivans." She looked at Julie again. "Was that a true story?"

"Why?"

"Just tell me if it's true." Madison concentrated on trying not to hyperventilate.

"It's true."

"Oh God." Madison plopped down into a chair. Leaning her elbows on her knees, she propped her head in her hands. "Oh. My. God."

Julie sat in a chair next to her. "Maddie, you're worrying me, hon. What's wrong?"

Madison took a deep breath and looked up. Before she could say anything, Julie squeaked, "Oh my God! You didn't!" At whatever it was she saw on Madison's face, her eyes widened. "Oh my God! You *did*. Both of them?"

Madison gulped. "Not…sex exactly. And not together. Um, I mean…" She sighed and felt her face heat with a blush. She wasn't used to being so frank about her sex life, even if Julie was.

"They each pleasured you."

"Yes."

Julie leaned back and a slow, satisfied smile curved her mouth. "They mean to mate with you."

Madison blinked. "Mate with me," she repeated.

"Uh-huh. When bond-brothers focus on one woman, they each have to show they're capable of satisfying her before they actually come together as a triad. Then, if all three decide to make the mating a permanent one, they go through a ceremony that solidifies the bond. Kind of like a wedding." Julie waggled her eyebrows. "So, did they? Satisfy you, I mean."

Madison thought her face might actually erupt into flames. At the very least, it could probably be used to heat a small country.

Julie laughed. "I can see they did. Lucky you." She leaned forward and took Madison's hands. "Are you interested in pursuing it further?"

Madison stood and began to pace again. "How can I, Julie? I don't know them. And I only plan to be gone a couple of weeks. I do have a life to get back to, you know." She pushed back the sadness she already felt at never seeing these two exceptional men again.

"Nothing says they can't be part of that life, honey." Julie stood. "Travel between Reivas and Earth only takes a few days. Give it a chance, Madison. You'll regret it if you don't."

She was tempted. Very tempted. And curious about something else. "What about you? You're marrying the ruler of the planet. Will you have two husbands?"

A sly smile crept over her friend's lips. "I'll have the same…rights and privileges of any other married woman on Reivas. Until we have an heir and a spare, though, my second won't be allowed, er, access to my pussy. But he can have all of my mouth and my ass he wants." As Madison's blush flamed anew at her phrasing, Julie winked. "It could be worse, you know."

"How's that?"

"You could be sharing the same man with another woman. There are cultures that do that."

The thought of sharing Gaelen or Leax with another woman sent a surge of jealousy through Madison that surprised her.

"See?" Julie grinned and punched her lightly on the shoulder. "Go for the gusts."

"Gusts?" Madison frowned, then her eyebrows lifted as understanding dawned. "Oh, you mean gusto. Go for the gusto."

"Yes. Don't just sit around and let life pass you by. Be adventurous."

Chapter Four

ಏ

Gaelen stood on the bridge, his hands clasped behind his back, feet slightly spread, and gazed at the view screen. It was not on, but he knew what he'd see if it was activated. Stars screaming by as they traveled at hyperspeed toward Reivas. He felt someone come up beside him and, glancing out of the corner of his eye, saw it was his bond-brother. "You've been busy, Lee," he murmured, a slight smile tilting one corner of his mouth.

"As have you." Leax mimicked his stance, only he rocked his hips back and forth, just the slightest of movements, but it was enough to fire Gaelen's blood.

Mystros, but he wanted to be fucking Madison's sweet, warm cunt while Leax took her in the ass. He'd never felt this strongly toward a woman before, knew Leax hadn't either. It was what Gaelen's father had termed "the sweet call"—that physical and emotional pull of a mated triad to one another. Males nearly always felt it immediately and too intensely to ignore. "I've spoken to Madison," he said, trying to push aside his carnal thoughts.

"And?"

"She ran out on me."

"Well. That's not too promising."

"I didn't misread her interest in me," Gaelen murmured. His erection grew as he remembered her slender hand on his cock. He stared straight ahead and tried to think of something else, anything else. But his thoughts kept straying back to Madison, her eyes closed, lips parted, moaning in passion. Giving up, he muttered a curse and adjusted his cock beneath his too-tight uniform.

Leax chuckled. "I didn't mistake her interest in me, either," he said. "She's not used to us, that's all."

"If we're to return her home as soon as the ceremony's over, she won't have a hell of a lot of time *to* get used to us." Gaelen scowled. He needed more time with this woman, time to discover more of her than just her bravery and beauty. "Chardon, you have the bridge." He turned and walked to the maglift, Leax at his heels. "We'll be in my quarters if you need us."

"Aye, sir."

* * * * *

Gaelen paused outside the door to Madison's quarters and rubbed his sweaty palms over his uniform. Mystros! He hadn't been this nervous going to see a woman since…never. He was so agitated he just knew he was going to fuck this up. He should've had Leax do this part. His bond-brother had a natural charm women responded to.

Just as he raised his hand to press the intercom panel, the door to the princess' quarters swooshed open and Madison stepped out into the corridor. She was laughing, and held up one hand in a gesture he'd never seen before—forefinger and thumb making a circle and the other fingers straight up.

She turned and saw him, and her smile fled. She crossed her arms and walked toward him. A blush pinkened her cheeks, but she bravely met his eyes. "Gaelen. Were you looking for me?"

He nodded and cleared his throat. "Leax and I would like to talk to you."

White teeth came down on her full bottom lip and she gnawed on it. The longer he stared, the harder she chewed. He reached out and freed her abused lip with his thumb. Cupping her cheek, he leaned down. "If anyone's going to bite that lip of yours, it's going to be me."

187

He gently bit down on her lip, then sucked it into his mouth. She gasped and leaned into him. That was all it took. His lips closed over hers. He meant to be gentle, to take things slow, but when her tongue invaded his mouth, thoughts fled right out of his head. So did all the blood, rushing away to his cock.

Without taking his mouth from hers, he grabbed her ass in both hands and lifted her, grinding his pelvis against hers. She let out a little whimper. Her hands slid into his hair, gripping tightly as she kissed him just as hard. She wrapped her legs around him, aligning her cunt perfectly with his throbbing erection. He staggered backward, then turned and made his way to the door to his quarters. He let go of her just long enough to pass his hand over the entry panel, and as soon as the door opened he stepped inside.

"I see the bonding has started without me." Leax's voice was low with arousal and dark humor.

Gaelen tore his mouth away from Madison's. He saw Leax sitting on the bed, his back against the wall, long legs stretched out in front of him. Gaelen gazed down into Madison's face, smiling at the unfocused, passionate look in her eyes. "We got a little carried away."

She turned her head, another blush darkening her cheeks. "Hello, Leax." With a slight clearing of her throat, she put her hands on Gaelen's shoulders. Her legs slid down until her feet were on the floor.

"I take it Gaelen, as usual, just jumped right into the fray without any discussion." Leax swung his legs around and rose to his feet, stretching slightly. The front of his uniform was undone to his waist and Gaelen saw his bond-brother's erection had returned, the tip of his cock protruding from the opening.

"She was biting her lip," Gaelen defended.

Leax grinned. "Ah." He walked over to them and stood behind Madison. Wrapping his arms around her waist, he pulled her against him and slowly pumped his hips against her ass. "We need to talk before we…do anything else."

Her eyes drifted closed. She curled her fingers around his wrists. "Then stop doing that," she muttered, even as Gaelen saw her start to grind her ass against Leax.

Gaelen stepped forward and curved his palm over her cheek. She nestled into his hand. "We need to talk to you about the bonding."

She sighed. "Julie already did."

He exchanged a look with Leax. "What did she say?"

Leax's hands slid up to her hair. He released it from the braid and combed his fingers through the heavy tresses. Then his hands cupped her breasts through her clothing, his thumbs languidly sweeping back and forth over her stiff nipples.

Madison moaned, her head falling back onto his shoulder. "She said...*ah*...it involves two men and...*oh*...one woman."

Gaelen slipped his hands under the skirt of her sundress. Leax moved long enough for Gaelen to take her dress up and over her head, then he went back to strumming her nipples. "Did she say anything more?" Gaelen asked, his voice rough with desire.

"That sex between three people doesn't make a bonding, and that the ceremony making it official doesn't have to be permanent." She shuddered and her eyes flickered open. Her head rose from Leax's shoulder. Gaelen traced her skin along the waistband of her panties. "If the bonding doesn't work—ooh!" She jerked as Gaelen dipped his fingers into her folds. She was wet and hot enough to burn him alive.

"If the bonding doesn't work?" Leax prompted, bending his head to kiss along the curve of her neck. He unsnapped her bra and dropped it to the floor.

"Then it can be dissolved."

"That's right." Gaelen knelt and pulled her panties down her legs, encouraging her to step out of them. Juliska had told her true, but if the princess hadn't volunteered that a bonding hadn't been dissolved on Reivas in over two hundred years, he wasn't about to step forward with the information, either.

If he and Leax decided they wanted the bonding to be permanent, it would be up to them to love her enough to convince her.

He pressed a kiss to her belly and stood. "And are you willing?" he asked.

She nodded. Reaching out, she stroked one slender hand down his cheek. "I want to make love with you. With both of you."

He leaned in and kissed her, a soft mating of lips and tongues. While Leax continued to kiss her neck and shoulder, his fingers toying with her nipples, Gaelen went to the bed. He pressed a button on the comm panel and the bed mechanism activated, doubling the bed's width.

Leax swept her up into his arms and gently laid her on the soft mattress. He quickly stripped out of his uniform and slid over her, kissing her, his hands running up her sides, her back.

From a small cabinet near the bed, Gaelen retrieved a small bottle of savory-smelling lubricating oil and cloths, and handed them to Leax, who placed them within easy reach. Gaelen took off his uniform and climbed onto the bed.

"You guys always go commando?" she gasped.

"What's this 'commando'?" Gaelen leaned over her and placed a kiss on her belly, felt her suck in her breath at the touch. She spread her legs ever so slightly in invitation.

"It's...ah...where you don't wear underwear." She shuddered under the fingers that dipped into her slick folds.

"Then, yes. We always 'go commando'." Out of the corner of his eye, he saw Leax curl over her torso and start sucking one of her nipples. His bond-brother's hand curved around the other breast, the fingers plucking at the rigid tip. "Does it displease you?"

"Oh God, no," Madison moaned. "It pleases me very much."

Gaelen moved down, coaxing her legs further apart. He eased her thighs over his shoulders, tilting her pelvis. His fingers parted her plump outer folds. Lowering his head, he swiped the flat of his tongue from her opening to her clit. Mystros, but she tasted like no other woman. Tart like the juice from the *oyo* fruit, sweet like nectar.

He nibbled his way back down to her opening and circled the small hole with his tongue. She gasped and pushed against his face. With a low groan, he plunged his tongue in, as deep as he could get it, and flicked the tip against her inner walls.

Replacing his tongue with two fingers, he fucked into her with slow, steady strokes while he pulled her clit into his mouth and began to suckle. In a matter of moments, he felt her channel constrict around his fingers, her climax rippling through her.

Rising up, he settled next to her and when she turned her face toward him he kissed her, a long, slow, gentle kiss. Not of dominance, but of affection and deep-seated lust.

Her slender hand reached down and curled around his cock. "I want to taste you," she whispered against his mouth. Her blue eyes were dark with desire, the pupils dilated even in the dimness of his quarters.

Without a word he lay on his back. Leax moved aside and she scooted down until her face hovered over Gaelen's erection. Holding his shaft in one hand, stroking the hard length slowly, her lips went to his sac.

As her tongue twirled a sensual pattern over the sensitive skin, Gaelen twitched and groaned. "Take me in your mouth, sweetling," he muttered, his hands going to her head. "Suck them."

Her mouth obediently closed over one of his balls. He threw back his head and his eyes squeezed shut as the suckling motion shot straight to his cock. He felt her give a slight jerk and then she moaned. He opened his eyes to see Leax with his face at her pussy.

Madison took his cock head in her mouth and sucked, flicking her tongue against the sensitive flange. "Take more of me," he gritted out between clenched teeth. "More."

Her mouth opened wider and she slowly went down on his length. It only took a few minutes of the exquisite torture for him to haul her off him. When he came, it would be in the depths of her cunt, and he wanted time to savor the hot clasp of her body.

"Didn't you like it?" she asked, all innocence. But for the spark of feminine power in her eyes, he might have thought her serious.

"Too much," he said. "But when I come, I want to be inside you."

"As do I." Leax rose up, his mouth shiny with her juices. He swiped a cloth over his face, then put his hands on her waist. Against her shoulder, he whispered, "Are you ready to discover the joys of bonding?"

Chapter Five

ಐ

Boy-howdy was she ever ready.

One pair of strong hands settled under her ass and lifted her, guiding her onto Gaelen's long, hard cock. She whimpered a little at the fullness as she was speared ever so slowly and deliciously. When she was finally fully seated, her pubic hairs meshed with Gaelen's, Leax placed a hand on her back and urged her to lean forward.

Gaelen came up on his elbows and sucked one of her nipples into his mouth. She heard the pop of the stopper on the bottle, and a wonderful, spicy scent reminiscent of cinnamon and cloves wafted to her nostrils.

Leax parted her buttocks with one hand and dribbled a small amount of the oil onto her anal opening. She gasped at the warmth, moaning as it seemed to spread inward. He rubbed the oil around and slipped the tip of his finger through the tight ring of muscles. She'd never had anyone take her in the ass before and with Gaelen's thick cock in her pussy she had a moment of doubt. "I...um, fellas, this might not work," she said.

"It will work." Leax pressed his finger deeper and she tightened around it. He added more oil and another finger. She gave a small cry at the tight fullness and forced herself to relax. It was hard, her body already spiraled toward an orgasm. Gaelen moved his hips, thrusting just the tiniest amount, bumping against her clit.

"How're you doing, dearling?" Leax's voice was dark and sexy, and her excitement mounted. The smell of the oil grew stronger and she knew he'd just poured more onto his hand. He added a third finger and she babbled something, pretty much in a state of incoherence. As long as he kept doing what he was doing, she was fine with a capital fuck.

Gaelen switched to her other breast and pumped against her. Leax moved his fingers a bit faster and her climax roared through her. She shuddered and moaned, bucking over and under her two men, who held on until she was still.

"Mystros, you're so beautiful." Gaelen's voice held a note of awe.

"Ready to go on?" Leax pressed a kiss to her shoulder.

Incapable of speech, she nodded. He withdrew his fingers from her ass and then she felt the firm bluntness of his oiled cock. Her hips rose in anticipation, making Gaelen give a little growl as she slid up his shaft.

With the utmost care and excruciating slowness, Leax pushed the fat tip of his cock inside her.

"Oh God," she moaned. "Please."

He pushed more of his cock into her. Slowly, just as slowly as she'd been eased onto Gaelen's shaft, Leax slid into her ass.

And in and in and in.

The heat from their bodies and the flaming excitement of the act brought a prickle of sweat to her skin. Leax brushed her hair to one side and his tongue swiped a path along her shoulder blade. He bounced against her a little and she felt his cock slide in that last inch.

She gasped and moaned and shook. God, she'd never felt anything like this in her life. It burned and hurt, and at the same time felt so good she thought she'd die.

Even though she wanted to move, she held herself still, giving her body time to adjust. Time for her mind to adjust to the feeling of being so completely filled. Gaelen's cock in her pussy, Leax in her ass. They stretched her, widened her, and it was so decadently sinful.

It was pure sexual bliss.

And then they began to move. In tandem, a long, slow pull out, an equally careful glide back in. In, out. In, out. As their bodies built toward their own orgasms, their thrusts become harder, faster.

Madison wrapped her fingers around Gaelen's shoulders and held on. He reached one hand between their bodies and found her clit, rubbing it in hard little circles. Her orgasm slammed into her like a runaway freight train. She threw back her head and screamed, her body arching and bucking as she clenched around both cocks.

The men continued to pump into her, then they stiffened almost as one and rammed hard, holding themselves deep inside her. Hot streams of semen jetted into her pussy and her ass, and another climax rocked through her, smaller than before but just as sensually devastating.

She collapsed against Gaelen's chest. The two men rolled until all three of them were on their sides, Madison sandwiched between them and impaled on cocks still partially stiff.

A kiss was placed against her nape from Leax, one on her forehead from Gaelen. "Thank you," they murmured together.

She opened her eyes with effort, suddenly so very sleepy. "That was…" She sighed and slid her left arm under Gaelen. Her other arm wrapped around Lee's neck and she held her two men. "I don't think I have the words for it." She looked back and forth between them. "What now?"

Leax turned her face to his and kissed her, his tongue sliding against hers. When he released her, Gaelen repeated the caress.

"Now we rest," Leax said, wrapping his arms around her waist.

Gaelen murmured an agreement. "And then we do it again."

* * * * *

195

Twice more in the next few hours, Gaelen and Leax made love to her. A little surprised she could withstand so much—they were very demanding lovers—Madison lay quietly in the aftermath and watched them dress. Both men had taken their showers and now had to report back to work.

While she would love to have them stay and snuggle a bit longer, she knew they had duties to attend to. And she needed some time alone to sort this all out.

She'd gone into this with her eyes wide open and her mind fixed on the fact that nothing about it had to be permanent.

Except now…*now* she couldn't imagine *not* having these two men in her life. Could she give up all that was familiar and remain with them?

She wasn't sure she had an answer.

Her career was important to her; she'd worked hard to get where she was. She couldn't imagine not being a writer. It wasn't what she *did*, it was what she *was*. But just how much of a call was there for a writer of sci-fi romance on Reivas? And what about the family and friends she'd have to leave behind on Earth?

Leax bent down and kissed her, his mouth warm and tasting faintly of mint. He sat on the edge of the bed, bracketing her with one strong arm. "I can see you worrying, dearling. What is it?"

"I…just don't know what to do."

"You don't have to do anything, decide anything, right now," he murmured. She caught the glance he shot toward Gaelen. "Just know that I want you—*we* want you—with us. Whatever we need to do to make that happen, we'll do it."

She searched his face, then Gaelen's. "It's not that simple."

"It can be." His comm pip chirped and he sighed. "I have to go. But I'll see you later," he said, his hand stroking against her cheek.

"Okay." Madison was unsure of what else to say. *Be careful* didn't seem right, and *have a good day at work* seemed a bit inane.

As Leax left the room, Gaelen came over and sat beside her. His gaze was intent, dark with lingering passion and the beginnings of worry. "The attraction of bond-mates for their woman is an immediate thing, Madison. Leax and I both knew within moments of seeing you that you were meant for us." He scrubbed his fingers through her hair, rubbing against her scalp, making her turn into his touch. "Neither one of us will ask you to give up your life, your home. All we ask is that you make room for us."

Could it be that easy? The travel between the two planets was only a few days—she might just be able to have her cake and eat it, too. Caught up in her thoughts, she watched his lean fingers fasten his uniform, feeling her carnal hunger beginning to ignite once more.

He chuckled and wrapped one hand around the back of her neck, drawing her up for a hard kiss. "You keep looking at me like that and I'll be climbing back in bed with you."

She smiled, not at all put off by the notion. "Wouldn't Leax get mad?"

"Why should he?" Gaelen brushed a few strands of hair away from her face. "The bonding doesn't mean that all three of us have to have sex together all the time. You and I, or you and Lee, can come together as the need arises." He brought his lips down on hers again, tongue fucking forcefully into her mouth. When he drew back, they both breathed heavily.

"You need to go," she reminded him in a soft voice.

"Hmm." Gaelen brushed his mouth over hers once, twice. "Mystros," he moaned, leaning his forehead against hers. "You're like a drug. One taste of you only leads to wanting more."

With a low oath, he stood, straightening his uniform. His cock was a rigid length along his thigh. "Do you want me to get you something to eat before I leave?" he asked, his voice deep and harsh with suppressed need.

Madison shook her head. "I'll have something with Julie."

He nodded. He appeared about to kiss her again, but then his fists clenched and he spun on his heel and left.

Madison hugged her arms around her middle. She felt giddy and sad and so full of love she didn't know what to do. Her stomach growled. "Okay," she said, and climbed out of bed. "First things first. Figure out how to work the shower, then get something to eat."

And determine what she was going to do about the two men who had opened the doorway to the rest of her life. Did she take a chance and go through it?

Or did she do what she'd always done? Close the door and watch life pass her by.

Chapter Six

♔

Over the next two days of the flight, Gaelen and Leax spent every available minute with Madison, usually making love to her until none of them had the energy to move. The more time she spent with them, the more she was convinced they loved her.

And she knew she had fallen in love with them.

Once they landed on Reivas, things progressed swiftly. The planet looked completely different from what she was used to. Pale blue grass carpeted the ground, twin suns graced a lavender-colored sky, and most of the buildings were tall with graceful spirals reaching into the air. It was strange and alien and wonderful. Exactly as Julie had described it so many months ago.

The chapel where the wedding was taking place was decorated in deep purples and blues. Madison, wearing a dark green dress made of the softest of materials, sat between her two men, handsome in their dress uniforms. Julie looked beautiful and her husband-to-be, the Supreme Lord of the planet, looked so much like Gaelen they could be brothers. A second man in formal wear stood on the other side of the princess. The three held their hands out, one on top of the other, as the priest blessed them.

Madison's breath hitched. That could be her and her two men, standing before a priest. Becoming bonded for life.

"That's Juliska's other mate," Gaelen murmured.

"That could be us," Leax whispered in her other ear. "Imagine it, declaring ourselves as bonded mates in front of witnesses." He placed his hand on her leg and slowly stroked up her thigh until his fingertips brushed against her mound.

"Behave," she muttered. Wishing for once he'd be serious, but loving him because he was so carefree, she picked up his fingers and dropped his hand into his lap. "We're at a wedding."

He grinned shamelessly.

Madison turned her attention back to the ceremony to find it was over. The three at the front turned and faced their well-wishers, then started down the center aisle. As they reached the seat where Madison was, Julie's eyelid dropped in a wink and she mouthed, "Go for it."

Madison pursed her lips. This was what it came down to. Was she Marquette enough to take a chance?

Gaelen slipped his arm around her shoulders, and Leax put his hand back on her thigh.

Hell, yeah. *Semper fi* and all that shit.

* * * * *

Five days later, Madison stood securely in Gaelen's embrace and waited for the teleport unit to be activated. They'd just arrived back at Earth and were preparing to transport down to her house.

Leax stepped onto the platform and gave her a sexy wink. "Are you happy to be home, dearling?" he asked.

"Yes, I am." She reached out and took his hand. He gave her fingers a squeeze.

Gaelen pressed the comm pip on his collar. "We're ready when you are, Chardon."

"Aye, my lord. Stand by." After a slight pause, Chardon's voice came over the comm unit again. "Safe journey."

In seconds, Madison and her two men were standing in her living room. It was exactly as she'd left it, minus the Raiders who'd returned to their ship and left the quadrant, according to Leax. She walked to her answering machine and looked at the readout. Three messages which, when she played through them, were from her brother, asking her to call when she got back in town, and two from friends.

Strong arms slipped around her from behind and drew her against a warm, hard body. She leaned back, resting her head on Gaelen's shoulder.

"We don't have much time, love," he murmured. "We shouldn't waste it standing around."

Madison blinked back tears at the thought of being without these two, even if it would be only a short time. They would be leaving on a trade mission to Julie's home planet. As First Province of Drace, Reivas' largest land mass and the home of the Supreme Lord, Gaelen was responsible not only for governing the people there, but also for securing trade deals for them. This was an important trip.

Because she had her own obligations to fulfill, Madison was staying behind. She would finish her manuscript and get it off to her publisher, wrap up some things with her agent, say goodbye to her friends and, when Gaelen and Leax returned for her in a month, she'd be going back to Reivas with them.

But she couldn't completely cut herself off from her home planet. With the quickness of travel between Reivas and Earth, she'd be making frequent trips back to visit, and she still planned to write books. One day, perhaps, she'd tell her family why she was unavailable for weeks at a time.

The saying *a good man is hard to find* was true. Or was it *a hard man is good to find*? Whichever, she'd managed to find two of them, and she wasn't going to let them go any time soon.

She turned in Gaelen's embrace and cupped his dear face in her hands. Going up on tiptoe, she pressed her lips to his. He tasted sweet and decadent, and as tempting as sin. Over his shoulder, she saw Leax stripping out of his uniform.

When the phone rang, she jerked. "Who could that be?" She twisted and picked up the cordless phone. Before she could even say hello, she heard the panicked voice of her agent.

"Maddie? I'm so glad I found you at home! I need your manuscript *now*."

"I just got home, Kurt. I'll have it to you by the deadline."

"No. No! The publisher's got two copy editors ready to go on maternity leave, and a line editor's laid up in the hospital. They're asking for your stuff ASAP."

Madison heaved a sigh. Gaelen moved away from her and she turned to see Leax's naked backside moving down the hallway toward her bedroom. Her agent's voice faded into the background as she watched Gaelen bend and take off his boots, then his socks. He unfastened his uniform and with a newfound playfulness did a slow striptease, undulating his hips while more and more flesh came into view. When the material bunched around his waist, he gave a little shimmy and the uniform dropped to the floor.

He stepped out of the pooled material and sauntered down the hallway. Madison trailed after him, admiring the bunch and flex of his muscled backside, and stopped in the doorway of her room. Both men lay on the bed, a space in between them. Two thick, long cocks rose invitingly against their bellies.

"Kurt. Kurt!" She interrupted the frantic wails of her agent. "I'll get it to you as soon as I can, but at the latest by the agreed upon deadline." She trailed one hand down Gaelen's thigh, then spoke over the sputter of her agent. "Kurt, I gotta go. But wait 'til you read my next book. I'm thinking of calling it *The Triad of Love*." Madison disconnected the call and put the phone down on the bedside table. Keeping her gaze on the two men in her bed, she removed her clothes and crawled between them, relishing the embrace of her two naked lovers.

Her bond-mates.

Always.

About the Author

෨

Sherrill Quinn grew up in Northeast Ohio on the southern edge of the snow belt. After sloshing through too many winters of ice and snow, she moved to southern Arizona where she's lived since the year 2000. After twenty years building a career in Human Resources, she went back to her early love of writing and started a second career in erotic romance in early 2005.

Sherrill welcomes comments from readers. You can find her website and email address on her author bio page at www.ellorascave.com.

Tell Us What You Think

We appreciate hearing reader opinions about our books. You can email us at Comments@EllorasCave.com.

COME HOWLING

Denise Rossetti

ဆာ

Trademarks Acknowledgement

જી

The author acknowledges the trademarked status and trademark owners of the following wordmarks mentioned in this work of fiction:

Doc Martens: Dr. Martens International Trading GmbH

Chapter One

ଛ

In the reception area the street door opened, letting in the muted drumming of rain, the steady swish of tires on wet asphalt. A gentle thud as it closed and the noise cut out. Mrs. T's voice rose in inquiry, but Luc could barely hear the soft, liquid murmur of the client's response. A woman.

His cock gave the faintest little twitch. Down, boy. Wistfully, Luc thought of his new sister-in-law's bountiful tits and lush hips. Lucky Gabe. She was a great girl, perfect for his twin. He hoped they'd be incredibly happy.

And that she didn't run screaming when his brother Manifested for her.

He glared at the spreadsheet on Gabe's computer. The orderly lines of numbers sneered right back. Error? What fucking error? He clamped a big-knuckled hand over the mouse and sent the smarmy paper clip to electronic hell.

He had to get this mess straightened out by the time Gabe got back from his honeymoon. His twin had a morbid terror of the IRS and he loved Bogdanovich and Marinelli Employment Agency the way bikers loved their Harleys. It was everything Gabe had worked for and now Luc was screwing it up. For chrissake, how had something as simple as babysitting the agency for a week gotten so complicated?

Luc ran a hand through his thick dark hair and ground out a string of curses. The base of his spine buzzed with familiar heat, his temples ached. Not now, dammit, not now. The curses deepened to a rolling growl. With the ease of long practice, he disciplined his breathing until the urge to Manifest subsided.

He shifted his massive frame, Gabe's fancy office chair creaking with the strain. He wasn't much heavier now than he'd been in college on a football scholarship—working for his own construction company kept him in shape—but he was still too much the linebacker to fit most normal-sized places with any degree of comfort. Absently, he reached down to rub his bad knee.

Though...he'd fit just fine between soft thighs. His lips curved with memory. God, they'd had fun hunting in the dark together, he and Gabe!

The woman's voice rose. "I'd like to see Mr. Bogdanovich."

Luc rocked back so abruptly the wheeled chair slammed into the wall behind him. He barely registered the thump as the back of his skull collided with the building.

What was the name of that old-time movie star his Dad fancied? Lauren Bacall, that was it. This woman sounded like Lauren Bacall after a smoke and whisky binge. Deep and husky, the voice slid sleek fingers into his pants, burrowed into his boxers and cuddled his balls.

"Or is it Ms.? I don't care. What about Marinelli?"

There was a scratchy note to it, as if the woman was hoarse from screaming loud and long, head thrown back, shrieking her pleasure while she rode his stiff cock to a mind-numbing orgasm, then as he flipped her over, gripping her wrists to stop her thrashing so he could ram every last inch high inside her while she wrapped long legs around his waist and came and came as if the world was ending. No, fuck it, even better, her legs over his shoulders, her heels drumming—

He was halfway to the door of Gabe's office when he regained his senses. Whoa! Not only was he as hard as a freaking rock—on nothing but a couple of banal sentences—he was fully Manifest.

Grimly, Luc braced a hand against the door. He didn't need to look in the small mirror hanging behind it to know what he'd see. The flames flickering deep in his pupils, the bumps where the short, curved horns were trying to push though the dark waves at his temples. He winced, reaching into his pants to adjust himself. Not his cock.

His tail.

Jammed uncomfortably down the left leg of his chinos, the forked end nudged the back of his calf, a reminder of his lack of discipline.

Adrenaline was what did it, every time.

Forehead against the wall, he counted backward from ten, reliving the worst day of his life, willing control to come along with the memory.

The last game of the college season. He'd been on a high, knowing his chances in the NFL draft were better than good. In the last desperate moments of the game, he'd thundered down the field to tackle a wide receiver. The guy had lain there, panting, staring through Luc's facemask, straight into red, glowing eyes. Poor dude had fainted.

There'd been a family conference over that one.

At training the next day, he'd wrenched his knee. It hurt, but no more than his pride, his soul. He'd loved football. Still did.

Luc straightened with a sigh and tucked in his polo shirt. Then he hitched up his pants, opened the door and ambled out into the reception area. "Can I help you?" he rumbled and the woman turned.

Shit. After the satin-sheets promise in that voice... She peered at him over Mrs. T's curly gray head, her face shadowed by the folds of a muddy-brown scarf, her long body swathed in a shapeless shawl and a khaki skirt that drooped all the way down to a pair of purple Doc Martens. Bag lady chic. Luc's eyes narrowed. All he could see was the gleam of a pale cheek and the tip of her nose. It looked a little pink.

"I hope so," she murmured, but this time he had himself braced for the phantom fondling and it wasn't so bad.

He arranged his features into the smooth, professional expression he'd seen Gabe use. "It's all right, Mrs. T. You go. I'll take care of our client."

Mrs. T looked skeptical, but she glanced at the clock and slapped a sheaf of forms into his chest. "Fill out a TR-986b or an ET-23. One or the other. Not both," she said sternly. "And don't forget the buff page for Social Security. There's a pile of brochures in Gabe's second drawer if you need them."

Then she rather spoiled the effect by reaching up to pat his cheek. "Don't worry. You'll be fine." She grabbed her neon green backpack and a tartan umbrella. "See you tomorrow." Within seconds, she'd disappeared into the rainy afternoon.

"You'll be the last for the day. It's just on quitting time." Luc flipped the sign on the street door from *Open* to *Closed*, but he didn't lock it. And he made sure the woman could see every move he made. He knew what he looked like. Shit, he topped her by a foot. She was tall, but so reed-slim her waist couldn't possibly be much thicker than his thigh.

"This way." He indicated Gabe's office. Strange she might be, but she smelled—his nose twitched as the woman glided past him—mmm...damp and fresh. Female. Infinitely more entertaining than a spreadsheet.

The way she moved was so fluid, she seemed almost to float, even in the Docs. She wafted into the client's chair. Slim, pale fingers untied the scarf and drew it away.

Luc stared. He couldn't help it.

Everything about her was long—her neck, her jaw, her nose, the line of her cheek. She should have looked horsey, but somehow, the component parts added up to an unusual symmetry that grew more intriguing with every second that ticked by. Her eyes were long-lidded, long-lashed, her mouth wide and sweet. And her skin—the urge to reach out and trail a curious fingertip over her cheek was almost irresistible. It was ivory pale, almost translucent. He couldn't imagine her at the beach. Hell, she'd fry.

Tendrils of rust-colored hair waved around her face, kinking a little in the damp air. She'd scragged it back with some sort of tie and he couldn't see how much of it there was.

"Right." Luc grabbed a pen and waved a form in her general direction, willing her to turn her head just a fraction. "Let's get started. Your name please?"

The woman had been sitting with her feet together and her hands clasped in her lap. Now she looked directly into his face. "Are you Bogdanovich or Marinelli?" No makeup, none at all. Not even lipstick.

"Neither. I'm Luc Kaminski. Bogdanovich and Marinelli sold the agency to my brother five years ago."

"You're not Irish?" Her fingers writhed together like snakes, then stilled.

"Kaminski isn't a common name in Ireland," he said dryly.

"No." She seemed to be considering that, staring at him hard enough to make him wonder if he'd nicked himself shaving. "You don't *look* Irish."

Luc didn't think he looked like much of anything in particular, except big and dark. His bone structure, including the Slavic cheekbones, was part of his Kaminski inheritance, but his hazel eyes were the gift of his gypsy great-grandmama. Together, of course, with the ability to Manifest. Quite a package, when he came to think of it.

"Is not being Irish important?"

"Could be," she said cryptically, leaning forward to offer her hand. "I'm Maeve O'Brien."

Luc nearly gelded himself on the edge of the desk, he rose so quickly to take it. When his broad palm closed over her fingers, he grunted in surprise. "You're cold!"

"Oh well." She pulled her hand from his and a wonderful wash of color bloomed under the porcelain skin of her cheek. "It's cool out."

"Can't have you getting sick." Hell, he sounded like his own mother! Gritting his teeth, Luc came 'round the desk to stand at her side. "This is soaked," he said quietly, rubbing the fabric of her shawl between his fingers. "Give it here."

For a moment, she resisted and he thought he'd have to wrest it from her. But when she relented, it was with a little sigh that twisted something in his gut. Such a tiny sound, barely a breath, but eloquent of something close to despair.

Forget the bedroom voice. Jeez, she was a strange one.

But that red-brown brush of hair reached all the way to the curves of her ass. And without the shawl, he could see the sweet thrust of pert breasts pressing against fine, damp cotton. The skirt both draped and revealed the line of long, slim thighs. God, under all that hippie crap, she was built like a faery, a slender, magical creature out of a game-player's wet dream, the sort you got as a reward for reaching Level 12 with all your limbs intact.

And he was losing his friggin' mind.

Luc grabbed his jacket from off the back of his chair and handed it to her. "Put this on," he said brusquely.

"Oh no, I couldn't—"

He reached for the trailing edge of his Manifestation and let it out to play. "Do it, Ms. O'Brien," he growled.

She shrugged the coat over her shoulders, the delicious color still staining her cheekbones as the garment enveloped her. If there was a man in her life, the bastard wasn't doing much about looking after her. You'd think a man had never shown her a courtesy.

"Are you married? I mean—" He couldn't believe the stupidity falling out of his mouth. "There's a space on the form. Marital status."

"No." She shook her head, the tension coming off her in waves. "My therapist says I need a job. I promised her I'd try."

"Your *therapist*?" Terrific. Peachy.

"Yes." Maeve O'Brien sprang out of the client's chair and took a couple of restless steps across the room, the Docs clomping this time. She skewered him with a burning green glance. "I'm a qualified accountant. By correspondence." Returning to the chair, she gripped the back of it, her knuckles whitening. "I topped the class. I'm very good with numbers."

Luc shut his sagging jaw with a snap. Perhaps she was one of those—what did you call 'em?—savants. "You understand spreadsheets?"

She nearly smiled. "Meat and drink."

Regardless of what she said, no matter how prosaic, his balls tensed and his cock reared with wicked expectation. Majorly weird.

Luc picked up her chair and plonked it down next to his, in front of the computer. "Show me. Fix this bast—one."

Maeve cast him a doubtful glance, but she perched on the edge of the seat and frowned at the screen. Almost immediately, her brow cleared. "For heaven's sake, it's simple! What idiot—" Breaking off, she pressed her lips together and reached for the mouse. Within minutes, she was transposing formulas and shifting columns, humming under her breath.

He hadn't taken the time to learn, that was all. He'd rather be outdoors, doing, *building*, making something with his hands. Absent-mindedly, Maeve reached up to rub her shoulder. His hands. Hmm.

"Are you sore?" He drew a slow fingertip over her neck, from behind her ear to her collarbone, lingering over her pulse.

That got him a startled glance and a sharply indrawn breath. This close her irises were shot with green and gold. "Repetitive Strain Injury," she said and the three words sounded in his head like a sweet-toned bell. *Fuck me, fuck me, fuck me.*

Luc removed his hand, though he ached to pet and soothe. "I can help, if you let me," he said. Compulsion had never been one of his gifts, but he threw in a touch of Command. His conscience kicked feebly, but he squashed it. Poor little thing, the tension was coming off her in waves.

Very slowly, giving her time to object, Luc reached out and closed his whole hand over her slender shoulder. "Keep going," he murmured. "I'll rub."

He circled his thumbs and Maeve's lashes fell to half-mast. Her lips parted, all soft and pink, and Luc felt the flames leap in his eyes. Steady, steady. Touching her wasn't the brightest idea he'd ever had, but his hormones were leading the way, high-fiving each other as they went.

Leaning back, he let his fingers learn the texture of her skin, as if he read her soul in Braille. Cool and soft, with an underlying resilience he hadn't expected. Smooth as cream. He wanted to lick her from her head to her heels, like a tall vanilla ice-cream sundae. Oh yeah. With long pauses for all the sweetest morsels—especially the strawberry bits, all pink and slick and musky and tart.

Grimacing, he lifted off the seat so his tail could snake out down his leg, while his hard-on reared in the opposite direction. He glanced down. Thank Christ for loose-cut pants. The horns weren't such a problem. The stimulation had to be right off the charts for them to Manifest fully, but the red haze in his eyes… With his free hand, he fumbled on his sunglasses. Better she think he was a poser dickhead than the alternative.

Maeve let out a long, breathy sigh, as though she wanted to moan, but was too inhibited. Her long white fingers trembled as she clicked Save.

Luc pitched his voice so low it was a subterranean rumble, barely heard. Coaxing. Commanding. "What did the therapist say?"

Maeve didn't lift her gaze from the monitor. "She thinks I've got a form of Tourette's."

"Tourette's?"

The note of surprise in his voice shattered the spell and she turned to face him, flinching when she realized how close he was. Close enough to feel her breath against his jaw. This time, her flush was scarlet, painful.

"I…ah…wail…cry…weep. Loudly."

Luc stared, dumbfounded, and his erection shrank to a nub. He whipped off the shades. "You what?"

Maeve sat up straight. Her jaw bunched. "I can sense a recent death or the shadow of death to come." She bit out the words. "But only if the person involved has Irish blood."

"That's crazy."

Her expression shuttered and suddenly, she was just a tall skinny woman with dead-white skin and terrible clothes, sitting hunched in front of a computer.

Oh no. No way!

He lurched into speech. "Sorry. Honest, I'm sorry. I never heard of anything like that before."

"Neither had the therapist." The blood had even left her lips. "But she's wrong. It's not a syndrome, it's a *curse*." Jerkily, she rose. "This isn't any use. I can't possibly get a job, not with real people." She began to shrug out of his coat. "They hate me."

Luc clamped his hand over her wrist. "Wait." He concentrated so fiercely on Command that the horn spots on his temples ached. "Tell me about the curse."

He watched the battle in her eyes. How well did he know the mad urge to confess, the lust to be free of the fucking secret, to be all that he was, without shame?

Lifting her wrist to his lips, he pressed an open-mouthed kiss across her thundering pulse. She whimpered and her eyes flared gold with panic and arousal. "Tell me." He licked a trail up a blue vein. "*Tell me.*"

"I'm a banshee. All right? A fucking banshee." A huge gulp of air. "*And – I – don't – want – to – be!*" The last came out in a long, throbbing howl that was eerily convincing.

Chapter Two

ℬ

Luc Kaminski leaned forward and shut off the engine of his truck. The night-silence closed in like a tangible presence, broken only by the rustle of the wind in the trees behind Maeve's isolated cabin and the croaking of frogs courting in the narrow stream at the bottom of the garden. The rain had stopped and fresh, green smells teased her nose. Because of the cloud cover, the darkness was absolute. In the confined space, Luc loomed like a man-mountain, so potently masculine she couldn't get enough air.

Maeve huddled against the window, the precursor of a headache gathering behind her eyes. God, she was pathetic! It had been so sweet of him to drive her all the way out here, especially after… She winced. But he'd got all male and huffy when she tried to set off for the bus station.

Now all she had to do was thank him nicely for the lift, apologize for the…disturbance and stumble up the steps to her cabin. There were painkillers in the bathroom and a wide bed with crisp linen and a firm mattress. She opened her mouth.

"Well, that was a fucking disaster," he said mildly.

Apology be damned. "I told you how it is with me!" Words tumbled out of her. "But oh no, you had to prove it for yourself. God, the Shamrock Bar and Grill! And you say *I'm* crazy!"

Teeth gleamed as he smiled. "Nothing like a good brawl." His sleeve rustled as he massaged the knuckles of one hand. "You realize the biker you picked was the meanest guy in the place?"

"I didn't pick him, the Curse did. Because he had Irish blood," she muttered. "And anyway, he was a big softie. He'd loved his Nanna. There were tears in his eyes when he thought of her."

Luc chuckled without amusement. "Yeah, sure. Right before he tried to deck you." His voice had dropped to a chilling growl.

The Howl was such an awful thing to do to anyone. She'd had plenty of practice understanding reactions and the biker's had been pretty typical. "Think about it from his point of view," she said wearily. "There he is, out for beer and pool with his buddies when some weirdo gets right in his face. And what does she do? Does she come on to him? Oh no." The headache stepped it up a notch. "She jabs a finger in his chest, wailing about death, death, *deee-aaath!*"

"Maeve..." he said warningly.

The tears spilled over again. Her nose was probably running. "Embarrassing as all hell. Especially when she's gone and died, his Nanna Calhoun, the only one who gave a shit about him. And this creepy, ugly bitch is mocking, tearing her hair, howling her head off. And she won't shut up. What would you do?"

"I wouldn't try to hit her." He slid an arm around her shoulders and drew her across the bench seat and into his heat. "And you're not a bitch. Or ugly."

For an instant, she was tempted to snuggle into all that strength and warmth. Lord, he was perfect—not good-looking, not *precisely*, but with a fine, strong face. She loved his warm hazel eyes, the way the dark hair flopped over his brow. And his forearms drove her insane. All hair-dusted latent power, with thick wrists. Jesus, Mary and Joseph, what would he look like stripped? Moisture welled between her thighs and she pressed them together against the sweet, burning ache.

A defender, she'd never had a defender before. And he'd done it without a moment's hesitation. When the furious biker had lifted a tattooed fist, something red had flashed in Luc's eyes and he'd interposed his big body between Maeve and her would-be assailant.

The biker had tried to rush him, but Luc simply stepped aside, dropped his shoulder and tossed the guy over the bar. A heartbeat later, the man's buddies charged, a phalanx of mean dressed in stained denim. Luc shoved Maeve into a corner and snapped, "Don't move!" Then he'd slipped on his sunglasses— *sunglasses?*—drawn a deep breath and waded in, utterly cool, almost scientific in his precision.

A few minutes later, he'd reappeared, hair mussed and tufted all over his forehead, shades intact. He'd grabbed her arm and hustled her out into the street, the happy sounds of combat fading behind them.

And now he was even defending her from herself.

But she couldn't afford the weakness. No snuggling, no dependence. Luc couldn't help her, no man could. The Banshee Curse was hers, hers alone to bear. As it had been for every female in her family, every generation, all the way back to the ancient Irish kings.

Wail, wail the banshee.

Only love will set ye free.

Nor flesh, nor fury shall stay the Curse,

And mortal man shall make it worse.

Tied in an eternal knot,

Love ye need, yet love ye not.

Her lips twisted. Magic was a lousy poet, but depressingly accurate. Because the handful of times she'd grown desperate enough to take a lover, the Curse had ridden her even harder afterwards. Something as everyday as restocking the groceries became an experience fraught with terrified anticipation, so bad she'd resorted to shopping online. The price of pleasure was the isolation that had to follow. Not that the pleasures had been so fantastic, but oh God, the sense of *connection!* Sometimes the urge to touch and be touched grew so painful her body *ached* with skin hunger, until she cried with it, great gulping sobs she despised. Thank God for the Internet, for email and cybersex and erotic romance novels.

"Maeve? *Maeve!*"

She jumped. Luc had slipped the band from her hair and sunk his fingers into the thick mass of it. He used the grip to tilt her face up. "You're *not* ugly, you hear me?"

"Don't be silly. Of cou—"

The heat of his mouth seared the breath in her lungs. Every thought in her head winked out, leaving only a dark, quivering void of physical sensation. Luc nibbled at her lower lip, licking his way from one corner to the other, insinuating a playful tongue to tease hers.

Maeve moaned and her fingers clutched spasmodically at his shoulders, so blessedly solid in her grasp.

Abruptly the kiss changed, becoming ravenous, carnal. When Luc growled deep in his throat, her eyes flew open. God, he sounded positively feral! But his eyes were squeezed tightly shut, the extravagant sweep of his lashes silhouetted against his cheek.

Her brain reeling, Maeve slid her arms around his neck and hung on for dear life. Oh God, oh God, it was good! She pressed her breasts into the wall of his chest, relishing the pressure on tingling nipples. Luc grunted, easing her down across the seat, her legs falling open in an inelegant sprawl. He peeled his lips from hers to nip a trail down the side of her neck, tiny, stinging bites, while one broad palm closed over her entire breast.

Maeve arched and shook, torn between desire and feminine panic. Oh God, he was so big, so powerful. So fucking gorgeous.

"Luc?"

"Mmm?"

She turned her head so he could taste behind her ear and a nervous giggle bubbled out of her. "Sure you're not a vampire?"

He reared back, insult eloquent in the rigid line of his shoulders. "A blood-sucker? Hell, no self-respecting—" A pause. "Uh, sorry. That was a joke, right?"

Maeve sat up and straightened her clothes. Ah well, she might have known. Too good to last. Mentally, she gave the Curse the finger. Grief was a luxury she couldn't afford, not if she wanted to stay sane, but something keened inside her. *Lonely, oh so lonely.*

Luc jumped out of the truck and came around to her side. He opened the door, reached in and scooped her up as if she was a child. "My knuckles hurt like the dev— Well, they hurt," he said, his lip jutting like a little boy's. "Aren't you going to kiss 'em better?"

Maeve's heart turned a complete cartwheel, so vigorous it actually hurt her chest, and for a second she couldn't speak. She pinned a mock-frown on her face. "You got away with 'the dog ate my homework' in every grade at school, didn't you?" she asked as he strode up her porch steps.

Obligingly, Luc dipped so she could fit the key to the lock of her front door. "Only when the teachers were female." She caught the flash of a panty-wetting grin.

"Jerk!" She thumped his shoulder and he chuckled.

As he lowered her to her feet, sliding her down that wall of muscle, inch by excruciating inch, Maeve O'Brien came to a startling conclusion.

She was having fun.

Sexy, normal, pulse-fluttering fun. Jesus, Mary and Joseph. *Fun!* He'd seen her at her worst and he didn't seem to care.

Smiling, she snapped on a light and Luc winced. He whipped the shades out of his pocket and fumbled them on.

What the—? "Luc, your eyes are red."

"I have a condition." He cleared his throat. "I'm sensitive to light, very sensitive."

The dark lenses gave him a forbidding air, like a Mafia hitman, large economy size. But it wasn't as if she couldn't deal with weird.

"Do you believe me now? About being a banshee?"

"Yep." Luc nuzzled his nose into her neck, then shifted to lick the base of her throat. "You smell fantastic."

"But why?"

"Dunno. Shampoo?"

"Luc!"

He relented. "Maeve," he said patiently, "the world is full of strange things." He ran a hand through his hair 'til it tufted over his temples. "I'm sorry I laughed when you told me. Hell, I'm pretty out there myself." Slowly, his lips curved into a predatory grin. "I like your howl. Very musical."

He slipped the first button on her blouse and his voice dropped an octave. "Hearing it makes me hard, Maeve. It's a major turn-on. I want more."

Another button, while she stared at him, mesmerized. "But this time..." The third button. "I'll be inside you, as high as I can go, making you scream." Gently, he slid the blouse off her shoulders. "Again..." He bent his dark head and licked the inside curve of her breast, along the edge of her sensible cotton bra. "And again."

The tremors began in the long bones of Maeve's thighs and progressed up her spine, turning into a full-blown shudder along the way. She gurgled, deep in her throat, and Luc snapped the catch on her bra and drew it away.

Silence.

Luc swiped his tongue over his lips and all her intimate flesh quivered and wept. "Fuck, I love strawberries. C'mere." He dropped to his knees to suckle, pressing his palms into her back, holding her captive for his plundering mouth, tormenting first one nipple, then the other.

Maeve swayed, whimpering, her fingers buried in his thick hair. A wave of soft, dark heat flooded through her, weakening her knees. Desperately, she tightened her grip and the heel of her hand brushed something hard.

Luc mumbled an oath around her tingling nipple. Abruptly, he wrenched himself away and Maeve cried out, staggering.

"I can't do this," he muttered as he steadied her.

The shock of it held her paralyzed for a second. Then humiliation surged over her, followed by a storm of hurt. Too ugly, too weird. A scalding tide rose over her cheeks. "You what?"

"Not with the light on. Where's the bedroom?"

Maeve goggled. Her head whirled. "F-first left."

Luc sprang to his feet, lifted her long body as if it was weightless and hit the switch. As he navigated his way through the dark into her room, an incredible suspicion entered her mind. He was making an awful lot of excuses. Her heart went all soft and mushy in her chest. "Luc, you're not…not a virgin, are you?"

The mattress dipped as he sank down on it, keeping her plastered right up against that fabulous chest. When he chuckled, she felt the echoes of the reverberation clear down to her pelvis. Her clit gave such a hard twitch it forced a gasp out of her.

"Not so's you'd notice," he said.

"You're not…ah…" How could she put it? He needed to know she could cope, whatever his problem. "Not…um…shy about something?"

This time, he laughed outright, a magnificent male rumble of amusement. Even as she smiled in response, the tears prickled her eyes. How long had it been since she'd laughed, laughed right out aloud like that?

Luc ripped his shirt over his head. Then he grabbed her hands and slapped her palms over glorious slabs of muscle.

"Here, darlin'." Oh God, the luscious resistance and heat of his skin, the rasp of hair under her fingertips, the peak of a male nipple, fiercely erect. "Feel for yourself."

The sunglasses cut an impenetrable swathe across his face, but she heard his breath hitch at the contact. "Oh yeah." He pulled her hands down, down over rock-hard abs, over a trail of wire and silk hair, to his belt buckle.

Maeve swallowed. Luc transferred her trembling fingers to the front of his pants. Oh. My. God.

He pulsed through the material, filling her hand, furnace-hot and huge. She froze.

"Say something, Maeve."

"No," she gasped. "You're right, you don't have to be shy." Incredibly, with every word she spoke, his cock swelled a little more under her palm. It made her light-headed, giddy with lust.

"Keep talking." Luc sprang to his feet, the solid bulk of him blocking what little moonlight came in through the window. He bent to rip off a shoe.

"What shall I say?"

"Don't care." A thump as the second shoe hit the floor, followed by his trousers. He turned his head toward her, hands on the waistband of his boxers. His teeth flashed in a naughty grin. "Can you talk dirty, baby?"

"Um…f-fuck?"

Luc slid the boxers off, the jut of his cock a long, intriguing shadow against the wall. Maeve reached for him, unable to resist. "Nu-uh." He danced away without turning his back, surprisingly graceful for such a big man, and grabbed her foot. "Try for a sentence." His fingers got busy on her bootlaces.

Maeve's mouth opened and closed. He hauled off the first boot and began on the second. Eventually, she whispered, "Fuck me?"

A thump as the Doc hit the floor. "Christ, that's the one!"

Luc rose up, surging over her, a blanket of muscle and testosterone bearing her down into the pillows. One hand speared into her hair, holding her still so he could plunder her mouth, the other reached up under her skirt, hooked into her panties and ripped them down.

Maeve wrapped her arms around his neck and clung, lost in the flames, in the ardent velvet of his tongue. Jesus, Mary and Joseph, she wanted him as she'd never wanted anything in her life, wanted him with a greedy desperation that was terrifying in its intensity. A blunt fingertip slid over her labia, leaving delicious tingles in its wake. She kicked the panties off one ankle, letting her thighs fall apart and her hips tilt.

Luc slid the finger gently inside her and hummed deep in his throat when her inner walls clamped down on the intrusion. He freed his lips enough to mutter, "You make me crazy." He dropped a kiss on her throat, licked all around her nipple. "Not too rough?"

Maeve bucked, arching into the beautiful weight pinning her down. "No, no! Please, oh please!" Something warm—his other hand?—nudged her inner thigh, pushing her leg high and wide. Her head spun.

Chapter Three

ॐ

"Shit! Wait, wait!" Luc reached down with a long arm and fumbled something out of the pocket of his pants. Cellophane crinkled.

She beat on his shoulder with her fist. "Hurry, oh hurry!"

But he froze. "Do you trust me, Maeve?"

Maeve dug her fingers into his shoulders. "Do it," she grated. "Now!"

Luc set his hands to her waist and flipped her over, pulling her up on her hands and knees. "Gotta…" He reached past her and snapped on the bedside light. The sunglasses bounced next to her on the pillow. "Watch it…go in. Jesus."

He knocked her knees open with his, setting his cock at her weeping entrance. Maeve imagined it opening like a greedy little mouth, sucking him. She whimpered, wriggling backward, and the first inch surged into her, searingly hot.

"That's it, baby. Sing for me." Callused fingers pushed her bunched skirt out of the way, soothed over the curve of her ass. "Fuck, you're tight." Another inch.

Set free by his command, the music of the curse bubbled in her throat, emerging not as a mournful wail, but as a song of lust, a primitive paean to the joys of the flesh. Up and down the scale it ranged, as Luc flexed his hips, feeding her his ram-hard cock, inch by thick, delicious inch.

But when he pulled out and slid back in for the first time, the sensation was so exquisite, Maeve's throat closed completely. Luc bent forward and bracketed her clit with two fingers. He set up a hard, jolting rhythm in counterpoint, hitting something luscious deep inside her with every solid stroke, his balls slapping against her labial lips. "Howl," he groaned, his breath gusting warm over her ear. "For God's sake, let me hear it!"

He shifted his hands to her breasts, pulling her back into his broad chest, tugging her nipples. But somehow he was still tormenting her clit from inside and out, his cock jammed high and wide in her clenching sheath. How—? Arching over her, he controlled her completely, orchestrating her pleasure. Too much, it was too much, she couldn't think, couldn't stand it, she was going to shatter, to fly apart, to—

As she died, Maeve shuddered, threw her head back and screamed, full-throated.

"Fuck! Shit! Fuck, oh fuck!" Luc lurched forward, grabbing her hips. As his cock spasmed inside her, he groaned deep in his chest, the sound so hellishly sexy it set Maeve off again, in a series of rippling aftershocks, sweet as honey.

Her knees went and she collapsed into the pillows, gasping, Luc riding her down.

Their panting breath filled the silence.

He smoothed her hair aside and kissed her cheek. Reaching past her, he picked up the sunglasses. Another nuzzle, the cold plastic brushing her skin. "Maeve, can I stay?"

Her fingers gripped the pillow case. "You want to?"

"Oh yeah." He nibbled her earlobe. "I have plans for you, banshee girl."

If she was too needy, she'd scare him off. "Sure," she said, striving to sound offhand.

She hadn't realized how tense he'd been until she felt his chest relax against her spine. "Good." Gently, he disengaged himself. "Bathroom?"

"Next door, on the right."

By the time he'd returned, Maeve had wriggled out of the crumpled skirt and was dithering about a nightgown. Luc twitched it out of her slack fingers. "Skin," he said, as if he'd read her mind. "Just skin tonight."

* * * * *

Luc woke in the pre-dawn cool, his arms full of banshee, his nose buried in her hair and his cock nestled in the crack of her delightful ass. Mmm.

Shit! His eyes flew open. His tail was looped over a pale, flawless thigh, the hopeful tip nudging the patch of springy auburn curls hiding her delectable cunt. Cautiously, he raised his head and peered into her face.

The breath whistled out of him with relief, even as saliva pooled in his mouth. In the dim, watery light, Maeve was still dead to the world, her pink lips curved with what he hoped was the memory of pleasure, a jaunty procession of freckles marching across her nose, dusting her cheeks, every one of them deserving a kiss of its own.

His gaze tracked downward over her slim length. More freckles on the creamy skin of her breasts, nipples like pink candies, a smooth sexy belly. Hell, even the knobs of her vertebrae were sexy, the curve between her waist and hip like music. Dress her in sheer hose and killer heels, and those endless legs would stop traffic.

The job idea came to him all of a piece, closely followed by other images, all delightfully carnal. Gabe would be proud of him, on all counts.

But first... He wouldn't get through the day without the taste of her in his mouth, without a close-up inspection of all that warm ivory loveliness, every nook and cranny, especially the strawberry bits. Besides, he wanted her face-to-face, so he could ravish her mouth as he sank his cock into the glorious heat of her, all smooth and gloving and wet and tight and—

Not a hope. One look at his Manifestation and she'd pass out. Or run. Unless he could...

Uh-huh.

With infinite caution, Luc eased away. Maeve snorted in her sleep and he froze, holding his breath until she settled. It took him a good five minutes of tiptoeing from room to room, but he found what he needed in some sort of office. Looking around, he pursed his lips in a soundless whistle. Pretty cool computer setup. Top of the line, even he could see that. Come to think of it, everything in the place was best quality, from the antique furniture to the brocade curtains and Persian rugs. Expensive and elegant. So why did she dress like a thrift shop refugee? Thoughtfully, he picked up the scarf draped across the back of a leather chair, lifted it to his nose and inhaled. Pure Maeve, even to the muddy-green color she seemed to favor.

Raising his head, he caught a glimpse of his dark reflection in the window. Six foot five of muscle and bone and sinew, vibrating with the lust to fuck, cock strafing his navel, balls drawn up hard and tight. Scary enough for any woman, but when it was topped off with devil horns and a tail lashing around his calves... The fleshy pointed tip of it pulsed with desire, near as keen as his cock. Fiery as the pits of hell, red eyes burned back at him out of the hulking man-shape.

His lips went tight. Not exactly love's young dream. He twisted the scarf between his hands 'til it threatened to tear.

Then he returned to the bedroom, fished a handful of condoms out of the pocket of his pants and kneeled on the floor beside the bed, behind her. She lay curled on her side, one hand beneath her cheek. "Maeve, honey." He licked a freckle on her cheekbone.

"Mmm." She stretched and purred, reaching back with the free hand.

"Don't open your eyes."

"Luc?" Her lashes fluttered, but her lips tilted. "Why?"

"Because," He brushed the scarf over her eyes. "I'm going to lick you all over and I don't want you watching while I do it."

He watched her press her thighs together, smelled the tang of her arousal.

"Why?" she repeated.

"It'll be more intense this way. For both of us. Please, sweetheart. I won't tie your hands, not this time." Shit, that slipped out!

But Maeve flushed, a pretty wave of pink flooding over her breasts and neck. Her nipples ruched as he watched.

"You like that idea." God, she was perfect! A fierce wave of possessiveness swept over him. He wasn't letting her go, not until he was finished. His skin felt tight with hunger, too small for his body.

"Maybe," she whispered.

Luc adjusted the scarf and tied it firmly behind her head. Then he rolled her gently onto her back. "Hands over your head, Maeve."

Her lips parted, the lower pouting deliciously, but she did as he Commanded.

Luc stood at the end of the bed, his heart thundering as if he'd played four quarters against the Raiders single-handed. "Spread for me," he whispered.

An excruciating pause. She shifted her knees about six inches.

His cock bucked and Luc swore. Gripping his unruly organ at the root, he exerted a brutal pressure. "More," he gritted. "I won't eat what I can't see." As a threat, it was pathetically empty, but Maeve wouldn't know that.

She made a tiny mewling noise deep in her throat, and he'd set a knee on the end of the bed before he knew it. He thought he'd die, watching her run her graceful hands down over her belly, her hips, the curls of her mound. Long fingers gripped her thighs, drew them apart. Wide. Wider.

He could see every delicate feminine fold, all pink and ruffled, swollen and slick with arousal, with her clit sitting up out of its hood, all pert and firm as a berry, begging for his tongue. And two little holes, the dark, tempting entrance to her sweet cunt and the puckered rosebud of her ass.

Oh yesss!

Licking his lips, he lunged forward.

Half an hour later, he'd driven them both to the brink of insanity. Maeve was singing his name with every gasping breath, while his cock was so hard he could have used it to hammer nails, oily beads sliding free of the slit in the head. He'd resorted to jamming his tailtip so hard up against his balls, it hurt.

"Lube?" he rasped as he circled the tip of his tongue around her clit.

"Don't need it." Maeve's head tossed on the pillow, her hair a torrent of tangled auburn curls.

Gentle nibbles all down one pink, frilly lip. "Answer me, Maeve." Back up the other.

She flailed a hand in the direction of the bedside table. "Top...drawer. God."

Ah yes. There it was. Luc's brows rose. Together with an interesting collection of vibrators and... He peered. An anal plug?

Goddamn, he felt like singing. Could she get any better?

Not that he needed such a toy, not when he came equipped with his own.

Swiftly, he squeezed a good dollop of lube over the tip of his tail. It twitched and a shudder of anticipation rolled up his spine. When he rolled the condom over his swollen cock, he noted with mild surprise that his hands weren't quite steady.

"Hold tight, baby," he murmured, as he brushed the taut head of his shaft over her labia.

Her moan was music to his ears.

A single luxurious plunge and he was hilted to the root, his sac pressed right up against her. The sensation was so powerful he was convinced his balls were going to rocket up his spine and blow the top of his head off. He breathed hard through his nose, fighting for control.

Maeve squirmed beneath him and he clamped a hand on her thigh to keep her still. "Not yet. Wait."

With infinite care, he worked the slippery point of his tail around her asshole, while his cock vibrated with barely leashed impatience.

"*Luc!*" She bucked and the walls of her cunt clamped down like a fist on his invading flesh.

Around and around and around. "You like that."

"Oooooh! It's—oh, Luc!

He grasped one slender thigh and shifted it to his waist. Then the other. Ah, what a gorgeous angle. Another inch of tail slid into her ass, teasing the nerve-rich flesh around the entrance.

Maeve's lips parted on a long, throbbing cry.

He didn't think he'd ever felt so *alive*, not even the one astounding time he'd made an intercept and scored a freak touchdown.

Luc leaned forward and brushed his lips against hers. "Sing for me, darling," he rasped. Then he sealed their mouths together and took her howl into his body, rocking into the carnal silk of her with bursting cock and throbbing tail, slowly at first, then harder and harder, wrapping her up, holding her down, devouring, possessing.

His, all his.

Beneath him, Maeve clung and writhed, shuddering and crying into his mouth. Abruptly, she arched up hard, her spine bowed off the mattress. The inner walls of her cunt and her ass convulsed, a brutal milking that made him see stars. The banshee shriek started in her straining throat and rippled through her body as the orgasm took her and then it was screaming though him too, the seed boiling out of his balls and surging down his shaft in an excruciating tide that jetted out of him in long powerful spasms of pleasure.

For a few ecstatic moments, Luc went away. Somewhere fiery, dark and pulsing.

When he opened his eyes, Maeve was limp, blanketed by his still-shuddering body. Her arms lay loose on the sheet, the slack fingers curled into her palms.

Bloody hell. He hadn't killed her? He rolled away, so relieved when she breathed out he nearly forgot to check his skull for horns.

Maeve tugged the scarf down, her eyes wide and blind-looking, dazed. She pressed trembling fingers against his lips. "That was…it was…"

"Yeah." For the life of him, he couldn't think of another thing to say. Instead, he rubbed his bristly cheek against the top of her head. Then he went to the bathroom to dispose of the condom.

When he returned, Maeve simply held her arms out and Luc went into them gladly, snuggling her head against his shoulder. As the dawn brightened into morning, they lay tangled together, not speaking.

* * * * *

Luc picked up a spindly chair and studied it doubtfully. In the gilt and rococo atmosphere of the dress boutique, he looked huge and square, dangerous as a mountain wolf. Lord, he was sexy!

And so bloody stubborn.

She'd tried to talk him out of the makeover idea a dozen times this morning, but he'd been immovable. Maeve suspected he would have been perfectly prepared to carry her through the mall draped over his shoulder. As it was, Ivana, the proprietor of the shop, was an old friend of his. A former girlfriend probably. She fought to keep the sour twist from her lips. He'd arranged for the other woman to meet them at a staff entrance before opening time

Now Ivana leaned a trim hip against the counter, her shrewd dark eyes darting up and down in a thoughtful assessment. Suddenly, she smiled broadly, stepped forward and gave Luc a loud smacking kiss on the cheek. "From the skin out, you said?" She shot Maeve a sideways glance full of glee. "She's built like a dream, you know. What look are you after?"

Maeve tugged his sleeve. "Luc," she hissed. "*Luc!*"

He patted her hand. To Ivana, he said, "Business woman, but killer sexy."

"Luc, it won't work!"

His hazel glance pinned her. He raised a dark brow. "It'll have to. I've got a job for you, sweetheart, and you can't go dressed like that."

Maeve shook her head, trying to clear it of a frantic buzz that felt like a hive of agitated bees. "Excuse us," she muttered in Ivana's general direction. "Come here!" Wrapping both hands around his forearm, she dragged Luc into a corner behind a shoe display.

"Why won't you listen to me? As soon as it activates, the Curse makes anything…ah, modern…fall off me. Disintegrate." Tears threatened. It was so fucking *unfair*.

"You mean anything pretty."

"Yes." Her head drooped.

Luc's big hand closed over the back of her neck, warm and comforting. "That's shitty. How do you break the curse?"

"Can't. There's only one condition and it's impossible."

"So tell me."

Chapter Four

Strong fingers massaged her nape and the words she'd never said to a living soul fell out of her mouth. "True love, of course. But there's a catch."

Luc had gone very still. Rising on tiptoes, Maeve whispered in his ear.

"Wail, wail the banshee.

Only love will set ye free.

Nor flesh, nor fury shall stay the Curse,

And mortal man shall make it worse.

Tied in an eternal knot,

Love ye need, yet love ye not."

When she drew back, he was frowning, his eyes curiously blank.

"You see?" She shrugged and the desolation of it hit her all over again, a sucker punch of grief. Luc had been marvelous, wonderful, but he'd go. He'd have to. The man didn't exist who'd live with the Curse. "Only love can set a banshee free, but not the love of a mortal man." She tried to laugh, but it came out all wrong. "If I thought it'd help, I'd get a puppy."

"But didn't your parents love each other?"

"Sex doesn't count. I don't know who my father was." She tilted her chin. "A passing sperm donor."

Flags of color flew on Luc's well-defined cheekbones. Oh Lord, she'd embarrassed him. Slowly, he reached past her and took a shoe from the display. The leather was bronze, the heel a moderate stiletto. Around the ankle winked fine gilded chains, twisted together. So classy. So *her*.

"These," he rumbled. "Wear these."

"But Luc—"

His gaze seemed to *burn*, little flames leaping in his eyes. Without looking away, he slapped his credit card on the counter. "I'm going to get a coffee," he said. "I have some thinking to do."

Maeve opened her mouth to protest again, but he forestalled her. "I want to see you, dressed as you should be." He cradled her cheek. "So everyone can see how beautiful you are. And that you're mine."

Swiftly, he pressed a hard kiss to her lips and strode out of the shop, leaving her to stare after him, numb with shock.

"Come on, honey, we've got work to do." Still reeling, Maeve let Ivana tug her into a dressing room. "And no mirrors 'til I'm finished."

With the last of her strength, Maeve said, "All right. But I'm paying." It wasn't as if money was a problem. The share-trading she did on the Internet took care of that.

"Fine. Whatever," said Ivana. "Oh boy, this is going to be fun."

And in an odd, heartbreaking kind of way, it was. Maeve stood, obedient as a doll, letting the woman's chat flow over her head, letting her primp and fuss and exclaim. In the process, she discovered Ivana's husband was Luc's foreman and that they had three children, the youngest of whom was named Lucas for their best friend.

Half an hour later, the other woman said, "Close your eyes, Maeve." Warm fingers took her by the elbow and led her out into the shop proper. Wobbling a little in the heels, she followed, her heart trying to escape from behind her ribcage. Everything felt so strange—the wisp of apricot lace Ivana referred to as a bra, the matching panties and garter belt. How she'd blushed to discover Luc had specified garters and stockings.

Ivana had chuckled. "Men are all the same. My Tom hates pantyhose. And Luc said I wasn't to choose anything that would mark your skin. So no thigh-highs either."

Oh God, the slide of silk and satin over her body, the beautiful colors and firm fit. Ivana's fingers fluffed her hair. "Hold still." The careful application of a lipstick. "Okay. Now."

Maeve opened her eyes.

She almost turned to look over her shoulder.

The woman in the mirror wore a tailored suit in a shade of warm caramel. The teal blouse beneath it belied the sexy severity of the suit, the softly draped neck giving a hint of creamy cleavage. The cut of the skirt and jacket both camouflaged and revealed the hourglass shape of her figure. Endless legs sheathed in gleaming nude hose ended in the bronze stilettos, winking chains clasping her slim ankles. The colors made her skin glow like a summer peach, the green-gold of her eyes exotic and vivid. Her rust-red curls streamed over her shoulders, crackling with energy.

Oh. My. God.

Sexy as hell. And yet so professional. With absolute sincerity, she said to the beaming Ivana, "You're a genius."

"No she's not." Luc loomed behind her, armored behind his sunglasses, a Stetson jammed on his head. It looked a bit odd with the polo shirt and chinos. "Ivana's good, but all she's done is reveal you." She watched in the mirror as he curled a lock of her hair around his finger. She thought his hand trembled. "The real you."

Ivana giggled and fanned a hand in front of her face. "Whoa," she said. "Is it hot in here or what?"

"Let's go." Luc slipped an arm around her waist and made for the door. "Before I eat you alive."

Maeve stumbled and he steadied her, pressing her hard into his muscular body. "Where are we going?"

His teeth flashed in a cocky grin. "Patel's Curry and Spice. No Irish there."

Although it was only a five minute drive, they arrived in an icy silence. Luc had been furious to discover Maeve had paid for the new wardrobe herself and he'd shouted. A lot. Honestly, did he think sheer volume was going to faze a banshee? As they pulled up, she sniffed and hunched a shoulder.

Luc turned to face her. She could see her own tiny image in his dark lenses. "The immoveable force meets the irresistible object. I'm going to have to invest in insulation." His lips twitched.

Maeve's jaw dropped. "Insulation?"

He ran a considering finger into the neckline of the blouse. "So the neighbors don't complain. What color bra did you get?"

She batted his hand aside and he frowned. "Neighbors? What neighbors?"

Luc leaned very close, until they were nose to nose. Maeve's eyes crossed. She was beginning to hate those sunglasses. He drew a breath. "We have a future together, Maeve O'Brien." His voice was very low. "I don't know what it is yet, but I know it's out there. Waiting."

Completely flummoxed, Maeve stared. "I…ah…um." Her heart sank right down to her beautiful, fuck-me heels. Too good to be true. Then it soared, filling her temples with her thundering pulse until she thought she might faint. Dammit, she *deserved* someone like Luc!

He leaped down and came 'round to open the passenger door. He handed her down as though she was made of spun sugar. "Come and meet the Patels. They need a bookkeeper."

Her brain still scrambling to keep up, Maeve let him lead her into the dim, spicy-smelling warehouse. They found Mr. Patel in the office, elbow deep in papers, a harassed expression on his round, coffee-brown face. As soon as he saw her, he bounded to his feet and took both her hands in his, pumping vigorously. "Ah, dear lady. Just what I need! Mr. Kaminski, I'm in your debt."

"Delighted." Luc shook hands in turn. "Ms. O'Brien has only one requirement—a quiet office where she can work undisturbed."

"Of course, of course." Mr. Patel put a hand under her elbow and bustled her out into the warehouse. "Come meet my wife and my boys. This is a family company."

Maeve cast one last longing look over her shoulder as she was led away. Luc pushed the shades down his nose, peered over the top and blew her a kiss. "Ring me," he called. He waited just long enough to watch the introductions. Then he disappeared and she was alone with the rest of the world. As usual.

* * * * *

Luc glared at the phone on Gabe's desk, willing it to ring again. The first couple of hours had been hell. He couldn't get her pale little face out of his mind, the uneasy mix of hope and fear in her eyes. He'd checked the staff for anyone remotely Irish, made sure she had an office to herself. But still... The pen he was holding snapped between his fingers.

And he recalled quite distinctly the reactions of the Patel boys. He growled under his breath. Horny young bastards. One look at Maeve and they'd sat up straight, dark brown eyes bright with male appreciation. Nice-looking youngsters too, with flashing smiles and charming manners. He ground his teeth, knowing his eyes were glowing.

Her mid-morning call had been such a relief, he'd almost cried. He could still hear the thrum of nerves in that luscious voice, but she'd sounded much more positive. Halfway through the first-quarter accounts and setting things in order, her confidence growing with every minute.

The phone shrilled and he jumped. "Maeve?"

"No, it is *not* Maeve!" said a furious female voice. In the background, he heard a shriek, a crash, men shouting.

"Mrs. Patel?"

"Yes, it is Indira Patel and never in all my life have I seen anything like it!"

Oh God. Luc rose, gripping the receiver so hard, the plastic creaked. "Like what?"

"That, that…hussy!" A prolonged rebel yell that wasn't Mrs. Patel. Her voice faded as she turned away from the phone. "Charles, stop that! Find a blanket, quick, quick now!"

"What the hell happened?" His tail Manifested so fast his spine ached with whiplash.

"Before my very damn eyes, she's standing here in her scanties! And every man in the place is staring!"

A woman sobbing, long hopeless sounds that tore his heart out by the roots. A demonic rage exploded inside Luc Kaminski. His horns sprang to life, the points sharp and wicked. "Don't you yell at her!" he roared. "It's not her fault. Tell her I'm coming!"

Snatching up his Stetson and shades, he barreled out of the office, Mrs. T staring after him, open-mouthed.

Although he broke all the speed limits, the few minutes it took him to get to the Patels were an agony. Dickhead, dickhead, *dickhead*! It wasn't her fault, it was his. His fucking fault. Why hadn't he listened to her?

Poor little darling, so brave, so gorgeous. And she'd trusted him, his Maeve, trusted that he knew what the hell he was doing. But he didn't. He hadn't from the moment she'd walked into Gabe's office and turned his world upside down.

The fury and the guilt burned everything else to ash but that was good, because now the solution to Maeve's problem stared him in the face. The forever solution, if he had the guts to risk it.

He screeched to a halt outside the warehouse and pounded inside, fists clenched, ready for battle.

A round, brown robin in a blue sari, Mrs. Patel stood in front of Maeve, her arms spread like a human barricade, but who she thought she was protecting was debatable. Grouped in a semicircle around them were Mr. Patel, his three sons and an older man, a stranger with a neatly trimmed moustache and a clipboard. Their expressions ranged from affront to unholy glee to embarrassment, but every eye was firmly fixed on Maeve.

She was so much taller than Mrs. Patel, he could see the tears streaking her flawless cheeks, reddening the tip of her nose. She was clutching a blanket so hard her knuckles were white. But it wasn't any use, the ends were unraveling, the blanket growing shorter as he watched, reaching her beautifully formed calves, her knees... Hell!

She moaned a kind of litany under her breath, her lips pressed tightly together. "Death and sorrow, death and sorrow, death and sorrow. Ah, sorrow, sorrow."

His expression avid, one of the Patel boys murmured, "Oh yeah." Luc wanted to rip his throat out.

He grabbed the older man by the shoulder. "You Irish?"

The man's pale blue eyes opened wide. "I'm Patrick Reilly," he said with dignity, but he couldn't prevent his fascinated gaze from veering back to Maeve. "From Customs."

"Out." Luc frog-marched him to the door.

"But— What?"

"Go get a cup of coffee or something."

"Really, I—"

"Get!"

Reilly got.

Now for the Patel boys. Luc whipped off the shades and let the growl build in his chest. He stalked back into the room and clamped a big hand on the nearest Patel shoulder. By happy chance, it was the one who'd spoken. Luc squeezed with grim enjoyment and the young man's eyes flashed up.

"Holy shit!"

Luc lifted a brow. "Exactly." He gathered the Patel menfolk with a burning glance. "Anyone else like to stay?"

Heads shook in chorus. Within seconds, he was alone with the two women. "Maeve, you all right?"

"Oh, Luc!" With a rush, she was in his arms, clinging as if she wanted to climb inside his skin. "I'm so sorry," she gasped into his shoulder. "So sorry."

"Sorry's not good enough, young lady," said Mrs. Patel. "Never in all my life have—"

Luc cut her off. "Where's the office you gave her?"

"End of the passage, but what about—"

"I can't apologize enough, Mrs. Patel." Maeve lifted her head. "Just let me get my things and we'll go."

"With the money you're owed for the work you've done." Luc stared Mrs. Patel down. She gave a jerky nod.

He shepherded Maeve back into the tiny office at the end of the building, gathering pieces of clothing from door knobs and chair backs and even a light fitting as they went.

Very carefully, he chose the strongest chair in the place and sat down with Maeve in his lap. He tossed the remains of the blanket to the floor and was momentarily distracted by the sight of pink nipples pushing against peach-colored lace. Down, boy. Gently, he looped the bra straps back up her arms, but they flopped, the stitching undone. The panties had fared better. Pity. He kept his mouth shut about that.

Maeve hiccupped as he massaged the back of her neck. "It was Reilly," she whispered. "I walked out to ask Mr. Patel for the next quarter's books and there he was and...oh God, his uncle's in hospital, dying." She gave a woeful little sniff. "I don't know why you bothered, Luc. But it was so nice to feel pretty, just once."

His heart began a slow gallop, hard and heavy in his chest. "It was my fault, sweetheart. But don't worry, it won't happen again."

She sighed, the sound unutterably weary. "Of course it will. I'm a banshee. I'm Cursed."

"Not any more." Shit, he'd never been this scared, never had this sensation of the world poised on a razor's edge. He dragged in a huge breath. "I love you, Maeve."

Something in the air shivered as if life itself teetered, but she didn't move so much as a muscle. He didn't know what he'd expected, but all she did was blink. "You do?"

"I do."

"But you hardly know me!"

"Doesn't matter. I think I knew from the first kiss."

Her pretty mouth formed a perfect pink O. "Really?"

He smiled. "Really. And you love me, don't you?"

But she just stared, the gold flecks shining in her eyes. His heart sank. Shit!

Abruptly his arms were full of warm, willing woman, satin lips pressed to his, a sweet cajoling tongue, soft breasts crushed to his chest. Relief singing through him, Luc relaxed and let himself be kissed.

When they came up for air, she went back to the problem, as he'd known she would. Because she was good with figures and it didn't add up. Stroking a fingertip over his eyebrow, she murmured, "Luc, I can only love you as much as the Curse will let me. I'll do my best, but—"

If he had to wait another minute, he'd go mad. *Get it over with, you coward.* "I'm not a mortal man," he said.

She drew back. "What on earth do you mean?"

He tilted her chin with his fist. "Look into my eyes while I say it, Maeve. Look deep."

Without shifting his gaze from hers, he said, "Hear me, Curse or whatever you fucking are. I love Maeve O'Brien, the banshee." A pause for oxygen. "And I am not a mortal man."

The words rang in the small room, louder than he'd intended. This time the air rippled. Maeve gasped and every vestige of color left her face. "Your eyes are on fire!"

"Yes." Something rustled on the floor. "Fuck, look at that!"

Maeve followed his stare and let out a little shriek. A button rolled out of a corner and wobbled determinedly across the floor toward her crumpled blouse. Another emerged from beneath the desk, and another. Threads waved and wove, sewing the buttons back on with invisible fingers.

"Eek!" Maeve jerked as the straps of her bra repaired themselves. The zipper reinserted itself into her skirt, the sleeves of the jacket reattached themselves.

"God, Luc, *what are you?*"

Luc rose and set her gently on the desk. Then he went to the door and locked it. "I think it's time you met my great-grandparents."

Chapter Five

∞

This was crazy. Rollercoaster wild. She couldn't decide whether to laugh, run screaming or jump his bones. Maeve considered Luc from under her lashes. He was taking something out of his wallet. An old photograph.

"My great-grandparents Kaminski." He handed it over.

The couple gazed solemnly at the camera, the woman wearing an Edwardian gown, buttoned high to her neck, the man a suit with a stiff collar. Very proper.

Except…

A forked tail snaked out from beneath the woman's skirts to coil neatly around her buttoned shoes and out of her carefully coiffed hair rose… Maeve gasped. Horns! Curved and wicked, like a devil's. The man was as fair as the woman was dark and sternly handsome. Above his shoulders arched a huge pair of feathery wings. The light struck a gleam off the pure blond of his hair, the effect very like a halo.

"Theater. They were in theater," she said, her voice a thread. "These are costumes."

"No. You're a banshee, Maeve." Luc sounded impatient. "Have a little faith."

She peered at the photo. "Their eyes look funny. Must have been the flash."

"It wasn't. Look at me, Maeve."

Slowly, she raised her eyes. A red cast had invaded the warm hazel. Tiny flames leaped in his pupils. The fluorescent light gleamed off the points of the short curved horns springing out of his thick dark hair.

Luc pulled his shirt off over his head and kicked off his shoes.

"What are you doing?" she yelped.

"Showing you the rest." He got busy with his belt buckle. "Do you know I've never fucked a woman in broad daylight? Let alone the woman I love." His hungry grin had pure devil in it.

The pants dropped to the floor. He'd gone commando. Oh yes! Maeve licked her lips and his beautiful cock jerked with enthusiasm, his balls tightening. His tail coiled around his calf, swishing with impatience.

Wait a— *His tail?*

"God, what *is* that thing?"

A flicker of hurt crossed his face. "It's my tail," he said with dignity. "You liked it last night. And this morning."

Maeve thought back. His hands had been everywhere, giving her such extraordinary pleasure. But he must have used his tail as well, to be able to— Good heavens, he'd put it—

The apricot panties flooded. He was right. If she could cope with being a banshee, she could cope with a lover who was...whatever he was. Maeve slid off the desk and sashayed over to her personal devil. She laid both palms against his chest and his eyes flamed. "Can I touch it?"

"Shit, yes!"

As if it had a mind of its own, Luc's tail snaked up her arm. Wonderingly, Maeve stroked the warm, firm skin while he shuddered and clenched his fists. "Sensitive, huh?"

"Very," he gritted.

Maeve nudged him with her shoulder, pushing him back into the desk. "Better hold on then."

As she sank to her knees, Luc groaned, almost as musically as a banshee. Knowing he watched, she skimmed her lips over the taut, velvet head of his cock. Then she reached between his legs and grasped his tail at the root, stroking down, hand over hand, as she mouthed the first inch of cockflesh.

Arriving at the forked end of his tail, she sandwiched it between her palms and rubbed, sinking her mouth further down his shaft at the same time. Luc positively vibrated with tension. Fascinating. Maeve stroked with her thumbs, adding a lick under his cock head at each pass.

His hands clenched in her hair. "*Maeve!*" The word sounded so guttural, it was scarcely recognizable. She smiled and fluttered her tongue, feeling the big vein throbbing against it. The sensation of control was absolutely delicious.

What if—? Struck by a carnal inspiration, she drew the forked end up high enough to lay over his cock. Try this, you sexy demon, she thought, and sucked both in together.

Luc made a strangled noise deep in his throat and came up on his toes. "Fuck, fuck, fuck!" he gasped. "Stop! Fuck, I'm gonna—" He tugged at her hair and reluctantly she drew back, releasing him with two plops and a regretful sigh.

He stared down at her, his chest heaving, eyes molten. "Watching you is the sexiest thing I've ever— No, it's not. Hearing you come howling is." He inhaled, a deep, ragged breath. "Hell, I can't decide. Can you sing with your mouth full, banshee girl?"

Maeve flashed him a challenging grin. "Make me, devil." And she bent to resume the torture.

She heard Luc's dark chuckle a half-second before his tail slithered into her panties, forged through her curls and tapped her clit with wicked precision. "Ooooh!" she mumbled.

The sensation was not unlike a closed circuit. The harder she sucked, the more he stroked until she was moaning with every pass, lost in a delirium of pleasure, caught in the excruciating crossfire of the growing pressure behind her clit and the eroticism of the thick cock stroking over her palate.

She fumbled a hand up over his body, desperate for an anchor, and he clasped it in one of his and clamped over his heart.

"*Maeve!*" On the word, his hips arched and his cock spasmed, the warm jets splattering down her greedy throat. His tail convulsed, hitting her clit and sending her spinning into a maelstrom of electrifying sensation. She shrieked around the hard flesh in her mouth. Her vision grayed out.

When she came to, she was lying half on the rug, half on Luc's broad chest. "God, I love you," she said.

"Good." He lapsed into silence, a smug grin curving his lips.

Maeve reached up to rub her knuckles over one horn. Warm and hard. Luc purred and his lashes fell to half-mast, so she did it some more. He groaned. "You spoil me, sweetheart." He grabbed her wrist and kissed it. "I'm taking you to the Shamrock for dinner tonight, to celebrate. No more Curse."

"Do you think it's really gone?"

"Oh yeah." He stretched, a lazy ripple of muscle and bone and sinew that made her mouth water. "I felt it, didn't you? And your clothes put themselves back together. You can give Reilly your sympathies for his uncle before we go, if you want to be certain."

"Not a mortal man. Luc —" She stopped.

He cocked a dark brow. "Go on, ask."

"You're not really the devil, are you? I mean," she sat up, "you're not evil. I know you're not."

"None of us are. Well, no more than anyone else."

"*Us?*"

"My family. It's a genetic thing, but our records only go back to the great-grandparents Kaminski. Just like the original Romeo and Juliet. God knows what their families thought. But my Aunt Lili, who does all the family history, says they were happy. Mom named my brother after the old man."

"Gabe?"

"That's right. He's blond. I take after great-grandmama's side."

"Gabe, as in Gabriel?"

"Uh-huh." Luc feathered her nipple with a fingertip. When had he got her bra off, the sneaky devil?

Gabe and Luc. Gabriel and— An incredible suspicion entered her mind. "Your name's not Lucas is it?"

He grinned. "No."

"Lucian?"

"No, my darling," he rumbled, kissing her with devilish skill. "It's not."

Also by Denise Rossetti

ဆ

Gift of the Goddess
Tailspin

About the Author

ဆ

When Denise Rossetti was very young, she had an aunt who would tell her the most wonderful fairy stories—all completely original. Denise grew up, as little girls do, but the love of stories has never left her. It was only when she dared herself to write down the secret sagas in her head, that life become *really* interesting!

Denise remains an incurable romantic. She loves happy endings, heart-stopping adventure and the eventual triumph of good over evil. All hail the guys in the white hats, she says. Unless the ones wearing black are more...um...intriguing?

She lives in a comfortable, messy old house in the Australian suburbs with her darling husband of more-years-than-she-cares-to-remember. And yes, she knows how lucky she is. She has one of everything that matters—one husband, one son, one daughter, one dog, one cat and, thank heavens, one cleaning lady. Denise is small and noisy and dreadfully uncoordinated and tends to wave her hands around a lot, which can be unfortunate if the tale she's telling happens to have explosions in it!

Denise welcomes comments from readers. You can find her website and email address on her author bio page at www.ellorascave.com.

LYRAEL'S SACRIFICE

Jory Strong

Prologue

ဢ

Even in times of famine and drought, when the rains didn't come and the tribe members died along the long-horned cattle and the goats and the camels, when the desert swept in and reclaimed the land at the base of the forbidden mountains — even in those times, the girl children of the Azzura clan were offered food and water first.

They were protected and guarded, watched over as they grew to womanhood. Their skin was kept smooth and free of hair except for eyebrows and eyelashes above sky-blue eyes, except for the golden tresses which flowed like silken sunshine to below their knees and even to their ankles.

The last few years had been good and the tribe had prospered. Now the time had come to take the jewelry and hides and livestock to the far mountains and to the sea beyond. But in order to gain the wealth offered by those distant cities and ports, to use the riches to attract husbands and wives so new blood would be added, the tribe had to trek across the desert. They would need to avoid the Djinn, the spirits who hated all mankind, who killed with shifting sand and violent sandstorms. Who could sometimes be distracted, appeased by a gift — by the sacrifice of one of the Azzura.

The tent village was broken down in preparation for the trip. The camels loaded, save for a single camel and a single structure where seven women waited.

The tribal elders gathered around a fire under a sky containing both the setting sun and rising moon. Their deeply tanned faces were wrinkled, somber, their fingers gnarled by age and hard work.

They passed a cup made from an ancient skull, drank the bitter, dark brew it contained and felt the liquid burn through them. When the cup was empty, they danced as the younger men pounded on drums made of animal hides stretched across frames of bone. They danced until they were lightheaded, until they felt the god's presence. Only then did the drums cease and the eldest of them pick up the carved pieces of wood and cast them into the fire. His voice lifted in praise to the god for interceding when six of the tokens disappeared in hungry flame while the seventh lay smoldering on a bed of ash. It was a clear sign telling them which of the Azzura was to be offered to the Djinn so the rest of the tribe might travel through the desert safely.

Chapter One

ഇ

Lyrael waited in the small, enclosed shelter of sewn hide. Her sisters and cousins huddled together, clinging to one another, praying to the god that he would spare them—all of them. But Lyrael knew the god wouldn't grant their prayer. She had seen the black mountain panther in her dreams. She had watched him turn into a black *juudu* bird and land in a pale, skeletal tree, only to slither down its white trunk in the form of a black serpent.

She shivered and fear clawed at her chest. Her heartbeat vibrated through her like a sudden thunderstorm across the land.

In her dream the snake and the panther and the bird came at her summons and were angry that she had the power to whisper their name in the wind. *Asrafil*. That's what they were called. That's what *he* was named.

For when the deadly serpent reached the lower limb of the tree, he dropped to the ground and the sand swirled up in greeting, spinning around him, hiding him from her sight though she knew what he was. Djinn. The enemy of her people.

Lyrael gazed at her two sisters and the fear in her chest receded, allowing her a moment of happiness. By the time the tribe returned to their lands, neither of her sisters would be a satisfactory offering to the Djinn. They would wear short braids and have down-covered woman's mounds—just as she would have if she had not called Asrafil's name in the spirit dream. After this trip, she and her sisters would all have joined the ranks of the mated women, their places taken by girls moving from childhood to womanhood.

The drums and singing stopped. In the twilight silence Lyrael heard beasts stirring, camels being prodded to their feet to start the journey across the desert. She straightened as footsteps drew near the hide shelter. "They come," she said, not bothering to cover her face with the material that was fashioned into one continuous garment flowing from head to foot in a robe that sheltered her skin from sand and sun.

Her female relatives stopped crying but continued to cling to each other. They looked at her, hiding their fear, their hope, their guilt.

They knew of the dream though she had not spoken to them about it. She saw it in their eyes but didn't ask them how they knew. Any who dream-walked were given to the Djinn for fear their spirit travels would draw attention to the tribe, bringing death and additional hardship.

The flap of the shelter was drawn back. The women were told to step outside.

"You will come with me," Herachio, the tribal leader's son, said to Lyrael, his body tense, his eyes both sorrowful and fearful.

They had grown up together, had begun sharing glances lately as they tended livestock and saw to the chores necessary to survive their harsh land and life. Sometimes Lyrael caught herself thinking of a future where she and Herachio built a shelter and lived as a joined couple, though they had never spoken of it. Until an Azzura woman was freed of her obligation to the tribe, no male allowed himself to grow too close, to risk his heart or share confidences for fear of having his secrets and his life delivered into the hands of the Djinn.

Lyrael tilted her head slightly in acknowledgment of Herachio's words, in a silent promise that she would not disgrace herself by railing or fighting against her fate. For even in times of famine and drought, when the rains didn't come and the tribe members died along with the long-horned cattle and the goats and the camels, when the desert swept in and reclaimed the land at the base of the forbidden mountains—even in those times, she had taken the food and water offered knowing this might one day be required of her.

She turned to her female relatives, kissing each of them as they passed by her on the way to where the camels carrying their family belongings waited to begin the long trek to the mountains and sea. And when the last of them had rejoined the tribe and the young men had started to break down the final shelter so it could be loaded upon the only unburdened camel, Lyrael followed Herachio into the forbidden mountains.

He took the common pathways at first, those allowed for hunting, those the god had claimed from the Djinn. Then he took the less common ones—the lands in between, where the god was said to still fight the Djinn on behalf of the tribe. And finally Herachio led her into a narrow crevice, the symbols carved on either side of the stone marking it as taboo to all save those who had been granted permission by the elders.

Lyrael's breath grew short and she stumbled in the dark, rock-strewn place. She almost went to her knees in fear because the spirit-presence was so powerful in the tiny space.

Herachio hesitated long enough for her to gain her footing, to regain her dignity and honor. She would not disgrace herself by going to her death crying and cowering.

The hot breath of the desert rushed past them. They climbed upward, a gradual slope at first, then a steeper one with glimpses of the night sky.

She shivered when they finally exited the rocky passageway. Her attention went immediately to the tree she'd seen in her dreams. It was like a pale, skeletal hand glowing under the full moon, its limbs bare of leaves and flowers, its trunk smooth and foreign to this land.

There were bones scattered on the ground near it. Terror made its first inroad into Lyrael's soul. She imagined the other Azzura who had been brought here before her, who had been sacrificed to the Djinn for the good of the tribe.

She bit her lip to keep from crying out, from pleading. Her breathing grew harsh as she fought the need to flee before Herachio could slit her throat as they did the goats they sacrificed to the god.

As if sensing where her thoughts lay, he said, "There is food and water in the calabashes. There's enough to last for seven days."

She noticed the calabashes then but wondered if they were empty, his promise of food and water a lie meant to comfort her, to distract her so her death would be achieved without pain or fear. None of the Azzura knew what it truly meant to be sacrificed to the Djinn. No woman taken ever returned.

In the dark of the night, when the elders slept, the girl children of each new generation whispered. They scared themselves with tales of grisly bloodletting and madness, of spirits who could appear human but whose skin burned like a firestone and whose eyes flickered with flames. The Djinn were beautiful and deadly beings, alien with their slitted pupils and features that mesmerized. They were demons who hated the god and took delight in tormenting those the god had created.

At the base of the tree a stake had been driven into the ground. Attached to it was a length of braided rope, its weave tight and strong. The sight of it made Lyrael think of the times she'd crafted just such a rope and used it to tether a calf so its mother would remain nearby and easy to milk.

Beyond the calf-rope was a neatly folded blanket. To the side were several calabashes, gourds with only a minimum of woven fabric surrounding them, as though whoever created them wanted to leave no trace the Djinn might follow.

Herachio directed Lyrael to sit underneath the tree and pull up her robe so he could lash the rope to her ankle. When it was done, he brought a firestone out and used it to build a small flame, and from the flame, to heat a thick piece of root from the *gego* tree until it glowed red.

He pressed the hot root to the calf-rope, burned the knot so it melted and smeared, creating an inescapable shackle. Then he ground the red tip of the root into the sand until it cooled and blackened. Afterward he put it back in one of the hidden pockets of his robe and retrieved a necklace. Where most necklaces were strung with beads and carved fetishes, this one had only a single disk made from the dried and flattened fruit of the *jukaabe* plant.

Herachio slipped the necklace over Lyrael's head. The deadly yellow fruit lay against her chest, providing her with a way to escape.

She glanced up but Herachio wouldn't meet her eyes. Without a word he stood and waked away, leaving her to the night. To the Djinn.

She shivered and scooted over to the base of the tree, looked inside the calabashes and found water and food. For long moments there was only the harsh sound of her breathing and the panicked thundering of her heart. But slowly those sounds faded, to be replaced by the call of night birds, the singing of insects and the rustle of both predator and prey as they moved around in search of food.

Lyrael huddled against the tree. Its smooth surface was warm against her back, as though it had soaked in the sun's rays during the day and now held on to the heat. The feel of it through her robes calmed her, gave her strength so that she didn't scream and reach for the *jukaabe* fruit when the sand in the distance began to swirl angrily, to rise to the height of a man and move toward her, a golden funnel gaining speed and power, a deadly force that could easily kill.

Asrafil rushed toward the Azzura woman. The sandstorm was as much a display of power and anger as it was a test of her courage.

This woman had whispered his name in the spirit world and summoned him to her. Him! Who was a prince of the Djinn.

He stopped abruptly in front of her. The wind from the storm concealed his form even as it whipped and tore at her robes. She lifted a hand and he stilled deep inside himself. He waited to see if she would be like one of the nameless females who had been brought here in the past, who had failed the first test by reaching for the *jukaabe* fruit and dying by their own hand.

The sands continued to swirl around Asrafil, cloaking him. His control of the fine granules was so complete that the pale gold grains didn't attack the beautiful sky-blue eyes now darkened with fear and glistening with courage.

Her hand moved past the necklace to clutch instead at the cloth covering her nose and mouth, keeping her face hidden from him. The show of bravery pleased him, stirred him. It replaced some of his anger with curiosity and the hope she would not disgrace him among the Djinn by having the power to summon him but not having the will to face him.

Her fingers trembled as she kept the wind from pulling the cloth away from her skin. Her body shook but she did not cower away from him or cry out or plead for him to spare her. Nor did she pray to her god to save her.

Anger returned with thoughts of the mortal's god. Asrafil's rage pulled more sand from the ground around them. Two of the calabashes containing her food went tumbling into the darkness, leaving a trail of hardened bread and dried meat behind them.

She whimpered, a small sound of distress. Yet still she did not cower in the presence of his anger and power, in the violence of the sandstorm around them—a rage brought on by the hate he bore her creator for coming upon the land of the Djinn and claiming it in bloody combat and ruthless conquest, for driving the surviving Djinn into hiding and naming them demons.

In the face of her courage Asrafil saw the touch of Djinn in her. It was a piece of his kind stolen when the daughters of the alien god's creation plucked all of the fruit from the oracle's tree and ate it.

The winds swirling around Asrafil slowed. The grains of sand dropped one by one as his desire to see what this female looked like increased.

With the curiosity came worry. That he would find her appealing, alluring. That he would come to care for her and crave the ecstasy of merging his body with hers, only to stand helpless and disgraced as she died before entering the city of the Djinn as many, many others of her kind had done before her.

It was his decision which of the three tests to administer first and he chose to further test her courage by presenting a terrifying visage. He preferred to end things before they began if that was her choice.

As the sands dropped away the moon reflected off the shiny black scales of a serpent. His massive body was coiled, his torso lifted in the air, the hood on either side of his face flared as his tongue flickered in and out, tasting the Azzura's essence in the air and finding her utterly desirable, utterly terrified.

Chapter Two

🙰

Lyrael was paralyzed by the sight before her, so frightened that her fingers twitched involuntarily as if to reach for the *jukaabe* fruit.

Have courage, Lyrael, her mother had whispered, her wet cheek pressed to Lyrael's when the tribe's elders sent for the virgin Azzura women. *Your vision is the strongest born to us in two generations. Have courage and you will find a place among the Djinn.*

Lyrael lifted her chin, reminding herself as she did so that even the youngest of the calves and goats sacrificed to the god struggled against death. She had seen this serpent in her dream walk. She knew the Djinn whose spirit was linked to hers could take this shape. Words formed in her thoughts but remained frozen in her throat so that only the whisper of his name escaped. "Asrafil."

The giant serpent swayed and she thought of the cobras she had seen in the bazaar, how they moved back and forth, charmed by the music of their keepers. "Asrafil," she repeated, her voice stronger.

The heat of the tree against her back surged into her. She felt connected to it, as if she could sense where its roots sought water deep in the ground, where its branches stretched heavenward, not reaching for the skies but shouting that what had been stolen would one day be reclaimed.

A sandstorm swirled. It rose from the serpent's coils and gained in speed as it lifted to hide the shiny black scales, the hood with its strange markings, the desert-colored eyes with their exotic pupils.

This time when the sands dropped away a man stood in place of the serpent. Lyrael's breath caught not only at the size of him, but at the sheer beauty. He towered before her with muscled arms crossed over a naked chest, his lower body hidden by flowing trousers, his feet bare.

Unlike the men of her tribe who kept their hair sheared close to their heads, Asrafil's midnight hair was worn in a thick braid that snaked down his back and past his buttocks, coming to rest against his thigh at the same place her own did.

Heat moved through Lyrael's face and she was glad the robe hid her reddened cheeks when her eyes encountered the bulge at the front of his trousers. Its size and position revealed his carnal interest.

Asrafil's erection should have terrified her, and yet the heat from where her spine pressed against the trunk of the tree moved into her womb, her woman's folds, the swollen knob she sometimes stroked during the dark hours of the night when the breathing around her in the tent told her that her family members were asleep.

She dropped her gaze to the ground and battled the unexpected reaction of her body to him. Her cheeks grew more flushed as moisture escaped from her slit and dampened her robe. It took several attempts before she could look up again, this time moving past the heavily muscled thighs and aroused penis, moving past the chest and arms to linger on his neck, either side of which bore the same swirling marks that had been on the serpent's hood.

He wore gold in both earlobes, small loops fitted tightly around the lobes. His skin was bronzed, his face the same color as his chest and feet, as though he walked in the sun unhindered by a robe.

His mouth was a tight, straight line and Lyrael shivered at the sight of it. She had the urge to press her lips to it and coax a smile from him.

As she watched, his mouth grew firmer. She wondered what he was thinking, if he was growing angry or if he intended to pleasure himself on her and then kill her — to entertain himself as her tribe traveled in the night, putting distance between themselves and the Djinn.

Once again Lyrael's chin tilted upward in a show of bravery and resolve. She was connected to this Djinn. It had to be so for her to see him in her dream and to know the encounter had called him to her, would have called him to her people as they traveled across the sands if the elders hadn't left her here. She forced herself to meet Asrafil's gaze and look into his exotic eyes with their oddly shaped pupils.

He smiled then, a small curl of masculine lips. She found her heart filling with joy, with sunlight.

"I am pleased," he said, speaking for the first time. His voice was a deep rumble that made her think of the giant, predatory cat he could become.

Asrafil crouched in front of the woman and despite himself he was more than pleased. She had spoken his name twice and he had felt the invisible tie between them strengthen. Her connection to the Djinn was strong, but it would have to be. He was a prince of his race, a creature of fire, and she had brought him to her. She had called out his name on the winds of the spirit world and he had not been able to refuse her summons.

His cock already burned for her. He wanted to quench the flame by sheathing himself in her wet woman's flesh. The scent of her arousal was an intoxicating perfume clinging to him, filling him, expanding within him so that his earlier anger at her power over him was pushed aside in favor of exploring her. Her show of bravery gave him hope that she would pass the remaining tests and enter the city of the Djinn to become his *sorja*—the wife of his heart and flesh and spirit.

In the time that followed the desecration of the tree, it had only produced a single fruit. When the most powerful of the Djinn seers had eaten the fruit, he had seen the day when the Djinn would reclaim their world. But to regain it, they would need these Azzura women whose ancestors had stripped the fruit from the tree in a day and eaten something meant to last the Djinn for centuries.

Asrafil had seen her fingers twitch in the presence of the serpent, had felt a stab of sorrow at envisioning her placing the *jukaabe* fruit between her lips and ending her life. But he would not have stopped her. Only those Azzura who passed the tests were welcomed and valued by the Djinn.

"What are you called?" Asrafil asked, knowing that by accepting her name he took a part of her inside himself. He would forever feel her loss should she fail the tests he must administer.

Her eyes flashed with surprise, curiosity, wariness and all three reactions were like fingers lightly teasing over his shaft.

"Lyrael."

The name pulsed through him. It echoed, claimed, resonated deep within as if combining with his own name to form a melodious chord that gave her more power over him. For an instant his earlier anger returned, stirring the sands at his feet. But when she looked away from him he felt loss instead of satisfaction.

There was no turning back. The seed planted long ago had grown roots and woven through time until it came to fruition here. Now. In this offering left by the mortals underneath the tree.

Asrafil grasped the rope keeping her tethered and followed it beneath the folds of her robe until he reached her bound ankle. He encircled it, marveled at how dainty she was. Pleasure flowed up his arm from the first touch of his skin to hers. Satisfaction settled in his belly at the way she accepted his touch. Her eyes and the scent of her arousal communicated that she found his attention pleasing.

She was nervous. The race of her heart gave her away, as did the wild flutter of her pulse against his palm. But it was a virgin's nervousness fueled by a woman's knowledge of what he would eventually want from her. Asrafil's cock jerked in anticipation of seeing what was now hidden.

With a thought the rope burned away from her ankle in a smokeless fire, making Lyrael gasp and try to pull out of his grasp. He tightened his grip and she once again relaxed, accepting symbolically that it was he who now held her bound, not the dictates of her tribe. When she met his eyes, he rewarded her with a small piece of knowledge. "The Djinn are creatures of fire. We were created at the beginning of time, when this world was molten rock and nothingness."

Asrafil stroked the fine bones of her ankle and then released her, shifting his weight back onto his heels and once again crossing his arms. His crouched position made his cock and balls press against the thin material of his trousers. "Remove your robe," he said. "I wish to see you."

She met his gaze immediately in a silent test of his will. But when he didn't yield, she stood, her fingers trembling as she unwound the *jamri* cloth and let it drop away to reveal her face and the sunlight gold of her hair.

He'd known she would be beautiful. All the Azzura were. But he hadn't anticipated the way his heart would sing at the sight of her face, how strong the desire was to pitch forward and worship at her feet, to pay homage by kissing up her body and pledging his own to her.

A lesser Djinn might have yielded, might have taken his cock in hand and begged for her acceptance, or simply fallen on her like a beast. Asrafil stiffened his spine in both a subtle display of how much he had to offer her and a silent command for her to continue disrobing.

Lyrael shivered, not from cold, but from the heat swirling inside her. He'd said the Djinn were creatures of fire and she felt the flames of desire licking across her bare cunt to settle in her womb and nipples.

She could barely keep her eyes away from the place between his legs. He had taken the form of a man, but he could easily rival a bull.

She licked her lips. Nervous. Uncertain. Afraid—not of him, at least not at the moment, but afraid of his reaction. No man had ever seen her naked body.

He shifted and the sands once again swirled at his feet. Her hands went to the length of woven rope at her waist. She unwound it seven times before letting it fall to the ground.

For a moment her robe remained closed, but as if he'd commanded it, a wind stirred, parting the cloth and revealing a line of skin from her throat to her bare mound. Lyrael shrugged the garment off and it slipped away, settling in a soft pool around her feet.

"Come to me," Asrafil said, barely able to keep himself from grabbing her and pulling her underneath him, from freeing his cock and taking her even though there would be nothing but pain for her if he did so without preparing her first.

Lyrael lingered for only a moment. Instinct guided her to remove the necklace and place it on her dropped rope, to offer him her trust with a demonstration that she wasn't so afraid of what he would do to her, what he would ask of her, that she would choose death rather than obey him.

She closed the short distance between them and gave a soft whimper when his hands went to her hips so he could pull her onto his lap. His crouched position made her thighs splay so her bare mound and swollen woman's flesh were visible.

Lyrael bit down on her lip to keep from uttering another sound as the heat of him burned her like erotic fire. The sheer fabric of his loose trousers did nothing to hide his strength, his powerful muscles, the temperature of his skin—hot like the desert sands during the middle of the day.

"Unbind your hair," he said and she obeyed, first uncoiling the long braid and then freeing the strands so her hair flowed down her back and past his thighs like a golden curtain.

"You please me," Asrafil said once again, his eyes leaving her face to roam downward.

Her nipples tightened into hard pink buds when his gaze settled on them. Their size and shape and color were like the *daakol* flower found only in the mountains.

"Do you pleasure yourself in the night when no one is awake to hear you?" he asked, his voice low and rough.

"Yes," she whispered, shivering as his lids dropped to partially cover his eyes.

His nostrils flared. "Show me."

Chapter Three

ॐ

Lyrael's cunt pulsed with the command. Her silken folds grew slick. They parted like a flower kissed by the sun and ready to blossom.

She licked her lips and he hissed, reminding her of the serpent that had swayed in front of her. Lyrael's gaze dropped to her splayed thighs, to her aching woman's flesh positioned only inches away from his male organ.

His excitement and interest were obvious, revealed by his fullness and by the wet spot where his cock leaked. He hissed again and took her hand in his, guided it to the place they were both looking at. His fingers covered hers as they gathered her arousal then stroked over her clit.

Lyrael cried out. She grabbed his shoulder with her free hand in order to steady herself. Her cunt spasmed. Her wet fingers were forced over the swollen knob a second time.

"Again," he commanded, taking his hand from hers though it settled on her thigh, ready to force hers if necessary.

She shook as she circled her erect clit. She panted and cried and clenched her buttocks as she obeyed his command, stroking herself as she did in the nighttime when everyone was asleep.

Lyrael resisted the urge to fuck her fingers into her slit until finally the emptiness in her channel couldn't be ignored. Then she pressed a single finger in and sought the hidden place that would make her body release and send ecstasy flooding through her.

Asrafil growled this time. The sound rumbled through her and made her want to rub her body against his. It made her want to go to her hands and knees, to offer herself to him as she'd seen animals do.

His fingers covered hers again. This time they forged into her, stretched her, burned her with their heat and their width.

Lyrael whimpered and hunched forward. She placed her head on his chest as the painful pleasure of having him invade her tight channel made her helpless, needy. He let her hand escape so he could press another of his fingers inside her. His movements quickened as her cries grew sharper and her body yielded, adjusted, accepted that he commanded it, that he controlled the rhythm and the pleasure.

"Now," he growled, "scream your pleasure now." And she flooded his palm with arousal as her sheath convulsed around his fingers, milking them as if they were a cock.

Asrafil rubbed his cheek against the silken blonde of Lyrael's hair. He reveled in the way she clung to him, shook from spent passion. Only the iron will of a Djinn prince kept him from revealing how deeply her obedience and acceptance of his touch affected him, how much he hungered for her.

Desire roared through him, burning with a heat that rivaled his Djinn core. He wanted to thrust his cock into the very place his fingers had been. He wanted to feel her slick, tight sheath fighting him, welcoming him, clutching him in fear that he would leave her body.

With a thought he could take another shape. He could become a lesser man with a smaller organ. But this was the form he favored. This was his truest manifestation when he chose to look almost human.

Asrafil brushed his lips against her hair, the caress light so she wouldn't notice the affectionate gesture—the mark of how weak she was already making him.

He placed her on her knees as he stood. It was deeply satisfying to see her naked at his feet, her arms around his legs, her face tilted upward in a submissive pose. She would call him master if he demanded it.

The thought sent a jolt of desire through his cock and up his spine. She might have summoned him in the spirit lands and brought him to her, but he was the one who would rule in the physical world, not her.

He freed the hidden binding of his trousers and let them fall to his feet. He stood for a minute as she measured him with her eyes, the nervous wash of her tongue over her lips making his penis jerk and leak in anticipation.

Asrafil crouched again, his knees spread, his cock jutting upward, hard and hungry. His heavy balls hung underneath, full of Djinn seed.

Lyrael licked her lips again. She thrilled at the way his body tensed, at the way his penis pulsed as though it wanted to feel her mouth and tongue on it.

She glanced at his face through lowered eyelashes. His eyes were slitted and his lips a straight line. She wanted to please him. She wanted to give him a release to equal the one he had pulled from her body. But she wanted to see him smile at her, to know she was more than a cunt to fuck, more than a human to amuse himself with.

She dared to stand. To put her hands on his shoulders and lean forward. To press her lips to his and touch her tongue to the seam of his mouth in a silent question.

He went completely still and for an instant she thought he would reject her, rebuff her. But then his hands went to her hair, holding her to him as his mouth opened and his tongue thrust against hers.

He tasted of desert storms. Of ancient power and molten rock. Of the very beginning when there were only the Djinn.

She held on to him as he became her world. Her breath. The beat of her heart. As he showed her with his tongue that he was the one who would always command, always dominate.

Lyrael was gasping for breath when he finally freed her. She was so lightheaded from the kiss that she sank to her knees and put her forehead on his thigh. Slowly she became aware of the nearness of his cock.

Asrafil growled at the first brush of her lips against his thigh. His hands clenched in her hair as everything inside him demanded that he force her mouth to his penis.

He could order her and she would obey. He could use his strength and make her take his cock into her mouth.

His rigid organ and tight balls didn't care how or why, only that they knew pleasure and gained release. But he cared. He wanted her to give to him freely, to offer this without compulsion as she'd willingly put aside the deadly necklace before coming to him.

Fire streaked through him when she turned her head and licked over his foreskin. It burst over him when she circled the head of his penis first with her tongue and then with her lips before drawing him into her mouth and sucking.

"Lyrael," he said, his voice breaking, his heart thundering as exquisite sensation whipped up his spine. He panted as she allowed him to push deeper into her mouth, to begin fucking in and out, trusting that he wouldn't hurt her in his passion.

Never had he dreamed he would find such ecstasy with a mortal woman. But as her lips and tongue caressed his cock, as she took him willingly into her heated depths, Asrafil could not hold back the sounds of his pleasure. He could not stop himself from praising her, guiding her.

His world became her wet, silky mouth. In and out he forged, his breath coming in short pants until his balls tightened, burned, warned of impending release.

Asrafil wanted to fuck into her channel, but now he was afraid to do so. He was afraid that until the first lava-hot rush of semen erupted through his penis he wouldn't be able to maintain his control. He feared that once he was inside her tight sheath, his cock held in the fist of her inner muscles, he would forget himself and rut on her like a crazed beast.

"Lyrael," he cried out, throwing his head back as the pull of her lips became more demanding, as she took him even deeper into her mouth and swallowed as though she wanted all of him.

His buttocks clenched and he fought the urgency. He fought the release—not because he wanted to deny himself the pleasure, but because he wanted to delay it.

The air carried the heavy scent of their arousal. The moon bathed them in light so that each touch, each expression was revealed.

She whimpered and struggled to take more of him, seemed to feed from the pleasure she was giving him. Asrafil found it intoxicating, a rush of power that could easily become an addiction—one that could easily be his downfall.

He tried to retreat emotionally by reminding himself she had yet to pass the remaining tests. It was too late. Each stroke of her tongue deepened the spell she cast on him. Each pull of her lips became a call he couldn't refuse.

"Now!" he growled in warning, giving in to her summons and letting orgasm come. His seed poured into her in a hot rush that left him curling over her, using her for support.

Liquid fire poured down Lyrael's throat. Its taste was spicy, like the *juura* fruit. It's effect on her was devastating.

Need streaked through her breasts and cunt. Desire overwhelmed her and she continued to suck hungrily, to desperately swallow each drop Asrafil fed her from his body.

Even when he softened she kept his penis in her mouth and reveled in the moans he made, in the way he panted above her. She only released him when the fingers tangled in her hair drew her away from his organ.

Lyrael licked her lips and Asrafil groaned. He grew hard again before she could look to his face and view his expression. He nudged her to her back and she went willingly. She spread her legs and showed him her wet inner thighs, the swollen cunt lips already parted to reveal her slit.

Asrafil was dizzy from the pleasure she'd given him. He was drunk from the submissive display before him.

He wrapped his fingers around his cock and it pulsed against his palm in urgent demand. The sight of her bare mound and parted woman's flesh were a lure he couldn't resist.

He leaned forward and buried his face between her thighs, licked along her glistening folds and swirled his tongue over her clit. Her arousal was a sweet nectar that went to his head, each taste making him hunger for more.

He pressed his tongue into her sheath, fucked her with it as she thrashed beneath him. Her moans and whimpers fed his lust.

Fire streaked up his cock and he pumped his fist in time to his tongue's forays into Lyrael's slick channel. He stroked the length of himself as he plundered her slit and swallowed her juices.

She pulled her knees toward her chest and the change of position allowed him to claim more of her, to spear his tongue even deeper into her wet core. He thrust hard and fast until finally she cried out his name and came.

Satisfaction filled Asrafil at the way she sprawled, boneless from the release he'd given her. Her breasts quivered as she panted, her thighs remained splayed, her soft, swollen folds still open, an invitation for him to seek them out again.

Something primitive stirred inside him. Something he'd never experienced before, the desire to mark a female with his seed.

He leaned over Lyrael and continued to stroke his cock, to fuck through the ring formed by his fingers. His buttocks began to flex each time he reached the tip and his palm glided over the slick head. White-hot flames licked at his skin as the need to come built until it couldn't be denied. He gasped as semen jetted from his cock and splashed onto Lyrael's bare mound and silken abdomen.

She cried out and arched as his heated release coated her skin. She whimpered and shivered and called his name. Even then it wasn't enough for Asrafil.

With a growl he freed his penis. He grabbed her hand and forced it to his seed. He used her fingers to spread his come, to massage it into her flesh and mark her with Djinn fire.

Lyrael begged as liquid flame burned through her cunt. She pleaded for him to fill her with his cock. Whatever he had done to her, she knew the fire burning her from the inside out would only be quenched by having him inside her. "Please," she whimpered, her need so intense that tears rolled down her cheeks.

There was no fear in her when Asrafil settled himself on top of her. He guided his straining cock to her entrance. "Easy, my beautiful Azzura," he whispered against her lips when she encircled his waist with her legs.

Her hunger was so great that she was ready to impale herself on his huge male organ. "Easy," he repeated, kissing her gently, binding himself more thoroughly to her with each press of his lips to hers. The intimate sharing of breath was the sharing of spirit among the Djinn.

"Easy. I am large and you are small."

He palmed her buttocks with one of his hands. He controlled her movements as he held himself above her and carefully pushed his cock into her. Despite his efforts to prepare her, despite the arousal that flowed freely from her slit, Lyrael's sheath was a tight fist that he fought against, pressed against until it slowly parted.

He caught her whimpered cries and swallowed them as her channel squeezed him mercilessly. Her slick flesh burned him and he wanted to cry out from the torturous pleasure of working his way inside her.

His buttocks clenched and his neck muscles strained with the effort. Sweat coated his body in a fine sheen. Ecstasy. It was everything he'd feared it would be when she whispered his name upon the night winds and summoned him to her.

Asrafil groaned, unable to hold sound back any longer as his balls pulled tight and Djinn fire streaked through his penis.

She scraped her fingers down his back and pressed more tightly against him, shuddered underneath him and his body echoed the movement.

"Lyrael," he whispered against her lips. He was panting from the strain of working himself into her virgin channel. Possessiveness inflamed his heart. She would never know another male.

"Please," Lyrael begged, burning from the heat of him. Needing him to mate with her, to fill her womb and channel with his seed.

She turned her head slightly and used her tongue to trace the swirling patterns tattooed into his neck. He thrust in reaction, a hard stab that made her scream. The pleasure riding the thin edge of pain.

Lyrael touched her tongue to his tattoos a second time and his body jerked. His cock forged even deeper and he tensed, gathered himself, reminded her of the serpent he'd been earlier, coiled and ready to strike.

She licked him again and this time he surged all the way into her. He thrust through the barrier formed by her inner walls and completely filled her.

Asrafil stilled and she looked into his face and became ensnared by the alien eyes with their slitted pupils. "You will not disgrace me," he said. His words confused her but he gave her no time to question him or to think further on them.

Asrafil's mouth captured hers. His tongue stabbed into her mouth, rubbed and twined and tasted as his hips began flexing, as his cock slid out and then back in. He penetrated her over and over again until there was no thought, until he once again commanded that she scream her pleasure and come at his summons.

She cried out his name as liquid fire poured into her. Her release was an ecstasy that shimmered through her. It took her like heat rising from the desert sands and disappearing into the night sky.

Asrafil rose with Lyrael in his arms. He used his power over wind and sand to free them both of the tiny grains that clung to them. When it was done he sent the wind scurrying to the folded blanket left for her and watched as it tumbled and unfurled and flattened to form a bed.

She had passed the first test. Tomorrow there would be another, and perhaps a third. But for tonight they would sleep beneath the oracle tree.

Chapter Four

Lyrael opened her eyes to the call of the *huudi* bird, the sunrise bird. Her first thought was to roll from her mat and dress quickly so she could beat her sisters to the easiest of the goats that needed milking. It was a game they played every morning. But the bone-white limbs of the tree above her and the male arm across her naked breasts were a stark reminder of her sacrifice.

She would never race with her sisters again or joke and laugh as they filled their calabashes. They would never again whisper of a future where their hair was worn in short braids and their woman's mounds were no longer bare as tradition required of the Azzuras who might one day be sacrificed to the Djinn.

Sadness welled up inside Lyrael. Her tears escaped to wet the sand.

She reached over and placed her palm on the tree. Once again heat surged into her. Only now she recognized it as Djinn fire and knew this tree belonged to them.

Next to her Asrafil stirred and rose onto an elbow. He traced her tears with the pad of his thumb, followed them to the sand before his fingers stroked along her neck, over her shoulder and down her arm. His hand finally came to rest over hers.

She felt the tree respond and caught glimpses again of its roots reaching deep into the ground. She'd thought they sought water, but now she saw they grew from an ancient place created at the beginning of time—when this world was molten rock and nothingness as Asrafil had spoken of, when the Djinn were created from fire.

Asrafil closed his eyes and nearly wept as the tree touched him through his Azzura female. The past lay before him in a twisting trail that spanned centuries. Once the seers of the Djinn had come to this tree and viewed what had been by fasting underneath its pale limbs. They had glimpsed what might be by eating of its fruit. But when the women created by the alien god stumbled upon the tree and stripped it, they had stolen the Sight from the Djinn.

Without the fruit of the tree, the Djinn were stranded in the present with their need for vengeance. They were left with only memories connecting them to the past, only their intention to reclaim their land calling from the future and pulling them forward.

Asrafil leaned down and pressed his mouth to Lyrael's. He willingly shared a part of his spirit with her and let the ancient Djinn fire flow from the tree to meld their fates together.

He was forbidden from speaking to her of the tests. From speaking to her of the city of the Djinn or telling her how and why the long-dead elders of her tribe had been tricked into offering the Azzura as sacrifices.

He could share his body and bring her pleasure, but he was forbidden to speak of the tender emotions she stirred in him, of the future he hoped to have with her. He could make no promises to alleviate her fears or doubts. The choice to live or die remained hers until the third test was done.

Asrafil deepened the kiss. He swallowed her whimpers and responded by rubbing his cock against her silky mound. She had charmed and ensnared him, first by her courage and then by her beauty. She had bound him to her by calling his name on the dark winds and then by accepting him, by voluntarily putting the necklace with the poisonous *jukaabe* fruit aside and yielding her body to him, submitting to him.

Lyrael's thighs parted in silent invitation and Asrafil slid his cock into her wet channel. He moaned into her mouth at the snugness of her sheath. She burned with Djinn fire, with the small flicker of it that all the Azzura carried inside them as well as with the flame seared into her with his seed.

Asrafil acknowledged to himself that her heat and need and connection to him had turned the blaze inside him to an inferno that chased away his caution. He would die with her if she failed one of the tests yet to come. He, who was a prince of his people, would follow her spirit to wherever it fled should she choose death.

He kissed her as he thrust his cock in and out of her slick sheath. He shared his spirit, his flesh, and longed to share his heart and his future with her.

His hips pistoned forcefully as he neared release. His cock and balls burned with the need to come.

She responded as she'd done the night before. She clung to him and whimpered, came for him when he commanded it. Her cries filled his chest with masculine satisfaction even as she milked him of his seed.

Their hands remained on the tree and he could feel these moments being woven into the history of the Djinn though he could glimpse nothing of the future. "Lyrael," he whispered, not wanting to move into the day but knowing it was required.

"I need to get up," she finally said, her gaze shifting away from him in sudden shyness.

Asrafil rolled to a sitting position. He let her disappear into the purple-gray of the predawn as he examined the contents of the calabashes and found fresh fruit. He cut the fruit into small pieces by pressing it against the rim of one of the calabashes, then he set each chunk on the lid of another food container. When he was done he rose to a crouch and waited for Lyrael's return.

Lyrael's breath caught at the sight of Asrafil. She had been so flustered by her need for a few minutes of privacy that she had not thought to reach for her robe. And now, as the purple faded into the yellow-gray that warned of the sun's nearness, she was still naked, as was Asrafil.

His masculine beauty and exotic features made heat curl in her womb. They made her pleasure knob stiffen and her breasts grow heavy.

He crouched as he had the night before, with his knees parted and his large sac hanging underneath his cock. She shivered and her cunt clenched in response to the sight of him.

Asrafil's gaze found hers and the force of his will pulled her to him. She knelt before him, willing to take his male organ in her mouth and swallow his fiery come if that's what he wanted of her.

He cupped her face and she nuzzled his palm. With a desperate yearning she wished his features would soften to offer a hint of his thoughts, his feelings.

His cock was rigid again. Huge and thick. The foreskin was pulled back to expose the flushed, wet head.

Lyrael leaned in and licked across his glistening tip. The sharp intake of Asrafil's breath and the spicy *juura*-fruit taste of him made her nipples tighten to painful points and her clit throb.

She reached between her legs to touch herself only to be halted by his growled, "No."

"No," he repeated, stopping her when she would have pressed her lips to his cock in order to appease him. In order to gain his permission to play with her woman's knob and ease the need raging through her.

"Place both of your hands on my thighs," Asrafil said.

She licked her lips and looked at him through lowered eyelashes. She watched in satisfaction as his nostrils flared when she placed her palms on either side of his straining cock.

His muscles bunched underneath her hands and his penis grew fuller. The heavy veins on its underside pulsed wildly. She stroked the skin of his inner thighs with her thumbs and his cock jerked in reaction.

"Enough," he said. His voice was a harsh command and yet the sound of it had arousal coating her swollen cunt lips as her chest filled with feminine pride and hope. He was Djinn and held her fate in his hands. She would live or die at his whim, but she was not completely powerless against him.

"I'm hungry," she whispered, letting the provocative words settle over him. Watching as flames roared to life in his slitted pupils.

"Then I will feed you," Asrafil said, his fingers tightening in her hair when she would have leaned forward to caress his cock with her lips, his other hand reaching for the fruit she hadn't noticed before.

Asrafil fed her from his hand. He struggled to hide what it did to him when she licked the juice off his skin and sucked his fingers into her mouth. She tempted and tormented and teased him with each offering of food, defied him subtly even as she obeyed him openly.

The Djinn were beings of fire. They were primal and deadly and serious, their passion hot and fierce and all-consuming.

He wanted to take her again, to take her repeatedly. He wanted to enjoy the unfamiliar playfulness as well as her submission. He wanted to burn her with Djinn fire and let her strip him of his control so that his emotions lay bare to her. He fed her the last piece of fruit instead, though he allowed his fingers to remain in her mouth as the scent of her arousal assaulted him, mixed with the heated smell of the desert.

With a thought, a small sandstorm swirled to life near where her robes had fallen the previous night. It passed over the necklace with its deadly dried *jukaabe* fruit and brought it to Asrafil's hand before the grains of sand fell harmlessly to the ground.

Without a word he pulled his fingers from the wet temptation of her mouth and clasped the necklace around Lyrael's throat. Then he rose to his feet and stepped away from her, called the sand again, wrapping himself in it and leaving.

Lyrael's heart thundered in her chest. She watched the sandstorm gain in mass and become large enough to bury a caravan as it sped away from her. She shivered and prayed to the god that none of the Djinn found her family or her tribe as they traveled to the distant mountains and seaports.

At the far end of the valley the sandstorm vanished. At first Lyrael thought Asrafil sought a few moments of privacy as she had earlier, but when he didn't return, a chill settled in her chest and she was glad to have the sun's rays caressing her skin.

Despair and doubt threatened to overwhelm her as fear had once done. Had she meant nothing to him after all? Had he merely amused himself? Had she pleased him enough that he had decided to spare her life? Or was this the reason why she'd been left food and water for seven days? Because he would return at dusk for that period of time before his interest in her waned and she was left to die, her bones joining the others scattered around the tree.

She stood and gathered her robe, only glancing away from the place Asrafil disappeared long enough to shake the sand from the material. She gave up her vigil when she was covered from head to toe and the belt wrapped seven times around her waist in order to hold the robe in place.

Lyrael drank then. Long pulls from one of the calabashes as the sun beat down on her.

The skeletal tree offered no protection. She knew she should break some of the smaller branches and stick them into the sand in order to form a rough shelter out of her blanket. But the thought of desecrating the Djinn tree in that manner made her heart ache and her stomach roil in protest.

Her eyes scanned the mountain where she and Herachio had emerged. Nothing looked familiar. She could search for hours trying to find the hidden tunnel and deplete her water with the effort.

"What am I to do now?" she whispered, casting her words to the wind though her visions rarely came when the sun reigned.

Lyrael closed her eyes and pressed her palm to the smooth trunk of the tree, seeking comfort and finding the answer she'd sought instead.

Djinn heat poured into her as it had before, swelling upward from the deep roots of the past and pushing Lyrael into a vision of the future, showing her a black mountain panther who watched and waited. Who could not answer her call or aid her as she crossed the hot sands. But who would take the form of Asrafil and welcome her if she came to him, followed him.

Lyrael tried to ride the vision further as she could sometimes do in the spirit dreams, but the shining white of the tree's branches blinded her to the images beyond what had already been shared with her. She stroked the smooth trunk in a silent offer of thanks, then opened her eyes and looked across the sands to the place where Asrafil had gone.

There were no handles on the calabashes left for her as there were on the everyday vessels used by the tribe. There was no way to travel with two or three of them over her shoulder, though she could fashion a sling from her belt and carry a lone vessel containing water.

Fear skittered through her as she pictured those last minutes with Asrafil. He had placed the necklace on her and given her a way to end her life as Herachio had done.

Lyrael gathered her courage and her resolve. She had set aside the necklace and gone to Asrafil willingly the previous night, not because she sought to trade her body for her life, but because their spirits had found each other and touched in a dream walk. She may have summoned him initially. But she felt bound to him even before he encircled her ankle with his hand and burned the calf-rope away, freeing her from the dictates of her tribe and claiming her for his own.

Chapter Five

ಐ

Asrafil watched from his perch on a rocky ledge. The sun beat down on the black coat of his panther form. What had taken him only moments to accomplish was taking Lyrael hours. And yet she came to him. She battled the desert heat and shifting sands in a demonstration of her willingness and determination to walk at his side.

This was the second test.

Asrafil did not allow himself to believe she would fail. He did not allow himself to flinch when she stumbled and went to her knees, each time lingering there a few moments longer than the last time before struggling to her feet. He did not look away as she took the last drink of water before abandoning the calabash.

When she reached the mountain, he stood and revealed himself. He gave a low, rumbling growl then turned and disappeared into the cave behind him.

The desert crossing was only part of the test.

Exhaustion made Lyrael's arms heavy weights at her sides. Her happiness at seeing the panther leaked away with the tears rolling down her checks.

Once again she gathered her resolve and drew upon the vision she had seen when she touched the Djinn tree. Slowly, painfully she climbed to the ledge and faced the cave entrance. She saw the tribal marks etched into the stone at the sides and top—warning that any who entered would be killed.

Lyrael was too tired even to fear. She wanted only what the vision had promised, to be held and welcomed.

She stepped into the cave and saw the panther above her, crouched as though he would spring. "Asrafil," she whispered, going to her knees as the giant cat leapt from his rocky perch.

Sand gathered and swirled, appearing out of nowhere to become a fierce sandstorm, dropping almost immediately to reveal Asrafil. She whimpered when he gathered her into his arms and kissed her gently. His tongue rubbed against hers as though he were seeking forgiveness, reassurance. She granted him both. Exhaustion and happiness made her boneless as he carried her deeper into the cave.

Lyrael fell into an exhausted sleep to awaken as cool water flowed over her naked body. She startled to find herself once again outside under a blue sky. But this time she was shielded from the sun by palm trees, saved from its heat by a breeze over oasis water.

Asrafil cupped the water in his hand and brought it to her lips. He repeated the process over and over again until her thirst was quenched.

"No," he told her when she would have escaped his lap and splashed water over her body.

He picked up her discarded robe and dipped one end of it into the cool water. He washed her thoroughly, cleaned her of sweat and sand, his touch so intimate that a different kind of heat filled her.

"You are beautiful," he whispered, abandoning the end of the cloth and picking up a date. He pressed the fruit to her lips, fed her as he'd done earlier, stopping only when she refused to open her lips and take any more.

Asrafil shifted her on his lap then. He held her as he'd held her before, with her legs splayed, his cock rising between them. The golden curtain of her hair flowing over their thighs.

Lyrael leaned into him. She initiated the kiss as her hands traced the muscles of his arms, his shoulders, before moving around to capture his braid.

Asrafil shuddered under her carnal assault but didn't stop her when she slowly undid his hair. She had not passed the third test yet. But in his heart she was already his *sorja*, the only one allowed to free his hair from its braid. The only one allowed to touch him so intimately.

"Lyrael," he whispered. His cock became trapped against her abdomen when he pulled her to him as his unbound hair flowed over his back in a sensual wave.

She clung to him, touched her tongue to his, thrust and parried in the wet heat, her fingers combing through his black hair and lightly scratching his back. It was an ecstasy of the heart, the spirit, the flesh.

Asrafil let her torment him. He let her stroke and tease and entice. He endured the burn in his cock and balls.

He wanted to spend the day with her here, underneath the date palms. But they were so close to the city of the Djinn. So very close. And he longed to be home, to spread her buttocks before the scribes and fill the last of her virgin openings with Djinn seed so her name could be written in the Book of the Djinn beside his own.

Afterward they would retreat to their bedchamber in order to make love and talk. They would be able to share their thoughts and feelings, to get to know each other in a way that was forbidden until she was his *sorja* in fact as well as in his heart.

Need rode him but he resisted the urge to cover her body with his own and thrust his penis into her welcoming slit. He'd been mesmerized not only by her woman's folds as he'd bathed her, but by the breasts he'd yet to suckle from.

With a groan his hands went to her arms. He pulled them behind her back so she arched, her nipples like pouting buds begging for attention. He lowered his head, wet first one hardened areola and then the other with his tongue. He pressed his lips to them in a gentle greeting before giving them an open-mouth kiss as his tongue swirled over them.

Her cries were sweeter than the song of any bird. The arousal leaking from her slit and coating his penis where their bodies touched was more erotic than any heated oil.

"Please," she begged him and he relented. He began suckling, his tugs becoming fiercer, his growls joining her whimpers as her swollen cunt lips spasmed against his cock like a hungry mouth trying to draw him inside.

Lyrael threw back her head and shamelessly offered her breasts to him. She rubbed her feverish cunt against him and offered her heart, her soul. He seared her with his heat, engulfed her in the flames of passion and she wanted to burn forever with his Djinn fire.

Tears rolled down her cheeks. Not from loss or exhaustion, but from the need for him. Her whimpers became cries. Her breath grew short as his teeth joined his tongue and lips in claiming her breasts. He bit and suckled, no longer a gentle exploration but a fierce, dominant claiming. She was shaking by the time he lifted his face. She was willing to do anything he asked if only he would fill her empty channel with his cock, his seed.

Asrafil devoured her with his eyes. Nothing in the centuries of his existence had prepared him for this. For her.

The sight of Lyrael shaking in passion, her thighs spread and her cunt glistening, her nipples marked by his desire as her eyes begged him to possess her—it satisfied him even as he knew he would crave it over and over again.

With a low growl he removed her from his lap and positioned her on her hands and knees. He covered her with his body and gloried in the sight of his night-black hair draped over her, touching her skin before pooling on the sand.

He impaled her in a single hard thrust, gave her more of his weight so she folded onto her elbows. He took her as the black panther would take its female. In a rough, fast mating that culminated in a scream as he gripped her shoulder with his teeth and pumped his seed into her.

Afterward Asrafil curled around her as they lay on their sides. He held her back tightly to his chest and felt her heartbeat thunder where his palm caressed her breast.

For the moment she was quiet, content, but he knew conversation would come if they lingered here. And as much as he craved it, needed to hold her in the afterglow of passion and share the history of the Djinn and the true reason for her sacrifice, it was forbidden. They were too close now for either of them to fail the other — her by choosing death, him by deviating from the path the ancient seer had set out for the Djinn who would claim the Azzura women.

Asrafil allowed himself a few moments of bliss, of tenderness. He stroked her breasts and belly, her bare mound and thighs as he explored her ear with his lips and tongue.

How easily he had lost himself in her. Become the servant as well as the master.

This was why the tests were so harsh. The Azzura women could just as easily destroy the Djinn as be their salvation.

"Lyrael," he whispered against her ear. His fingers explored her wet slit. His cock was hard again. When she would have turned in his arms and offered herself to him, he denied her. He forced himself to release her and rise to his knees.

He dressed her himself this time. Wound the robe between her legs, knotting it in various places so it would not slip from her body the short time it would be on her. She opened her mouth to question him but he hardened his features and put his finger on her lips in a command for silence.

When he was satisfied with the robe, he placed the deadly necklace on her. Then he stepped away and called the sand, glad the third test would be over in a heartbeat.

Lyrael watched as the sand gathered into a familiar storm, this time lifting high into the air. He would appear as the black *juudu* bird. She knew it with certainty.

In her dream the snake and the panther and the bird had come at her summons when she whispered the name *Asrafil* in the spirit winds. They had been angry then, and she had been afraid. But now her body hummed with pleasure and her heart sang from the tender way he had held her, the thoroughness in which he had secured her robes. He would not hurt her.

The sand fell away to reveal the bird hovering above her. She gasped at the sheer size of it but she did not flinch as it dropped from the sky with its sharp black talons extended in front of it. She did not scream when it grasped the cloth of the robe and lifted her into the sky, though her heart raced with the fear of being so high above the ground.

His wings beat the air and their speed increased. The desert valley with the oasis became a place of the past as he soared above the mountains her tribe knew were still claimed by the Djinn.

Lyrael's breath caught in her throat as he began to dive. Her hands balled into fists and a whimper escaped as fear tried to consume her. Many times she had witnessed the *juudu* bird kill its prey by hurtling it against rock.

The mountain raced toward her. At the last instant she closed her eyes. Felt her heart stop as her mother's words passed through her. *Have courage and you will find a place among the Djinn.*

And then her heart began beating. Her body burned with Djinn fire and she opened her eyes to behold the city of the Djinn with its golden domes and spires.

Asrafil flew across white sands until they reached the city. Then he gently placed her in a courtyard where four Djinn waited. They were tall and muscular, their hair braided to reveal the intricate tattoos on their necks, their only clothing the same flowing trousers Asrafil had worn the first time she saw him as a man.

The Djinn were gathered around a raised circular dais. The image of the skeletal tree was carved into it, touching the edge at each place they stood—north, south, west and east.

This time Asrafil did not call the sand but shimmered like heat rising from the desert as he changed into a man in front of her. He cupped Lyrael's face and brushed his thumb over her lips to keep her silent when she would have spoken. Pride and desire filled him as he gazed at her. The first test had been one of courage. The second a show of willingness and determination. The third a test of trust.

Now there would be no more tests.

Had they been in their bedchamber, he would have welcomed her to the city of the Djinn with kisses and heated touches and whispered words of love. He would have worshipped every inch of her until they were both shaking with the need to join. But they could not seek privacy until she'd been claimed completely.

There was no advantage in lingering or in allowing the scribes to witness how enthralled he was with his Azzura female. Asrafil removed the necklace and it turned to ash in his hand. He reached for her robe—pausing to shake his head in denial as her face flamed and her mouth opened as though to protest the presence of the scribes.

He undid the knots he'd put in the material in order to ensure her safety as he flew with her. When they were free he gently pulled the garment from her hands even as she tried to keep herself covered with it.

Asrafil destroyed the robe as he'd done the necklace. He scooped Lyrael into his arms and stepped onto the dais, moving to its center.

He lay her down on the image of the tree, positioned her arms on the limbs that touched the east and west, pressed her wrists to the warm stone so she would know she was to keep them there. He bent her knees and splayed her thighs, knelt between them but did not rebuke her when she whimpered in protest. Shyness colored her face and breasts even as her exposed cunt wept and parted.

A scribe held out an urn small enough to fit in the palm of his hand. Asrafil dipped his fingers into it, coated them before rimming her last virgin entrance. She startled at the touch, whimpered again, but she did not disgrace him by disobeying his silent commands or by trying to evade his touch.

He worked his fingers into her. Stretched and prepared her until she was arching, displaying her arousal with the juices that coated her lower lips and inner thighs.

Asrafil draped her knees over his arms so she was completely open, completely helpless as he pressed his penis to her back entrance. He leaned forward and covered her mouth with his—unwilling to share any more of her with the scribes than he had to—he swallowed her cries as he forged inside her dark channel.

Lyrael shuddered as he pierced her. Cried out as his length and width seared her nerve endings and made it impossible to remain still. She pleaded with her body for him not just to sheath himself in her forbidden passage, but to claim it as he had done the rest of her, to fill it with his seed.

He growled into her mouth and began thrusting. The rub of his pelvis over her swollen clit and the taking of her virgin ass was an unbearable pleasure. The presence of the watching Djinn faded as Asrafil become her entire reality.

She yielded to him. Let him demonstrate how easily he could command her body and summon her pleasure.

She screamed in release as he poured himself into her. She begged for him to take her again even as he left her forbidden channel.

Asrafil gathered her into his arms and stood, his attention directed at the scribes.

"Let the name Lyrael be written in the book of our people. Her mortality was sacrificed by her tribe and now she is one of us. She is Azzura Djinn. One who belongs to the past and the future. To the tree of the oracle. Place her name next to mine as *sorja*, the wife of my heart, my flesh, my spirit."

When Asrafil stepped from the dais and strode away from the four scribes, he looked down at Lyrael and allowed her to see what he felt for her. Her heart filled and her eyes glistened as she looked into his eyes and found a love hot enough to rival the fire which created the Djinn.

Also by Jory Strong

‽

About the Author

଼ଠ

Jory has been writing since childhood and has never outgrown being a daydreamer. When she's not hunched over her computer, lost in the muse and conjuring up new heroes and heroines, she can usually be found reading, riding her horses, or hiking with her dogs.

Jory welcomes comments from readers. You can find her website and email address on her author bio page at www.ellorascave.com.

Tell Us What You Think

We appreciate hearing reader opinions about our books. You can email us at Comments@EllorasCave.com.

Why an electronic book?

We live in the Information Age—an exciting time in the history of human civilization, in which technology rules supreme and continues to progress in leaps and bounds every minute of every day. For a multitude of reasons, more and more avid literary fans are opting to purchase e-books instead of paper books. The question from those not yet initiated into the world of electronic reading is simply: *Why?*

1. ***Price.*** An electronic title at Ellora's Cave Publishing and Cerridwen Press runs anywhere from 40% to 75% less than the cover price of the exact same title in paperback format. Why? Basic mathematics and cost. It is less expensive to publish an e-book (no paper and printing, no warehousing and shipping) than it is to publish a paperback, so the savings are passed along to the consumer.

2. ***Space.*** Running out of room in your house for your books? That is one worry you will never have with electronic books. For a low one-time cost, you can purchase a handheld device specifically designed for e-reading. Many e-readers have large, convenient screens for viewing. Better yet, hundreds of titles can be stored within your new library—on a single microchip. There are a variety of e-readers from different manufacturers. You can also read e-books on your PC or laptop computer. (Please note that Ellora's

Cave does not endorse any specific brands. You can check our websites at www.ellorascave.com or www.cerridwenpress.com for information we make available to new consumers.)

3. *Mobility*. Because your new e-library consists of only a microchip within a small, easily transportable e-reader, your entire cache of books can be taken with you wherever you go.

4. *Personal Viewing Preferences.* Are the words you are currently reading too small? Too large? Too... ANNOYING? Paperback books cannot be modified according to personal preferences, but e-books can.

5. *Instant Gratification.* Is it the middle of the night and all the bookstores near you are closed? Are you tired of waiting days, sometimes weeks, for bookstores to ship the novels you bought? Ellora's Cave Publishing sells instantaneous downloads twenty-four hours a day, seven days a week, every day of the year. Our webstore is never closed. Our e-book delivery system is 100% automated, meaning your order is filled as soon as you pay for it.

Those are a few of the top reasons why electronic books are replacing paperbacks for many avid readers.

As always, Ellora's Cave and Cerridwen Press welcome your questions and comments. We invite you to email us at Comments@ellorascave.com or write to us directly at Ellora's Cave Publishing Inc., 1056 Home Avenue, Akron, OH 44310-3502.

THE
☥ ELLORA'S CAVE ☥
LIBRARY

Stay up to date with Ellora's Cave Titles in
Print with our Quarterly Catalog.

TO RECIEVE A CATALOG,
SEND AN EMAIL WITH YOUR NAME
AND MAILING ADDRESS TO:

CATALOG@ELLORASCAVE.COM

OR SEND A LETTER OR POSTCARD
WITH YOUR MAILING ADDRESS TO:

CATALOG REQUEST
c/o ELLORA'S CAVE PUBLISHING, INC.
1056 HOME AVENUE
AKRON, OHIO 44310-3502

Cerridwen Press

Monthly Newsletter

News
Author Appearances
Book Signings
New Releases
Contests
Author Profiles
Feature Articles

Available online at
www.CerridwenPress.com

MAKE EACH DAY MORE *EXCITING* WITH OUR

ELLORA'S
CAVEMEN
CALENDAR

www.EllorasCave.com

erridwen, the Celtic Goddess of wisdom, was the muse who brought inspiration to storytellers and those in the creative arts. Cerridwen Press encompasses the best and most innovative stories in all genres of today's fiction. Visit our site and discover the newest titles by talented authors who still get inspired - much like the ancient storytellers did, once upon a time.

Cerridwen Press

www.cerridwenpress.com

Discover for yourself why readers can't get enough of the multiple award-winning publisher

Ellora's Cave.

Whether you prefer e-books or paperbacks,

be sure to visit EC on the web at
www.ellorascave.com

for an erotic reading experience that will leave you breathless.